To:
George & Elaine

NO ONE CAN KNOW

Love,
Adrienne LaCava

ADRIENNE LaCAVA

Copyright © 2013 Adrienne LaCava
All rights reserved.
ISBN: 1491228067
ISBN 13: 9781491228067
Cover photo © Bettmann/CORBIS.

Publisher's Note:

This is a work of fiction. All of the characters, organizations and events portrayed in this novel are either products of the author's imagination or are used fictionally.

For Mom, who inspired the love of story in all of us.

The very word "secrecy" is repugnant in a free and open society; and we are as a people inherently and historically opposed to secret societies, to secret oaths, and to secret proceedings. We decided long ago that the dangers of excessive and unwarranted concealment of pertinent facts far outweighed the dangers, which are cited to justify it.

President John F. Kennedy,
Address to American Newspaper Publishers Association
April 27, 1961

PROLOGUE

NOVEMBER 19, 1963

CIA operative Gabriel Haines was ordered out of Guatemala to lie low. Not one to question commands, he grabbed a ride on the next transport back home to Texas. Tensions in the southern hemisphere were steadily worsening and, in the months since Kennedy fired Company Director Dulles, it had seemed like a fuse lit somewhere in Central America. Haines was glad to jet out of there.

Strapped into a raw metal jump seat, he suffered five hours in a 1000 KG fuselage stuffed with cargo. The big planes might hold a lot but they sucked for comfort, and by the time they put down at Lackland Air Force Base, his spine hurt as much as his ass. Spies aren't the jet-setting martini drinkers civilians like to imagine—they're mostly just weary hitchhikers tramping around off-the-record.

Haines's personal HQ was near the northern edge of San Antonio. He'd rented a seven-acre parcel of land with a barn on it, prompted by the impulse purchase of a mare named Bella. It was almost midnight when he finally reached the property so he whistled twice as he approached, and Bella's enthusiastic whinnies encouraged a wide, happy smile on his mug. He knew country life defined his future. He'd been raised on a farm and loved the lifestyle. Destiny must have put the irresistible palomino in front of him to hurry things up. A conversation last week with an old Army pal might be destiny calling, too. At forty-five years old, the idea of retirement from the Company wasn't so far-fetched for Haines, especially given his most recent orders.

The stench of sour hay and manure filled the barn and had him opening shutters and doors. A stable hand from a neighboring farm tended Bella daily, but she deserved more than this neglected old place. Haines breathed in the fresh air and relaxed his guard as he moved toward Bella's stall.

A stoic demeanor made Haines an exceptional spy, but he'd never for a moment withheld emotion around Bella. And while only a handful of people in the world knew he even had a first name, nobody—*nobody*—knew he talked to his horse.

"Come on, girl. How about a rub down?" he said, leading the beauty out of her stall. Bella whickered, causing creases to appear on his face, deep enough to hold a peanut. Not many people got to see his dimples, but time with his horse was good therapy and he was going to enjoy it. He only had twelve hours before he'd head out again, for a personal mission this time, that meant a short ride up to Dallas and back. He'd prefer to hang with Bella a few days first, but a plan was taking shape that could very nicely provide him with a way into retirement. He just had to make a deal with a good friend to make it happen.

Haines glided a coarse brush over Bella's golden coat and she leaned into the pressure.

"If this meeting goes right with Tucker, girl, it'll mean greener pastures for both of us."

She lowered her head in a solemn nod.

Dallas lawyer and famed hotshot Tucker Massey happened to be one of the only people in the world Haines would call a friend. Tucker knew Haines was ready to get out of the game and offering him the job of foreman at his newly restored cattle ranch was just the ticket. Haines wrestled with some natural skepticism at first, but allowed himself to imagine the possibilities of a simpler, freer kind of life.

Bella pawed the dirt and whickered again, happy with the prospect too. Big girl had a wise soul.

"Fifty thousand acres," he said with a soft whistle that put her ears flat. "Imagine that. We'll ride every square inch, I promise."

Static shot from a transistor radio hanging from a peg, startling Bella. He shushed her gently, fiddled with the dial and restored country music to the breeze. Nashville songbird Patsy Cline had been scheduled to appear in San Antonio on Saturday, but she'd died in a plane crash a few months earlier. The music world still grieved and the radio DJ promised her hits back-to-back all night. Haines hummed along and filled a water bucket at the spigot.

"On a moonlit night by the Alamo..."

Without easing into it, he poured some water over Bella's flinching back and her big head dropped and rolled into an eleven-hundred-pound body shake before he could jump out of the way. All six feet of him dripped. Taut and toned muscles reshaped the cotton shirt he wore. He laughed hard and wiped his face on the shirttail.

Haines's heritage was hard to detect, but anyone could see he was built like a plough horse. His mother was full-blooded Negro and best guess on his father's side was Italian, according to his grandfather. The resulting skin color and cranial features were ambiguous, and interesting. The sight of him could scare the timid, but drenched and laughing as he was, he presented no threat.

Instead, he could almost be mistaken as comforting. Haines's dream of days ahead, when he and Bella could just take off and ride, untethered, not worried about people noticing or remembering him, softened his hard exterior because, when he finally got to cut Bella loose on a ride, let her lead "Bella style," he'd let loose too—with a natural, world-class yuck that vibrated meadow grass and made wildlife scamper.

"Sure will be nice to stay put in one place, won't it? Not hide anymore?"

It's all he'd been doing lately, and he was tired of it. The direction of Company business didn't suit Haines anymore. America's so-called intelligence-gathering organization was unrecognizable. Its leaders had become a bunch of facilitators, or so it seemed to Haines. Operations had gotten politically ensnarled and too many rogues were out there pulling triggers unsupervised. It was time to get out.

Besides, he was sick of the danger, if truth be told. No James Bond to begin with, he now wore a slice of healing flesh that made a crossroads of his right eyebrow. An accidental casualty on his last assignment after liquored-up Spaniards with blades went at it—in the cantina—over a senorita. Talk about cliché. But it got him out of Guatemala. Distinguishing marks were dicey on a spy's face, though. He'd need to see a doc if plans with Tucker fell through. Besides an identifier, facial scars could be a "tell" if they discolored when the wearer fibbed. But Haines didn't mind the new marking himself; he could actually use it to his advantage.

A clean split from the CIA required careful handling and a good cover, like injury and a tailor-made, irresistible job offer. Disagreement with the Company could be deadly, but this kind of reasoning they just might get behind.

He leaned toward Bella's flinching ear as though she had a say. "Don't let this be a tease."

November 22, 1963

On his last morning in Dallas, Haines woke with the chickens. Not real chickens, though; Kat's was a room-and-board place filled with oil-field hands who thrived on greasy, starchy breakfasts. A man had to get up early not to miss out.

Still dark outside, thunder rolled while he dressed, and rain patterned the tiny steamed-up window of the second-floor room. He might have to catch a cab to the train station at this rate, which was normally a pleasant twenty blocks he'd rather walk. Unlatching the single pane, the chilly air outside carried a heady fragrance into the space. He leaned over the basin in front of him and slapped water on his face.

In the mirror, his usually wicked, sharp eyes glared back muddy and derisive. A thundering herd of mustangs was loose between his ears. He arched his eyebrow and winced as the cut along his skin stretched. It'd be a wonder if Tucker's head didn't hurt as bad, even without the wound. The two of them had nearly overdosed on whiskey the night before, drinking 'til the wee hours, shooting pool in a crappy dive near Kat's. They'd also alternated shots of tequila. Celebrating. It was official.

Haines smiled to know he was foreman of Tucker's vast, scenic ranch. Perched atop Texas Hill Country, Tucker said the property offered up the best the state had to offer, from high bluffs to rambling creeks, game-filled woods and lush pastureland. Haines imagined it'd be like the rolling hills of Kentucky where he'd ridden and played as a boy.

Pink light peeped through the clouds outside and brightened the room for a moment. Allowing a surge of high spirits to strike, he took a deep breath and ignored the old skeptic in his head that poked holes in the plan; pushed away fears of severing all his old ties.

The Cold War's no place for geezers.

The truth was, the Company didn't need him anymore, and he didn't need the Company.

Scents of breakfast wafted in and his stomach whined its response, jerking him out of his reverie. He pulled on new cutter-heeled boots and headed downstairs to chow.

• • •

A small television, with rabbit ears held together by tinfoil, sat on the open windowsill. Scattered sun was forcing itself through the clouds now as TV newscasters shouted appropriately through the boisterous, crowded dining room. Catching the president's name on the air, Haines realized the broadcaster's topic was the presidential motorcade that had been set to go through downtown Dallas later that day.

Haines thought the signs were good that Kennedy would follow through. Last night he'd huddled up with Tucker and counted the insiders they'd recognized around town, trying to figure it out for themselves. His old friend had connections, serious connections that went all the way to Vice President Johnson and the White House. Tucker had alluded to preparations, commented on extra security activities he was involved in, and complained because the presidential itinerary kept changing.

Haines tried to tune out the news chatter the best he could and ambled the length of Kat's legendary buffet, salivating along the way to the stack of warm plates and flatware. Oil-field crews knew their comfort food, and Haines knew there was no better remedy for a hangover than Kat's buttermilk biscuits floating in cream gravy with chunks of her spicy, house-made pork sausage; embellished grits, too, with extra-sharp cheddar cheese and tiny bits of fresh jalapeño. Haines garnished the substantial pile on his plate with crispy bacon strips, found an empty chair and succumbed to the medicine.

But the newscaster's voice crept back in while he ate. According to the TV—and contrary to earlier predictions—citizens had enthusiastically welcomed the president and first lady to the great state of Texas in earlier stops at San Antonio, Houston and, just that morning, in Fort Worth.

The Dallas newspapers, however, had surely lacked restraint in publishing fanatical, right wing hate rhetoric the last few days. Haines wondered if it was Company work. Around the globe every day, propaganda specialists molded public opinion, sanctioned by the National Security Council and Joint Chiefs of Staff. Depending on the intended spin of the matter and the customs of the targeted audience, select professionals marched into media control rooms representing "national security," and nobody refused them anything. He'd watched them retool inconvenient news plenty of times. But Dallas had been the only major city in the country to prefer Nixon in 1960. Could be its newspapermen didn't need help spinning disfavor.

Hearing laughter and applause from the TV, Haines focused for a moment. The president was speaking at a breakfast in Fort Worth and had just told the crowd that being in Texas was like their trip to Paris, where he'd introduced himself as the man who accompanied Mrs. Kennedy around. "Nobody wonders what Lyndon and I wear," he added.

Laughter from the ballroom's two thousand guests roared onscreen. It looked like the suave and sophisticated Mr. Kennedy intended to charm the locals right out of their little ole pants, and shoot the finger to his foes. Haines sent the president a mental thumbs-up and decided if it didn't start raining again he'd catch the parade before heading back to Bella and the barn.

Politics at work had forced him to be a closet fan of Jack Kennedy's—nearly every military and intelligence professional outright despised the commander in chief. To them, he was a commie-loving traitor. Haines saw him as a war hero, though, with different ideas about diplomacy, a man who believed, as Haines did, that America could be secure without aggression. Tension in the ranks got extra ugly after Kennedy fired Director Dulles. Dulles had led Central Intelligence for a decade. And Kennedy inherited Operation 40, including the Bay of Pigs plan, from Eisenhower. He didn't agree with OP 40's missions in the Caribbean, but canning Allen Dulles hadn't helped internal relations any.

Staring at his empty plate, Haines felt heavier—both physically and mentally—but less booze-soaked. He returned to his room to shave. With the sun now winning against the rain, a finch squatted on a branch by the window, trilling her melody over and over. Haines grinned at himself a moment. He was really retiring, leaving the Company. Getting out.

About damn time.

The brinksmanship and visceral strife got under his skin severely. Treasonous talk was commonplace and people were acting with bitter carelessness. *Oh yeah, and we have the bomb.* He'd begun to see himself as part of a machine that could recklessly cause the extinction of humanity.

Leaning over the basin again, he wet his scalp, daubed the soapy foam on, and continued shaving with practiced efficiency. He wore bald well—and *yessir*, Ranch Man looked good.

So did the day. Clouds had moved on east and left behind a brilliant morning. He settled the bill with Kat and stepped onto the porch. Dressed in dark Wranglers and a white western-fit shirt, the unmasked Haines—just Haines—picked up his old, buffalo-hide duffel and set out for town.

Crisp autumn air felt scrubbed of pollutants by the rain and complemented his unusually sunny disposition. The city almost smelled *good.* He turned west to pick up Commerce Street when disorder snagged his attention. Wet paper that looked like handbills littered the street, stuck to windshields and pavement everywhere. He lifted one: "WANTED FOR TREASON" it said in bold print over front and side views of an unsmiling Mr. President. *We're not in Kansas anymore.* A similar propaganda piece had taken up half a page in the *Morning News*, attributed to the notorious right wing John Birch Society or something.

Haines sneered at the paper and moved on, remembering his conversation with Tucker last night.

They'd stood around the bar's single pool table shoved in a corner, and had just uncorked a new bottle of aged whiskey. Both of them had tossed back a redundant shot, already three sheets.

"You remember Mike Gilroy?" Haines had asked, though he knew Tucker remembered their squad mate from World War II.

"Yep. I think I saw him at the automat in my office building Tuesday, buying a sandwich."

Haines nodded. "He walked past me yesterday on Akard Street."

They'd exchanged a look, a breeze from somewhere setting the fake Tiffany shade over the pool table swaying.

During their years together in the war, Tucker had led a military intelligence unit that spent almost two full years in Italy. Tucker and Haines were the guns, Gilroy their spotter. The trio—plus a pair of specialists in plastic explosives and a sole radioman—made up the special ops team. But he and Tucker didn't talk about Italy. Ever. Even inferring it, there, over the pool table, had made the atmosphere prickly.

Tucker put a hand to the lampshade and studied his play options on the felt.

Their squad, assigned the code KODIAK090, had dissolved and split up soon after D-Day. "What happened to Big Mike after '45?" Haines asked.

"He stayed with the company awhile, on the inside I'm thinking. Dropped off my radar around '54 I'd guess."

The men of KODIAK090 had shared experiences capable of evoking soul-wrenching pain if a man let his mind dwell there.

Details and faces could never be truly forgotten, but each soldier, in their way, had to get past the experience and move on. Tucker got himself a law practice in Dallas and a leadership role with the Texas Democratic Party. All too easily, Haines had slid into employment by the postwar OSS, which soon morphed into the CIA or "the Company." His chameleon-like ability to blend and superior command of the Spanish language, including a dozen dialects, kept him on assignment nearly 365 days a year.

"He's not the only shooter in town," Tucker had said, speaking to the floor.

"I know."

Watch your back, Mr. President.

Reaching the towering shadows of the city's heart, exhaust fumes were stronger and sunshine created humidity that held the stinky, brown haze low to the ground. Sidewalks were clogged with placard carriers and parade goers, everybody moving the same direction. Newspapers had published the motorcade route that morning, an approximate fifteen-mile loop out of Love Field in north Dallas. The limousines would start out south on Cedar Springs, turn right onto Main Street and travel westward through downtown, then cut back north to the Trade Mart for lunch and a speech. Approximately one hour later, the Kennedys would be transported, in a quieter manner, back to Air Force One.

Squinting in the late morning sun, Haines walked north a block to pick up Main, where he joined an even denser crowd.

It made sense that details of a presidential visit had to be kept under wraps until the last minute. Tucker had said Vice President Johnson's security people griped because nobody would confirm until yesterday that the envoy would even stop in Dallas, let alone stay long enough for a parade. The metroplex teemed with security and Intelligence suits all week, he'd been told, and over that pool table last night he and Tucker had identified six professional assets milling about Dallas.

Stopping under a tobacco store awning, Haines looked around. There'd been talk of snipers foiled and bagged in Chicago three weeks ago. Some loner set up in a nest directly above the presidential motorcade route. Secret Service and CIA have their own sets of rules, but Haines expected the windows in buildings overlooking the route to be ordered shut, particularly at points where the vehicles would slow down. He also figured Secret Service snipers would be assigned rooftops, with spotters watching holes in the perimeter. But windows were still open in buildings all along Main Street, and it was almost show time.

The celebratory atmosphere seemed honestly adoring, at least, in the traditional way of welcoming a hero, so Haines reined in the urge to study shadows. He let the ebullience of the crowd and the ideal weather carry him on.

His plan was to catch the 1:20 out of Union Terminal over to Fort Worth and hop a cab to the base where he'd get a ride back to San Antonio, eventually. He and Tucker decided he'd buy a new pickup and horse trailer there, fetch Bella, then take up residence at the ranch. Four days, tops. A brand new stable, corral and cowboy quarters were waiting for him, and Tucker excitedly insisted they start breeding livestock right away. Haines knew weeks of research had to be done beforehand, but he itched to get started. *No reason to delay things now.* In his mind, he smiled.

Reaching Houston Street, he paused to study the nightmarish, gothic structure of the city's early courthouse, Old Red. It faced a grassy park with reflecting pools and statuary called Dealey Plaza, where three major streets came together marking the west side of downtown. According to the publicized route, the president's car would be forced to almost stop at the corner of the one-way street where Haines was standing and take another sharp turn a block later, in order to reach the freeway's northbound on-ramp. Union Terminal was two blocks south, so Haines staked the corner. It was the best spot to see the charismatic couple up close.

The increasing din signaled limousines were near and people started bunching at the curb. Gargoyles peered down from the roof of Old Red and Haines stepped over near the low shrubs that lined the building to stash his duffel. Positioned under the street sign, a group of mouthy pre-teen schoolgirls alternated giggles and ear-piercing shrieks, but he had no trouble seeing over them. Everything vibrated and the energy revved, with all heads craning toward thunderous advance bikes.

Police officials in the pilot car took the sharp turn in front of him first, tasked with spotting any trouble coming up. Next, a group of noisy motorcycle cops rumbled past, then an unmarked car that would be the Lead, carrying big wigs of the Secret Service and probably the local sheriff's department. Haines glanced northward at the criminal courts building where the Dallas County sheriff's offices were housed, and it looked like a battalion of deputies stood at parade rest. All of them faced Houston Street, poised for inspection.

He swept his gaze along the buildings in range. A push against his shoulder made Haines lean back to let an excited fan pass, and he noticed a man in shirtsleeves and dark glasses moving away, only to turn back midstride and tip his head *hello*. Haines stared in dreadful recognition at a face from his days in Florida—a notorious Cuban exile, Horace Ortiz.

The line of freshly waxed limousines crawled toward him now and Haines refocused on the spectacle. People of all walks, stacked ten bodies thick, cheered wildly as the president's convertible eased through the turn. The young girls shrieked like he was Elvis. Mrs. Kennedy came into plain view and Haines didn't hold back a broad, dimpled smile. Drop-dead gorgeous and classy as a queen, she seemed amused by the crowd and their undeniable affection. By her side, sunlight glanced off the Irish in Jack Kennedy's hair. Haines recalled their security code names, Lancer and Lace. *Truly, beautiful people.*

He considered the wisdom of an open car then, realizing agents weren't riding the running boards as they should. Secret Service detail hung behind the limousine and Haines puzzled over the assumed breach in protocol. The immediate crowd was peeling away to keep pace with the president's car, some crossing to the grassy plaza infield or running to catch the glamorous pair at the next turn on Elm Street. Uninterested in the other limos, Haines collected his duffel and turned toward the train station, away from the crowds. He felt the rifle report before it registered audibly.

Stepping tight against Old Red, he fought any acknowledgment of disaster, though apprehension pushed against his breastplate. The schoolgirls wailed and their heartfelt terror gripped

Haines with dread. Another rifle report jolted him with an echo. Counting, he swept the scene.

Dear God, Mrs. Kennedy on deck—tires peeling in smoke, celebrants prone. Uniforms and dark suits merging like ants with weapons drawn, charging uphill in two directions.

Haines turned away and locked eyes on his boot tops. All the suspicion about guns in town came together suddenly. The United States President had just been shot at, possibly killed. *Why was Mrs. Kennedy out of the car?* Haines realized he needed to get out of there before he was seen, before he could be brought into any investigation. Knowledge would quickly be assumed because of his Company credentials, never mind that he wobbled in shock.

Willing his feet into motion, he suppressed the abrupt, sickening sense of personal loss and took a side street in search of a cab.

June 1964

ONE

Ivy Jean

PROSPERITY, TEXAS

Ivy Jean Pritchard considered the fate of the world while sunning like a lizard on her favorite rock. The wide, smooth plank of stone had plopped down nicely, half in and half out of her creek, and despite a recent growth spurt, she could still fit her tall, thin body across it.

Lying on her stomach, she watched as a school of minnows darted and swarmed in an eddy below her, and wondered if they could feel worry. The way they skittered around made it seem like they did. Her shiny, dark hair was loose from its usual ponytail and made a canopy of shadow for them.

She caught her reflection in the water and scowled. Every since a boy from school had called her "Daddy Longlegs," she'd fought a less flattering idea of herself. He'd meant a spider that is all legs. For her entire life, she'd wanted to be a petite brunette, the way she'd heard her mother described.

Too bad, her older brother Wade had taunted just last month. She had their mother's shiny, dark hair but their dad's long legs and narrow hips.

'Daddy's long legs' ain't even funny.

Ivy Jean was twelve years old and felt all out of proportion. In fact, the whole world seemed to be that way these days. Her father, Vincent, ate up newspapers and TV broadcasts like they were barbequed ribs, but Ivy just thought the news made people nervous for no reason. She sighed and looked around her at the woods, hoping her friend Julie would show up like they'd planned.

The creek near her house in Prosperity had served as Ivy's playground for as far back as her memory went. *Requiring strict obedience*, her father warned daily, referring to his rules for hanging out there. True, in a wet summer the water levels might reach the bottom of Ivy's cutoffs if she stood in the middle, but most of the time the creek was a shallow stream, five strides across at its widest. It flowed, with a lazy trickling sound, through a wooded swath that divided crop fields at the edge of town. Now thick with oaks and cedar elm trees—and all the underbrush that comes with them—generations of junior explorers had worn a labyrinth of paths and crafted dozens of hideaways in their midst. Whether the woods were labeled 'magical kingdom', 'alien planet', or 'war-torn village', the trees were picked to serve as friend or foe. If Ivy got to name the game, they'd shelter knights and princesses battling for their queen.

Before leaving the house every day, Ivy Jean crossed her heart and promised her father she wouldn't even put a toe in the creek unless other kids were there.

"A person can drown in a teaspoon of water," he'd remind her like clockwork. Even though she could swim well since age four, Vincent said the solemn promise was a rule of play.

Her brother always called their father "Vincent," but only between the two of them, never to their father's face or in public. Wade cautioned that Vincent was "our elder, a war veteran, and generally deserving of respectful address by his children." She'd told him he sounded like Jem speaking of his daddy, Atticus Finch, in her favorite movie, *To Kill a Mockingbird*, and Wade had given her an all-business frown.

Wade William was Ivy Jean's only sibling. When she was three and he was eight, their mother suddenly died, so when it came to things that mattered only to them, the impersonal reference to Vincent not only seemed natural, but necessary. Discussions between her and Wade were private, after all. They were a team. Obedience to the Vincent Code proved it.

But since her brother up and joined the army, Vincent had gotten pure-D weird. It had been a drizzly morning in March when they'd watched Wade climb on the Greyhound bus that'd take him to Fort Bliss, Alabama. *A place called Bliss filled with tanks and guns*, she'd laughed. Wade had called it irony.

From that day on, it seemed their tenderhearted, if stern and absent-minded, father had transformed into some mean old Scrooge. He constantly snapped like a wounded dog she couldn't predict anymore. He muttered to his newspapers and carped about what they said. And he argued with her about the stupidest stuff.

She chewed the sweet end of a wild oat, concluding that Julie wasn't going to show and pondering feelings of lonesomeness. Her brother might be friendless in the Army camp, just like her there in Prosperity, and that made her sad. She hoped her letters were enough to help because, for some reason, Vincent didn't write his own letters to Wade. Instead he'd just scribble a note at the end of hers. Sometimes Ivy Jean wished for more family.

Sitting up, she put her sneakers back on. They were the dry-goods store's version of Keds, but Vincent promised that her next pair would be the real things. Not that it would matter. She'd still feel awkward and tall.

Julie must be opting for Photoplay magazine and phone calls with boys, Ivy thought. Ivy liked celebrity gossip okay, but thoughts about what boys were thinking or saying about her caused distressing pressure on her chest. And no sooner had Wade left than she had gotten her period. Vincent nearly blew a gasket at that news, and she had to agree: it's an icky, life-changing process. And now she was supposed to get boobs, too? She looked down at the front of her shirt and frowned.

What does Vincent know about that?

Ivy Jean was a product of the Atomic Age. That meant being plugged into troublesome adult matters almost constantly, and it was why she liked playing at the creek so much. Bomb shelters and red phones and real people gunned down on television were everyday things. *Everything* could change in the blink of an eye. Like the president getting shot in Dallas last fall.

My own mother got shot in Dallas!

The stories weren't related, but the subject matter made her long for excitement of a friendlier nature. Get her mind off exploding bombs and invasions in Florida.

She stood and decided to go home for lunch. As she crossed through a sorghum field, the sweet summer air around her went still, like they say happens when storms are brewing a twister. Ivy Jean looked up to find just one dark little cloud parked between her and the sun.

TWO

Haines

DAHL HOUSE, BODEN, TEXAS

Life at Tucker's ranch agreed with Haines and Bella, although it took them several months to get there. It was June now and assassination matters in Dallas weren't much clearer, but Haines felt further away from that, and all of the "old" life, every day.

After the president's murder that awful Friday, he had taken to immediate radio silence and disappeared, the same as any operative within a day's drive of Dallas had, unless they had a clear, official purpose to be around. All the questions and finger pointing demanded it. Being recognized by Horace Ortiz during the motorcade might have been coincidence, but having also seen Gilroy and other known guns around the city made Texas a hot zone while the smoke cleared.

Haines had used a non-Company-issued passport, made his way on civilian airways to islands in the Caribbean he'd read about and, for the first time ever, slipped off the Company grid.

Implications of his coincidental presence in Dealey Plaza didn't materialize into any detectable signs of trouble while he was in the islands. For a couple of months he'd fished the remote Abaco chain with a local crew, waiting for facts to emerge that never did, and thought of Texas and Bella every day.

While watching Kennedy's funeral on television in his room, Haines didn't stifle tears when the riderless horse passed, in its slow, prancing progression behind the caisson; the president's boots turned backward in the stirrup. Nothing said fallen hero like the riderless horse.

Though he was what seemed to be worlds away from reality, Jack Ruby's cold-blooded murder of the President's alleged assassin shocked the deepest corners of the globe. Distraction drama was a familiar ruse to Haines, but the average American seemed to be buying it. With Lee Oswald's demise, Haines knew they both were fall guys and all hope for a solvable crime had vanished. There could never be a trial to prove, or disprove, the "lone" gunman's crime.

The small hotel where Haines had taken a room served breakfast on the veranda. It was his favorite hour of the day when he could linger over coffee and the newspaper. One morning, a personals ad in the *New York Journal-American* caught his eye:

```
KODIAKOHNINEOH: Job waits. Sunny here.
```

It had to be Tucker, trying to track him down, Haines had thought.

But it could be Gilroy.

The same ad had appeared every Monday and Friday in the *Journal-American*. One night late in January he'd gotten drunk, the first time since Dallas that he'd tied one on, and in that weak moment he'd called his old friend to answer the "ad."

Finding out Tucker was, in fact, responsible was a huge relief. The ranch was more than ready to stock, he'd told Haines. "For calving in the spring we've got to get some beasts having sex, chop chop."

Tucker had pitched it well and Haines was sorely tempted to come back to reality. He'd not allowed much thinking about their plans or his decision to leave the Company since the assassination. Everything had changed with that.

"It's time to stink things up with some cow shit," Tucker had pled. "Let's get this show on the road."

Haines laughed at his friend's way with words, but he'd withheld enthusiasm and asked for more time. Then he'd filled a string of long days dragging nets while purposeful measuring filled his mind.

First, before ever setting a compass on Tucker's ranch, he'd need to set wheels in motion to officially retire from the Company. Stateside was just a mess in his circles. He could deal with questions from Company management, or the law, because his reasons for being in Dallas were not relevant to the Kennedy case. But if there'd been a conspiracy to kill the United States President, inside job or outside job, an agent with knowledge of how such things could happen, who was in Dallas to see it go down, was in danger. All clues and supporting evidence had to be snuffed, completely erased in the case of conspiracy, prosecution simply could not happen. The signs of walking the cat—code for covering up a mess—were easily recognizable to Haines, even in the establishment press; he just didn't know who, or why…yet.

If the mob had been behind Kennedy's killing, and they knew Haines had been in the crowd, he'd be a fool to reappear. Same story if it were the Company's doing. Speculation was all over the map, though, and Haines didn't know what theories to believe. A pesky voice in his head hissed *inside job*. Otherwise they'd have gotten to the bottom of it by now. Some staunch and fearless reporter would nail it; someone would talk.

Unless James Angleton was in charge…

Angleton led the counter intelligence division—the man invented smoke and mirrors. If those inside Angleton's tiny nucleus were the only humans who knew, and if they were behind the sanitizing, it might be kept quiet.

Soon after the hit on Oswald, when he'd read about Johnson's effort at settling the matter legally, Haines had heard another nail pounded into the coffin of true events. Chief Justice Earl Warren would preside, giving the situation judicial legitimacy and an eponymous label. But when Haines had seen the Company names of Allen W. Dulles and George Bush attached, it meant to him this Warren Commission of government insiders was the bait. Those walking the cat, the clueless agents out there blurring lines and fouling paths backward, were performing the switch. *Classic.*

All the more reason for Haines to exit his Company employ.

After measuring and weighing for a few more weeks, Haines had finally sat down and telephoned his superior at CIA headquarters.

"Haines. What have you been up to?"

"Hunting big game in the Rockies, up in Canada," Haines had lied. "Still there, in fact, and it's damn cold."

He had already decided any plans for settling in Texas were his business only. He'd fished for a mention of names. "Tragic about Kennedy. What do we know outside the newspapers?"

"Not much. I don't see it as our case."

"Do we have people on it?"

"I suppose, but nobody's talking to me about it."

Haines had detected impatience rather than evasion in his superior's words and supposed the Company wanted the matter settled like everybody else. He then got around to asking for official release from service, and by the time he had ended the call, his retirement paperwork was underway.

With his official departure arranged, Haines reasoned that lying low at Tucker's ranch was about as effective as in the Caribbean. His first day on the job as foreman was St. Patrick's Day. A lucky charm if ever there was one.

Tucker intended for the ranch—Dahl House, as it was called—to prosper. Everything the boss promised came through, backed by serious cash. Breed and origin decisions took more than one coin toss to settle, but the first steers were led to pasture less than two weeks after Haines arrived. Heifers were due that Tuesday and, with gestation being ten months, if they mated now the first calves would show up in April next year, when pastureland was lush. The timing was perfect.

Settled into the bunkhouse and loving his fresh start, Haines took a few measures regarding his job change. He'd always maintained a network of people across the country who'd helped him manage personal business—usually lawyers in small towns who had no idea who he really was or why he picked them, and who didn't care as long as payment was prompt. A P.O. box in Waco held his last bit of paperwork from CIA headquarters in Langley, arriving via law office in Watertown, SD, including a deposit slip for his final paycheck. It had been a sweet moment fetching that.

Also, just in case, he had reconnected with one more person who might prove useful. Henry Moss was a former Company guy who'd defected from CIA to the National Security Agency, or NSA, four years ago. Moss was the closest human after Tucker to being trusted as a friend. In 1959 they had teamed for eight weeks in Kuwait, helping the Brits through a tense period, and they'd gotten to know each other well. Moss now operated out of Fort Hood, a sprawling Army installation thirty miles south.

One night they met up to talk, smoking a bunch of cigarettes and drinking coffee from a thermos. Younger by a decade, Moss's tall good looks, blond hair and blue eyes never seemed to age, and Haines was pleased to see him.

Being the strong, silent type, Moss fit well with the NSA, the "listeners." They were the defense agency keeping the president plugged into communications, foreign and domestic. The men trusted each other and shared stories. Haines asked about goings on in Dallas after the assassination.

"Chaos reigned for weeks. Three consecutive and connected murders will cause some chaos, never mind one being the president."

Haines remembered a street cop named Tippit was the third killing, also supposedly Oswald's deed. "It's no wonder they had trouble deciding who caught the cases."

"The place crawled with law enforcement pros from all levels of the food chain, tripping over each other, all of them proclaiming they were in charge. Case management didn't exist, and most efforts at it were a humiliating embarrassment."

"Contaminating evidence and statements along the way," Haines knew. "Jesus, what a mess. Are they ever going to make sense of it?"

"The White House wants it accepted that Oswald did it; time to move on. The establishment press appears to be in agreement. There's just too much queer about it, though, relevant questions that have no answers, and some bulldogs out there won't let it die. One group of investigators actually making a bit of progress is the street reporter crowd, believe it or not," Moss said. "We've got a couple guys in Dallas—'investigative journalists.'"

Haines routinely checked his news sources and scrubbing activity in Dallas seemed ongoing. "One of the suburban papers suggests the number of seemingly small and "odd coincidences" that dead end a promising lead is alarming."

"No shit. It's got to be an impossible task by now for anybody actually investigating what went down. Here's an example: Drunken nightclub patron, known sot, tells a reporter how one or two hours before the assassination, he's arrested and driven to the police station. Turns out his arresting officer, and patrol car driver, was Officer J.D. Tippit." Moss paused for emphasis but Haines didn't get it. "Sitting beside him in the squad car was Jack Ruby."

Haines got it.

"The old sot saw Tippit and Ruby on television and started talking about it with people at work—"

"—Which is how the reporter picked it up," Haines finished.

Both men reached for the thermos, and Haines poured. "Eventually, DPD brought the guy back in. He said they put him in a room by himself, then two Dallas big wigs he could name, ordered him to forget about it."

Haines considered the significance of this.

"Forget it or be arrested on narcotics charges they'd make stick," Moss added. "Poor old drunk hasn't been seen talking to anybody since."

"Dead?"

Moss shrugged. "We may never know. No other Tippit-Ruby connection has surfaced."

The same kind of stories involving various law agencies continued "off-the-record" through the last of the thermos dregs. Haines had forgotten how entertaining and smart Moss was and, although it sounded like an elaborate movie script, it was pretty clear pertinent statements and leads to prosecutorial evidence were being systematically removed or contaminated.

But who's behind it?

That question lingered in the back of his mind while he worked the ranch but, overall, he found it remarkably easy to separate his life from the outside world and immerse himself in country living. He looked forward to the day when news of Dallas didn't matter anymore.

When a stud arrived for Bella, it was even easier to stay present. He was a huge, frisky chestnut from southern Missouri, further proof that Tucker Massey intended to put power behind every piece of his operation; right down to the horses his staff rode. Named

Blade, the horse came from extraordinary workhorse lineage and had been a pleasant surprise to look at. Haines would change his name if he could, finding the B pairing too cutesy, but sweet, golden Bella warmed to the stallion's energetic overtures right away. They made a pretty picture out in the pasture, nuzzling over clover.

Tucker's ranch truly could turn out to be the peaceful and fulfilling future Haines longed for. He owned a library card for the first time in twenty years and could name all the spring flowers on the hillsides.

Every dawn, he felt less like a spy in hiding.

THREE

Vincent

PROSPERITY, TEXAS

Vincent Pritchard didn't mean to spin gravel off the driveway when he left for work. Neighbors notice that kind of thing and talk. No doubt he owed it to a constant sense of life spinning out of control. He'd forgotten how to start the day expecting good things.

Tall and slight, Vincent never wore a hat or sunglasses, and the growing slope above his brow freckled early in summer. He was usually quick to smile but felt overwhelmed lately and mostly grimaced. Parenting issues weighed heavy on his shoulders, the same as if he carried around a sack of cement. That morning, harsh words with his youngest, Ivy Jean, had added guilt to the usual churn of unpleasantness.

The bank where he worked was only a two-minute drive away and he should have just walked. It might have helped him shake off the bad mood. Driving slowly, he noticed an old wood fence by the road looking like it might collapse under the weight of honeysuckle blooms, so he leaned his head out the open window and drew a deep breath of the powerful, sweet fragrance.

Vincent and his children lived on what everyone in Prosperity called "Creek Road" because it skirted the western boundary of town, running parallel to a tributary branch of Buckeye Creek. The road turned toward the highway at the center of town, where First Cattlemen's Bank sat waiting. He'd driven exactly five-eighths of one mile.

Stomach nerves had him swilling milk of magnesia out of a bottle from the glove compartment of the Pontiac. He parked and, turning his back to the building, pulled another chalky dose from the distinctive blue container. Weren't children supposed to get easier and less troubling as they grew up?

But no, two weeks ago, Vincent learned that his only son and firstborn, Wade William, had orders for Vietnam. President Lyndon Johnson had steadily and sneakily escalated U.S. involvement there, committing more and more ground troops to "the conflict." Johnson and his cronies were motivated entirely by greed; they manufactured weapons, for Christ's sake. Right in Fort Worth, thousands of new fighter jets were in development, at the taxpayers' expense. Johnson had turned away from Kennedy's course of non-aggression, given big oil its depletion allowance, and the Military Industrial Complex was getting even richer on what would soon be called a wartime economy.

Vincent belched and straightened on leaving the car, taking regular strides to the side door of the bank in case anybody was watching. If he wasn't mindful, his body tilted out of habit, compensating for pain where he stored some shrapnel from a hand-grenade explosion in World War II.

The war of *his* generation.

But this was Wade's generation and the boy had enlisted without a single word of warning. Zero discussion. That had hurt almost as bad as the act itself.

Vincent used his key to enter the windowless door and went about his morning routine as usual, but his mind was on other things, like poor little Ivy Jean. She was closing the gap to womanhood so fast and the worrisome truth of that had invited the idea of re-marriage to come up more than a few times. Thankfully, common sense returned pretty quick and convinced him that trying to fix his daughter up with a mother wasn't a smart reason to get married. But the thought of Ivy having menstrual cycles and wearing a bra, giggling over the prospect of romance? For God's sake. It left him gasping for air. Especially with Wade no longer at home to tip the scales in their favor.

Vincent fought serious doubts either of his children was ready to face the world outside of Prosperity, to be away from him. He was desperate to keep his family together and stomach flames accompanied the voice in his head taunting, *it's too late*.

The bank's monthly board meeting kept Vincent in motion all day, the same as every second Monday of every month. Responsible for a succession of reports, he scoured ledgers and compiled numbers, up and down from his desk, in and out of the vault, back and forth from the file cabinets, working straight through lunch. He did not attend the board meetings himself, but he re-verified all data after the secretary formatted his work and typed the summaries.

It was just a normal day at the office.

Until 2:50 p.m. when, like a specter born of vapor, Carla Summers stepped out of his past and appeared in front of him. It shook him, literally. Those ageless silvery eyes, in stark contrast to her glossy black waves, bored into him. Nine years. It thrilled every nerve in him to see her again.

Carla and his late wife, Gwendolyn, had been like sisters, inseparable since their first day as giggling freshmen at TCU in Fort Worth. Bashful, soft-spoken Vincent had tried to sell them basketball tickets on campus and they'd adopted him as their buddy and protector. The three of them became family. World War II had split them all up for a while, but their relationships somehow endured. He and Gwendolyn had fallen in love through letters and, right after the war ended in 1945, she'd agreed to marry him. They all finished school in Fort Worth but took jobs in Dallas and settled there. Carla had lived with them off and on. She'd dated but never seemed to take romance seriously… and then she had gotten mixed up with Vincent's younger half brother, Tucker Jack Massey.

Vincent loathed Tucker's brash confidence, his wealth, and all he stood for. When Carla became his mistress, it had seemed to trigger a whole series of fucked-up events.

Gwen had been killed, by accident, during a bank robbery in 1955 and, soon after that, Vincent removed his children from the city they'd always known as home, excised the influence of meddlesome, intrusive family, and re-crafted a more insular family existence for them. Carla had been perfectly willing to leave Tucker then, and had pleaded tearfully for Vincent to let her move in and help with the children. She was willing to walk away from the sorry asshole, no strings, but it hadn't mattered to Vincent.

He'd rejected her along with everybody else.

"I've missed you so much, Vincent," Carla whispered as she hugged him.

It felt surprisingly good to hold her, almost like holding Gwen again. Vincent broke the embrace at that thought and looked around warily. Nobody in First Cattlemen's Bank seemed to have noticed them, but there was no need to start gossip either, so he nodded to a chair by his desk. "Have a seat."

His cheeks flushed as he remembered Carla had come up vividly during one of his remarry-for-Ivy episodes. And there she was in the flesh. In all her classic, beautiful flesh, as if he'd conjured her up. He fetched them coffee and fumbled with sugar cubes, gaping openly as he watched her every move. She caught him and blushed.

"Christ, Vincent. Did you think I was dead or something?"

"No," he managed. "God, Carla, it's great to see you. What are you doing here? Finally had enough of the big bad city?"

Guilt struck him silent. She would have left the city nine years ago for him and his kids. She tilted her head and smiled. He mirrored the motion, open affection on his face. The awkward moment passed.

"How are the kids?" she said.

"Every bit the handful they were nine years ago." He suppressed an urge to ask, *How do I make sure they're ready?*

She looked at her lap, then up at his smiling face. "Can you get away for a bit?"

He blinked in surprise and she pretended not to notice.

"I'm dying to hear everything, Vincent. We have scads to catch up on and I have to get back to Dallas soon."

There was a tension in her voice—he could hear it. He wasn't sure what, but something was going on. "Sure, sure. We should have time together."

The relief on her face made the final decision for him. His board reports were ready enough. "There's a roadside park with a covered picnic table just off the highway." He pointed his thumb. "Two miles south. All these years, I've never once seen picnickers there." He checked the clock. "Fifteen minutes?"

• • •

A shiny new Corvette at the roadside park almost made him bypass their meeting spot, but when he saw Carla wave, he quickly pulled over, thinking his boy would go nuts for that car. Vincent shut the door of his old Pontiac—it was nearly new the last time he saw her.

He sat down at the concrete table across from her as she fidgeted, a smile on her face the whole time. A slight breeze lifted her hair away from her cheeks and she looked like an ad for some kind of beauty product. He'd forgotten how thick her eyelashes were and that she never freckled like Ivy Jean and Gwen did in summer. They always wore a tiny splash of spots across their noses. He smiled at the thought of Ivy Jean. *Will my little girl remember Carla?*

He spoke first. "Did you know Wade joined the Army?"

His boy would remember Carla; they had been bicycle buddies.

"I did!" she said. Her face lit up, then darkened. "Tucker said he might be shipped to Vietnam."

Of course Tucker was still in the picture.

"You must be worried sick, Vincent."

He nodded, wondering how the hell his estranged brother knew about Wade's orders for Asia. After a few minutes of small talk, Carla seemed to collect herself, as though preparing to leave, then looked him straight in the eye.

"I'm having Tucker's baby."

Vincent felt like she'd punched him right where the shrapnel still curled around his gut muscle. It didn't go over so well inside his head either. Disappointment, old hostility and hard-to-admit jealousy fought to dominate his reaction. And somewhere in there, a sense of insult wormed around over the private information fueling the gossip mill. But he forced friendly words out of his mouth and reached for her hand.

"It'll work out. You're a natural mother," he said.

"Tucker expects it to just go away."

It meaning the pregnancy, he supposed.

"He thinks it's my fault and expects me to 'handle it.'" She made quotation marks in the air with her fingers before reaching into her pocket for a tissue and blowing her nose.

"He threatened to leave me."

Both of them knew Tucker well enough not to be too fussed over mean words coming out of his mouth. And *of course* it was her fault. Nothing was ever Tucker's fault.

"I can't have another abortion, Vincent. I just can't!"

A dam burst inside Carla as she cried, and he pushed aside the shock that had shot through him at the word "another." He moved to her side of the table and held her around the shoulders. "Shh..."

Tucker, you fucking fool.

"I don't want him anymore," she blubbered on Vincent's shirt. Her face rested on his chest for a bit, then she sat up and blew her nose again. "I don't care what he does."

Several quiet minutes passed, then, sensing more emotion building, Vincent released her and leaned back on his elbows. Brilliant pinks and oranges were shaping up over the western hills. He felt her turning to face him.

"Vincent…Will you marry me?"

She spoke timidly, and his head whipped around, intensely wishing he'd dreamed it. Crocodile tears rimmed her pleading eyes. She eked out a smile. "It could be a sensible arrangement."

After starting to object a few times, Vincent listened. Yes, he had feelings for Carla. He loved her like family, but could they be happy being *married*? Whole words had trouble forming while he tried to get his mind around the practicality she approached the proposition with.

"Let me be sure I get this," Vincent said. "You think we can be a couple, a family, and raise this baby together, along with getting Ivy Jean through her teenage years…"

And Tucker?

"I'm afraid of bringing up a kid alone, Vincent. I'm not made of the same stuff you are. Besides, the Russians could obliterate us all in our sleep tomorrow. Why not reach for some security?"

Vincent drew in a breath. It was a valid point, but he knew better. "It won't work like you want it to, Carla. You know that."

And, just like that, he'd cut her deeply again. Instead of being open to possibilities, or even joking about her ideas, he'd discouraged it. He may as well have dismissed her like some outrageous clown. He felt awful. The whole episode had been a jolt.

Less than two beats later, she spoke again. "You're right," she said with a little laugh. "Saying it out loud makes the whole idea seem preposterous."

Her toothy smile and unwavering eyes put him at ease, then she stood and picked up her handbag.

"Can I come back and see Ivy Jean soon?"

FOUR

Tucker

<u>Dallas, Texas</u>

Most of the married men Tucker knew kept a string of women on the side, but for nearly a decade he'd kept only one—Carla Summers. Women came easy to him, like everything else, but he'd been faithful to her, more or less, all those years.

The gorgeous nut had gone too far this time.

They stood in the living room of her apartment in north Dallas, a cheerful place decorated with tasteful shades of white and sunny accents of yellow. Hundreds of light-hearted and unforgettable moments had happened there. When she wasn't pregnant.

Tucker had stopped by on his way to work in a frisky mood and was greeted by her snarling one. They were gaining steam with the same unreasonable argument about her keeping the baby.

"I'm leaving. We can talk about this later," he said, heading for the door.

"Wait. I need to tell you something."

He heard the stress in her voice and turned back.

"That beefy slob came back yesterday, asking me where you were during the motorcade."

Family connections to Lyndon Johnson had earned Tucker unwanted attention lately with some tenacious investigators and reporters. The beefy slob she spoke of was from the Department of Justice. He stood facing her. "And?"

"He said he didn't believe that I'd written about our early lunch that day and demanded my books and—"

"—Books?" he interrupted her, holding his breath.

"My journal," she said, rolling her eyes. "You know I write, Tucker, and it's none of their business."

"You said *books*, as in plural, Carla. Like secret diaries?" Tucker's mind reeled in multiple directions. She had no idea what kind of ammo she'd just given the enemy. Those guys *looked* like comedy cops, but their intention was to make trouble.

Frustration fueled anger and he attacked a neat line of yellow pillows on Carla's couch. Clutching them like hand grenades, he tore and twisted 'til one blew its wispy guts around in a childish display of idiocy. He glared at his mistress, sitting coolly in the chair, clutching one intact pillow, which he swore shivered. Carla stared out the window, unruffled. Worn loose, her black mane hid some of her face, along with the defiant look he knew was there.

He clicked off the television and stood over her. While he wasn't leading man handsome, Tucker had a thick head of hair, a formidable build, and the confident style of a wealthy man.

"Why did you keep this from me?"

She squirmed in the chair and glanced at him. "Because my writings are private, Tucker. You should get that. My life, my business? I've written a lot of things I don't intend to share."

No doubt many pages full of every sorry word she could dream up about him forbidding her pregnancies.

Did she really write up a tale about them being together during the motorcade? It would help defuse things, but if she wrote about them partying with the White House guys the night before, it could be embarrassing—and possibly lethal.

"Listen to me. There is so much tension in Dallas right now, and my family is being scrutinized because of our ties to Lyndon. Something like your diary in the wrong hands could ruin me."

Tucker's life was getting complicated. Earlier last fall, because his father arranged it, he'd been recruited by then Vice President Johnson's personal security chief, for an on-call, off-the-grid kind of arrangement—a secret squad of operatives, qualified men, who were unquestionably loyal to Johnson.

Then Tucker's old man had died, and while his passing had thrust Tucker into powerful business circles, Kennedy's death had shoved him onto the path of amazing opportunity. Lyndon Baines Johnson, his father's long time crony, had been jettisoned to supreme commander of the land. It could only mean good things for Tucker.

"Did you write about the night before the assassination, with the Secret Service guys?"

Carla sneered for a moment and didn't answer, but he wasn't sure what it meant. He'd been asked to arrange some entertainment. Involving her and a few choice, playful friends, had cost him a grand in cash, a diamond bracelet, and a week's worth of the silent treatment.

Since the assassination, Tucker had been interviewed six times by five different sets of "official" lawmen, each citing as reason his, or his father's, relationship to President Johnson. It was a confusing sequence of meetings, but none had felt overtly threatening, until lately. Now a string of creeps was digging around and Tucker had accidentally told one pushy investigator he'd been with Carla during the hit.

Not my smartest move.

In truth, November 22 had him serving as extra security around the VP's car, blocks from the sniper's nest, armed with a walkie-talkie and focused on persons herding around the fourth limousine when it passed a single intersection. He had nothing to hide, but Johnson's private squad was off-the-record—it did not exist.

"People are dying, you know," Tucker said, to make a point. "People who only have the slightest insight as to what went down, even if what they heard or saw don't matter."

She rolled her eyes. The air conditioner kicked in and her expensive perfume hit his nose.

"I mean it," he added, trying to ignore the rich scent. "A reporter doing a story on Jack Ruby is dead, and so is a stripper from his club who overheard discussions about a hit. And the number of deaths is growing. Hell, a city bus ran over a woman who knew something about Oswald's activities before work that day—are you listening to me?"

He could see she wasn't. He tucked his shirt back into his trousers, checked his appearance in the wall mirror, and said to her back, "Hand your book over to the man, Carla. It could be accepted as proof that I was here with you. I'll call in favors and keep it quiet, but I want the goons satisfied…and gone."

He spoke in a manner afforded influential men, and it wasn't an act. She didn't grasp the predicament, and it just pissed him off that she'd remain so obstinate—especially if her diary really was harmless.

Then the minx lifted her chin and snarled, "You don't want me to have a family of my own."

What? He sighed aloud. *Fucking pregnancy swings.*

He didn't have time for another battle over babies. Tucker's lips flattened. "You know that's not it. Your goddamn timing sucks."

"Tucker, I'm only pregnant, and this might be my last chance at motherhood. Maybe it's blessed timing," she challenged. "I can keep it quiet."

Tucker Massey and his family—not to mention his wife's family—were frequently in the newspapers and, lately, often on television. Joanne was a brilliant public relations strategist and, like him, felt LBJ owed their family something after Tucker discovered a ledger his father left behind, a secret accounting of tens of millions of dollars funneled to Johnson causes over thirty years.

Joanne steered their image matters and had already started pestering him about a post in D.C. She'd sternly warned him that appearing squeaky clean was imperative with the gossipers and the press. Negative publicity could be their downfall.

Of course, sensationalized news was all the rage and mongers skulked everywhere in the whole damn country now, disguised as legitimate press. And even if "they" would let a commonplace extramarital fling slide, illegitimate children were hot property. And *secret,* illegitimate children? That kind of knowledge was for sale at very high prices.

Carla's getting pregnant had been reckless. It floored him she wouldn't take the new birth-control pill. The greatest gift to mankind. *And population problem? Solved.*

"Were you wearing your diaphragm when this baby was conceived?" He snapped the dig at her. She'd been custom fitted for the best money could buy, courtesy of Tucker himself, but he knew blaming her would only inflame the row.

Carla stood and faced him. "I'll slit my wrists, Tucker Massey, so help me God, before I get another abortion for you."

"You know better than to play the suicide card," he warned, moving closer so they were nose to nose.

He'd been to war. Offing yourself was cheating.

"I'll abort the thing myself," she threatened and sat again. "Might as well rupture everything up in there while I'm at it, so we don't have this problem again."

Tucker didn't like where things were headed and tried to reason with her. "Listen, Carla, I love you. You know that." He actually crouched beside her chair. "You just cannot have a baby now. It's mine too, and I have a say."

She pushed at him and stood up again. "You idiot! You had your say when you didn't wear a rubber."

Her pretty face scrunched up. "I might get married," she said, adding softer, "I already asked an old friend."

Tucker wasn't going to take the bait on that one. He gathered his hat and jacket, knowing boundaries were being crossed.

"Tucker, you know I will not just go away. We aren't done talking about this."

"Don't threaten me," he said, tossing a glare at her as he slammed the door.

FIVE

Tucker

A day later, Tucker sat in his office, still brooding. Late-afternoon sun blazed through the glass of his giant window, thoroughly heating the darkly paneled space. From the fourteenth floor, his office overlooked the Trinity River's east fork—pricey real estate. But despite refrigerated air conditioning, the room was only pleasant until two or three o'clock on summer afternoons. Tucker shed his jacket, tossing his cufflinks on the desk, and rolled up his shirtsleeves.

The intercom buzzed, and his wife Joanne was announced. He took the call.

"What's up?" he said.

"Our delinquent daughter got expelled again, Tucker. We're at the ranch."

Tucker rubbed his forehead, confused. The last he'd heard, Joanne was shopping in Houston. She and Debra weren't supposed to go to the ranch until next week, after Deb's semester ended at the posh academy in San Antonio.

"The righteous Catholics at that damn school wouldn't let her stay another day," Joanne declared, wound-up and edgy. "Taking her back to Dallas seemed pointless, so we just came to Dahl House. We're just about done moving in. You're all that's missing."

"Good God. What did she do this time?" Tucker stared at the calendar on his desk and alarm crawled under his skin. It was Thursday. He and Carla had planned to spend the weekend at the ranch. That was pre-fight, but they'd never called it off. His wife and daughter weren't supposed to be there.

For two years, Joanne and the contractors at the ranch didn't work Saturday or Sunday, so every chance he and Carla had, they'd sneak off for a weekend in the country. They'd seen this weekend as their final chance to play before the family moved in for eight weeks.

"I don't want to spoil the surprise," his wife answered finally, "but it involves a motorcycle hoodlum, her trashy mouth, and smoking. And I'm not talking about Winston's."

Tucker sighed. His little girl had always been a feisty one, but he had to admit over the last year or so she had become increasingly disturbed and angry.

He half listened to Joanne ranting about Debra's embarrassing conduct and the "mortifyingly scandalous position" it put her in. Instead, he was trying to figure where his mistress might be right then, hoping she hadn't headed out of the city yet.

Joanne demanded he join them immediately.

"I'll call you back," was the only response he could think of.

"Listen to me, Tucker. This is not about your precious image. Or mine. Debra needs attention from someone with authority, and I mean someone she isn't pushing to commit filicide." She didn't wait for him to challenge her, and she wasn't gentle hanging up.

Any intended humor from his wife escaped him. She liked to cut his balls while she had him on the phone, then ring off in a huff, and her favorite ball-cutting topic was his ineffectiveness as a parent.

He lit a cigarette before picking up the phone again. The escalation of yesterday's fight with Carla still made his stomach roil. She was plenty pissed at him too, and probably wouldn't go to the ranch for a million dollars right now, but he had to make sure. He'd just call to let her know Joanne and Deb were there and officially call their plans off.

No surprise, the line was busy. He kept trying off and on during the next hour while reading through a brief, and taking and placing some business calls. After so many attempts to reach Carla though, the busy signal felt intentional. When another hour passed with no luck, he figured she'd taken her phone off the hook. *Playing fucking games.*

He stood to leave the office and drive by her apartment, even more pissed that she'd made the detour necessary. Gathering some work he'd take to the ranch, he considered who else he could send over to Carla's place in his stead, when a call came through on his private line. He willed her to be on the other end and spare him the trouble.

"Stan here," a deep voice said.

D.C. calling. Tucker sat back down. "Hello, Stan."

Secretly representing Lyndon Baines Johnson, president of the United fucking States, "Stan" spoke in familiar, chatty code. He requested Tucker's participation in "an event," á la an off-the-record mission, under the orders of "management," meaning you-know-who. There was no turning this one down. At 17:30, Tucker would be boarding a private jet out of gate five at Love Field. Further orders awaited his arrival in the great state of Mississippi, of all places.

A phone call from Stan was always a thrill, even if it did disturb his private life sometimes, though Tucker's assignments had largely been mundane—document retrievals actually, from a law office over in Fort Worth. But each call from Stan since Kennedy's assassination brought an extra surge of excitement because it put him one step closer to Johnson's inner circle, and maybe a post in his administration.

Finding Carla, getting secure word to her to not go to the ranch, just went critical. He'd be gone a few days and needed that detail cleared before departing.

He tried her number again, and this time it went straight to *beep, beep, beep* before he even dialed the last digit. He almost threw the chunk of plastic at the wall.

Instead, he called his secretary in to take a few memos and get her up to speed on cases requiring attention. After dismissing her, he unlocked a drawer at the bottom of a wall cabinet and removed a wide-mouth, leather bag. He had just over an hour before the plane left Love Field.

Eager to jet off on a mission for the president, he pushed worries about reaching Carla away as much as he could. He'd tried to reach her, and it hadn't worked—there was nothing more he could do just then. He tossed a carton of Lucky Strikes from his credenza in the bag and tried to remember where he'd put the phone number for the ranch. He'd better call Joanne. Most likely he'd be gone at least two nights, and in all cases he'd be under strict radio-silence, unplugged from the outside world.

His intercom buzzed, and Joanne was announced on the line again.

Evidently one of her pills had kicked in because her voice purred. "Tucker, there are a few things I want you to bring to the ranch."

He explained he wasn't coming yet, and she didn't hide her annoyance. After Lyndon became President, there wasn't any way to avoid letting her in on at least the skeletal details of his private security gig. Especially since she already knew about the ledger he'd found.

"Do you think this will finally be the one?" She meant an assignment that would bring him into LBJ's personal sphere, or at least result in a personal phone call from the man. A fair question, considering, but she sounded like his manhood was at stake.

"I couldn't say. You know how this works."

"I still don't understand why you don't just call up the president and speak to him in your artfully candid, Massey way—"

"—Honestly, Joanne," he cut her off. "Don't you think a million people are lined up for a piece of him right now?"

Some days she was just too pushy.

"Our daughter is avoiding consequence of her rotten behavior again," she whined. "You've got to get in the middle of this, Tucker. She is out of control."

He felt the gnarly finger of blame and forced himself not to react. "I know. I'll be there as soon as I can."

Tucker begged off with Joanne again, and begged in his head for Carla to finally pick up her phone and *un*-complicate matters. One last busy signal brought the receiver smashing down, this time so loud his secretary opened the door to check on him, which he angrily waved shut.

From his office closet, he pulled two folded and wrapped dress shirts, continuing to pack for his assignment. Out of the safe under his desk, he took a snub-nosed, holstered revolver, one box of shells, and a fake ID pack.

He would just have to deal with Carla Summers later.

But she's pregnant, crazy, and pissed off. She might show up at the ranch out of spite, or to kiss and make up. Who fucking knew?

From a note card in his wallet, Tucker dialed the number for his foreman, Haines, on the new bunkhouse line. Tucker needed *someone* to keep an eye out for Carla. Tucker let the phone buzz in his ear at least ten times before giving up. Haines could be anywhere on the property.

He rang for his car, picked up his suit coat and travel bag, and looked around the office. A picture of his family sat on the bookshelf near the door and caught his eye.

That's it, he realized suddenly. *Family!*

He sat back down, pleased with a possible stroke of brilliance, and dragged an old dog-eared address book from the back of his middle desk drawer. He picked the receiver up one more time. Squinting at a page in the book, he dialed his half brother's house in small-town Prosperity, Texas.

Vincent sees through bullshit, but I bet he's still soft on Carla.

SIX

Ivy Jean

<u>Prosperity, Texas</u>

The unexpected outburst from the telephone jangled Ivy's nerves. Then her dad stood up so fast that the dining chair he'd been sitting on flew back and hit the wall. Their phone table sat nearby, like everything in their small, tidy house.

```
TELEPHONE BLOWS MAN OFF CHAIR,
      CRACKS HEAD OPEN!
```

For some reason, random headlines flew into her mind all the time lately. Ivy reached over and righted Vincent's chair, wondering who was on the phone.

A stack of newspapers sat on the floor waiting to be read. It occurred to her that, for a man who didn't care to be part of the big wide world, Vincent couldn't get enough reports on it. The *Fort Worth Star Telegram* sat atop the *Dallas Times Herald*. It was a half-day's drive to either one of those cities. He also read the *Wall Street Journal* and the *Washington Post* on weekends, for heaven's sake. No wonder headlines filled her head. Vincent might as well wallpaper the house with the newsprint for how many papers sat around.

Her father kept his back to her and spoke at a low volume. She glanced at the stack of newspapers again. Something was definitely up.

I hope its not bad goddamn news about Wade. She shuddered at the thought.

Not even her brother knew she'd started cussing. To Ivy Jean, certain swear words were exactly right on certain occasions. It also felt good to see shock on the faces of kids at school when a so-called "good girl" started cussing an impressive blue streak. Why it was such a surprise though, Ivy didn't understand. Nuclear bombs could land in the backyard tomorrow and blow all of Texas to kingdom come and they'd never see it coming. *How could anybody say using colorful words was a goddamn sin?*

She hadn't tested her argument on any grown-ups yet.

Ivy looked over at Vincent, still talking softly into the phone, noticing in him the same bony posture and jutting hips that she had.

One more reason to cuss.

Cutting a piece of ham into small morsels, she thought about the unmarried women in their town who might fall for a guy like her father. The gal who owned the beauty shop and Eldon Helmsberger's aunt, who supposedly danced with Vincent at the VFW hall over in Priddy. According to Eldon, his aunt was a real "ooh-la-la babe." It was a rare Saturday night, though, when her father donned cowboy boots and smelled of Old Spice, leaving her with Wade, a jigsaw puzzle, and strict orders about not watching TV all night.

Ivy observed, as he stretched the phone cord as far as it could reach. His raised whisper and stiffened posture wasn't a good sign. He looked over his shoulder at her, clearly annoyed. Ivy started clearing the table, uncomfortable under his surveillance, but dawdled since the pronoun *she* kept cropping up. Ivy mentally squeezed her brain to think why *she* might be in trouble. If any of those brats at school told on her about her cussing, she'd make the kid's miserable life a burning hell.

But maybe the *she* pronoun meant *a woman*.

With a sinking feeling, she remembered that Mrs. Polk, the Swedish lady who kept their house and prepared their suppers, had caught Ivy watching soap operas. Racy TV and magazines—both of which happened to be *excruciatingly* exciting to Ivy Jean—came under a Vincent Pritchard Pet Rule, which meant serious punishment like a real grounding and no chance of early release. Ivy privately figured her father should get used to it, because all she had to do was look around and see that raciness and sex were everywhere.

When Vincent finally hung up, he volunteered nothing. Ivy carried the ham platter into the kitchen, noticing a jittery edge taking up space between them. Without looking at her, he took the dish and scraped the leftover bits in the wastebasket with a frown. Fear crept in, and patience was nowhere in Ivy Jean's chemistry.

"Who was that?" she demanded, gushing out breath she didn't realize she'd held. He tore a piece of tin foil off the box, ignoring her question.

"Have you ever been to a ranch, Ivy Jean?"

She wanted to stomp her foot but resisted the urge. He knew exactly where she'd been in her life. At least the call wasn't about her or Wade, but Vincent didn't have to try to be clever about it. She wasn't stupid.

She sighed. "Whose ranch are we going to and why?"

He opened the refrigerator. "They have a swimming pool and horses," he said, trying to sell the idea. "Could be a real western adventure."

Ivy suppressed an exasperated, but excited, "when do we leave?" Summer had been unbelievably boring so far, and Lord knew she needed a break from Vincent. But her father was not a spontaneous man, especially about trips away from home. She could hope, of course, this meant a *fun* change in him, but it didn't feel right. He was helping with her chore, for one thing. That plus his trying to be sneaky? Something was definitely going on.

"Well, actually, your uncle—my brother, Tucker—invited you to visit."

"You've been talking to Uncle Tucker? When in blazes did this happen?"

"Don't speak like that," he said, pulling out the dishpan from under the sink. He turned the hot-water tap on. Her father considered expressions like *blazes* to be swearing and unladylike, and normally Ivy was careful to be considerate of that since getting in trouble wasn't worth it. She'd *never* cuss in front of him under normal circumstances, but this news had truly stunned her, and her guard had slipped. The only reason she even knew she had an uncle was because Wade had told her.

Ivy pushed her too-long bangs out of her eyes and pressed them behind her ears; put both hands on her hips and glared. "You can't expect me to just say 'oh, that's nice.'"

"I don't know, Ivy Jean. Why not?"

Ivy thought she was getting used to uncharacteristic surprises from her father. Eventually he gave her an explanation, which she knew was incomplete, but she took it to heart. His brother needed help, it was urgent, and meant a few days in Dallas for Vincent… and a dreamy ranch adventure for Ivy…with her wealthy relatives. She'd never in her life felt like somebody's relative besides Wade's sister or Vincent's daughter. It was exciting. But Vincent hated Dallas. *Why would he agree to this?*

Her brows knitted with skepticism. "What kind of help?" she asked.

"That's not important."

Since she was the only family around at the moment, she'd hoped he'd confide in her more. He wouldn't like feeling so unimportant.

"But what's so urgent?"

And what if you don't come back? Momma never came back. What about me then?

She wanted to yell out her fears, but when Vincent's jaw clenched she knew he was done, so she saved herself from going hoarse. A person helping their brother was a good thing, she guessed, no matter what the reason.

"When did y'all get so chummy?" She expected one of his "watch yourself" looks because she sounded sassy, but he surprised her.

"For a long time I've been petty and selfish about matters between me and Tucker," he said. His jaw worked, and she could tell he was chewing the inside of his bottom lip, a definitive sign that Vincent was worried.

"Wade being away, somehow, makes it important for me to try and mend fences," he explained. "Family shouldn't get too far apart."

Ivy shifted her weight. Her father talking about feelings made her uncomfortable. She had little practice with it, and the night had already been too weird. She resolved to do what her father asked and kept the arguments in her head. She'd go along with the western adventure idea, having never been in a backyard swimming pool or on a horse that wasn't just to sit on for pictures.

. . .

In her small and tidy bedroom upstairs, Ivy packed some clothes in a scuffed-up, ancient, silvery-blue suitcase. June bugs whirred outside and attacked her window screens, same as they did every night, and Ivy wished she had pressured her dad for a new swimsuit. Her tank from last year was barely decent the way it fit.

A mother would know that.

Vincent called up to her that it was time to go, and Ivy shoved the last of her things into the case. As they drove away, the single lit window of their kitchen held her gaze from the backseat until the Pontiac rounded a corner and the house disappeared. Ivy recalled a sensation from church camp as slight panic crept in. Whenever her rowboat left the shore, it always took her a while to relax and enjoy the ride. But she always did. Wondering about what lay ahead though, and considering how fast her boring evening had changed, she thought maybe they'd been sucked into an episode of *The Twilight Zone*. This anxiety wasn't as easy to quell.

In the sparsely populated county, their car reached utter darkness in two minutes. Hundreds of bugs splattered dead on their windshield. Both front windows were open, too, so Ivy dug in the suitcase for her sweater, mixed feelings buzzing in her head. The at-first exciting idea of an extended family started to change: Daddy and Wade were her family, and they didn't need outsiders.

Eventually, Vincent turned off the highway and rolled up the windows because of the gritty dust from outside. By the third time he turned their car around on the narrow country roads—a tedious process of back-and-forth maneuvering—it was pitch black and they'd been driving for what seemed like hours looking for the damned ranch. Ivy lost count of how many dirt-road turns they'd taken but felt sure they'd been down the last one twice already.

LOST FAMILY DRIVES OFF BLUFF
IN REMOTE COUNTY

"Seems to me we might be lost," she said. "Haven't you been here before?"

"I haven't seen Tucker or his family in nine years." He turned the big steering wheel and ground the gears, huffing with frustration. "Never been to the ranch."

Ivy could not grasp it; eight years without setting eyes on his own brother? She couldn't imagine not seeing Wade for that long. "Will Tucker be at the ranch?"

Again, the car stopped and Vincent squinted at the impossibly crumpled road map under the dome light. He didn't correct her and ask her to call him Uncle. "No, I told you Tucker was called away, and that's why I'm going to Dallas."

"Then who's at the ranch?"

He put the map aside and drove on.

"Tucker's wife, Joanne. I hear she's fixed the old place up real fancy. They call it Dahl House."

"Like dolls live there?"

He spelled it. "A family name on Joanne's side. She inherited the place a few years back."

Dahl House. Ivy thought just going to a house that had a name promised high adventure. And inherited meant she's an *heiress*. Ivy wondered if Joanne would be kindly like Opie's Aunt Bee on television, or if she'd be a stuck-up snob. In the dark window, she smiled at her own reflection, hoping someday her head would grow into her teeth. They were straight enough, thank goodness, but had seemed to get gigantic overnight.

"Tucker's teenage daughter will be there, too."

At that news, Ivy moved the map and climbed over the seatback. She wanted to hear more about this cousin of hers. Horses, a swimming pool *and* a cousin was promising indeed. Friends at school talked about their cousins all the time and it always felt like she was missing something.

"I remember fiery curls and temper tantrums," he said. "She was six, I think."

Practically grown now, then—fifteen. "What's her name?"

"Debra. I don't remember her middle name." His eyebrows pulled together. "Tucker said she's had some trouble at school. You mind your place, Ivy Jean."

Ivy blew her bangs out of her eyes. "I thought my place was with you."

"You know what I mean. Joanne is pretty tolerant, but don't go assuming Debra's ways."

"What does *that* mean?"

"No daring behavior, Ivy. Okay? You know how to act. Make a good impression."

Ivy tried to imagine a redheaded daredevil, wearing something sequined maybe and prancing around a circus ring. Or maybe Debra was like Samantha's devious cousin Serena from *Bewitched*.

The car slowed again, and Vincent turned onto a road she didn't recognize. They entered a dense, dark spot, thick with cedar trees and tall oaks that seemed alive with noisy insects and tree frogs. Ivy rolled down her window for a better look. All of a sudden, the darkness opened up to a graveled drive that veered left and they were facing a *humongous* house, warmly lit like a beacon of safety. Ivy gasped. It looked like it was straight off the cover of one of those architecture magazines in the library at school, glamorous and looming.

We want a woman with an inheritance like this for Vincent.

A deep porch completely wrapped the square, two-story form, invitingly set with rockers and flowering pots. Ivy stilled a thrill because Vincent might see her approval as permission to not come back.

SEVEN

Haines

DAHL HOUSE RANCH

Haines uncapped a bottle of beer on the opener nailed to the cabinet and stretched out to absorb the most recent events there at the ranch. He sat in the unlit bunkhouse and watched the shadows of movement that the curtains made on the floor as the moonlight and a southerly breeze came in through the open window. His best thinking happened in the dark.

He looked around, squinting. The back end of the barn had been converted to cowboy quarters and still smelled of sawdust, but he didn't mind. He savored a pull from his cold beverage and a store-bought menthol-and-tobacco-leaf cigarette. Though he indulged in no more than five or six a month, he looked forward to each one of them.

He blew out another puff and recalled event number one: Tucker's family arriving unexpectedly the day before.

It was a good thing he'd already opened the main house. He'd been expecting Tucker on Friday, and at first had felt blindsided by the wife and kid showing up like that. Tucker had called later to explain that he'd also been surprised by their arrival. Honestly, though, Haines had concluded by then that it could be nice having other people on the ranch with him.

Event number two: Tucker wouldn't be coming out to the ranch for a while yet. His old friend was angling for presidential favor, it seemed, and wouldn't be able to leave the city for a few more days. Haines gathered it had something to do with the private security outfit he knew Tucker was involved with. Tucker had also mentioned "investigators" of questionable origin hounding him about where he was during the assassination. It was a dangerous time in certain circles. He hoped Tucker kept all antennae alert.

His wife, Joanne, hadn't acted surprised when the house was open and ready for her a week early. More likely she assumed a ready house just happened, like her ladyship returning to the manor, but she'd seemed pleased. He'd actually enjoyed the labor, turning on the utilities and all that. There wasn't regular reason for him to enter the main house, but he loved it when he did. Tucker had asked him to stock the kitchen, so most foodstuffs had been chosen for his taste, but the women had plenty of easy fixings.

Haines had carried some porch furniture outside from a pile in the barn, expensive wicker pieces. He'd hosed everything down and spent time testing out different arrangements in various parts of the deeply shadowed porch. The architecture of Dahl House reminded him of plantation homes in the South Pacific and Hawaii. The porch, or *lanai*, was his favorite spot on the homestead.

Haines savored another draw on his beer.

After setting the furniture, he'd gone back to the feed store where he'd seen flats of pansies for sale. The colorful touches of purple and yellow in the corner urns turned out downright artistic. He had just sat down to take a break when the lady's town car rounded the bend. Caught red-handed, so to speak, he'd stepped to the car to assist, recalling his role as stable boy on the farm.

Slender legs emerged first, then a manicured, extended hand.

"Mr. Haines," she'd said in greeting. Her subtle once-over as she'd stood made him feel oddly unsure.

He'd seen pictures of her in the papers—a classic blonde of Scandinavian descent who came across as regal, a real Grace Kelly sort. Much better looking in person, too. The slightest lift of her brow betrayed her surprise that *Mr.* Haines might be from ethnic descent.

"Tucker said you were a Kentucky horseman with fine lineage," she said in an alluring drawl. "I have kin in Kentucky."

Faint but distinct rounded vowels of a blue blood.

"I grew up at Kilhoran Farm, just south of Shelbyville," he said with perfect, indistinct articulation and a dose of dimpled charm. All Kentucky horse people knew Kilhoran Farm, and Haines's grandfather had served its owner, a revered federal judge, for fifty odd years, eventually retiring as stable master.

She strode past, giving him the eyebrow again. "How fortunate."

Haines started helping the driver unload the bags when a teenage girl emerged from the backseat, yawning. Striking red tresses and a sharp jawline made her instantly recognizable as Tucker's progeny. Still dressed in a schoolgirl uniform, her presence seemed to forewarn of disturbance and contests of will, like a restless filly. Haines hoped that whatever trouble she dished out didn't unsettle the peacefulness of the ranch.

"Daddy didn't tell us you were colored," were the first words Tucker's girl said to him.

Was he being oversensitive with these two? At least she didn't say *nigger*, though he almost countered with, "Do you mean caramel colored?" Instead, he flashed his dimples again. "Well, he probably forgot I'm half black. We've been friends a long time."

She didn't smile back but leaned in, conspiratorially. "No, probably because Mother would have thrown a shit fit."

Stepping back, the girl scanned for his reaction. "My mother absolutely would have said no way to hiring you."

Cultured enunciation, southern vowels that are more Texas than Kentucky. Defiant potty mouth… Authentic Tucker.

Joanne had interrupted from the doorway. "Mr. Massey won't be joining us just yet," she announced as if speaking to a crowd. "He's been called away on sudden, out-of-town matters but should arrive in a few days."

The teen had pranced up the steps in her short plaid skirt and knee socks, and disappeared alongside her mother into Dahl House.

Haines frowned, remembering the scene. His beer emptied, he gauged his ability to sleep and picked up another cigarette instead. He quickly put it back, denying the urge.

Later last evening, before calling it a night, he'd dragged a garden hose around to water some budding crape myrtle trees he'd planted along the sidewalk. The property had been dark except for a pole light at the bottom of a hill behind the main house, between the stable and corral. A few windows at Dahl House shined behind drapes, but that'd been all.

What had always been a footpath, according to Tucker, was bright with fresh concrete now, sidewalks straight and angular around outbuildings but given a nice ribbon movement in the section between the main house and barn. Crape myrtles were suited to the soil and climate, and would show brilliant flowers in late June. He'd thought color and shade along there would pull the space together visually.

Holding the hose at the base of a sapling, he'd wondered if Joanne approved of the trees, when Tucker's girl came strutting down the path, red curls bouncing in the moonlight with her gait, schoolgirl uniform swapped for a fetching green top and white shorts.

She'd gawked at his arms, shamelessly. "Where's my father?" she'd demanded.

Just wearing a T-shirt and dusty jeans, he felt underdressed. "I don't know." He moved and drew the hose around the tree. "Maybe working?"

Moving toward the far end of the tree line, he carried more garden hose ahead. She followed.

"He told me you were spies together in the war."

Haines maintained his poker face and jerked more hose along the row.

"You know where he is," she said. "I know you do, so tell me."

He chuckled at her bossiness. "War's over, miss. Besides, Lieutenant Massey never did, and still doesn't, report his whereabouts to me."

Debra planted her hands on her hips. "I heard about you," she said. "A hero in Italy and super-spy since."

Forcing a friendly smile, he said, "Your daddy exaggerates."

"What makes you think you can be a rancher now?" Her tone had changed to baiting, and he felt compelled to diffuse whatever tension was building between them. Tucker was going to have his hands full with this one.

"I grew up on a horse farm, and I've been studying the cattle business for a while. Do you dressage?"

He'd moved to another tree and hoped she'd accept his attempt to change the subject. Tucker told him his daughter lacked the discipline and poise to compete in the horse set, though, and that it was a source of strain between her and her mother.

So you dig at the girl?

"No," she answered conversationally. "I ride at the club to please my grandmother, but the open range is what I prefer. And I like it bareback."

Tucker had said her riding style was pure Calamity Jane.

"Have you cut loose out here?"

Her eyes widened. "Surely you realize our horses aren't here yet."

Tucker must not have told her about Bella and Blade, but he was running out of trees to water and decided not to mention them for the moment. "You're in for a treat."

As he began coiling the water hose, she executed a perfect pivot and tapped her low-heeled sandals away. He hadn't known what to think of the exchange but didn't let it get to him. Now, a day later, as he sipped his beer, he was still curious about it.

He'd stayed busy all day, assessing pastures to tighten up before setting livestock to roam, and hadn't seen much of either female. Fence repair would be the first job of the new hands Tucker had authorized. Throughout the day, he'd seen Joanne on the porch with a magazine or at the window in the library sipping an iced beverage. Once or twice during the day, he'd thought he heard noise on the wind of the two women screaming at each other, but he ignored it.

Until young Debra waltzed into the stable at about noon demanding to ride Blade, calling him "the stallion."

He guessed the missus had explained, and Haines was tempted to let the kid ride just to get her out of his hair, but he'd encouraged her to give him another day to prep the poor thing.

"The horse threw a shoe and picked up a stone, bruised his hoof," he'd said.

Against all odds, she hadn't challenged the lie. And there wasn't another peep from the main house after that. He'd labored outside until dark then pored over supply catalogs through dinner. Around nine o'clock, he'd just removed his boots and uncapped his first beer. Now on his second, the bunkhouse phone rang, but only once, rattling the Formica table where it sat.

He took another sip of beer and waited. Sure enough, thirty seconds later there were two rings, then quiet again. Moss, his NSA pal at Fort Hood, was signaling for a meet up. The simple, but specific, code implied importance, face to face, at rendezvous point B. Haines put his beer bottle in the refrigerator, pulled his boots back on and responded, per the plan.

Moss lived with his family in one of the small towns that dotted the hills between Tucker's land and the army base. During one of their coffee chats, when Haines confided in Moss that he'd been in Dealey Plaza when the President was shot, Moss had insisted on certain precautions. Haines made his way on foot to their meeting place, crossing pastures and a stretch of woods.

Over the weeks, Moss had proven useful getting him settled. He'd steered Haines away from ultra-prejudiced merchants in the very white, very Scandinavian settlements making up most of the county's population. Even with Haines's lighter skin and subtle features, it wasn't worth the risk of gossip or conflict, either of which might bring him unwanted attention. Moss had also introduced him to saddle and tack people, and a veterinarian who happened to farm a few miles away, and a feed store and grocer over in Gatesville. As long as Haines remained in Texas, Moss would serve as a vital conduit.

They met under a Corps of Engineers bridge, near the second cutoff to Massey's ranch off the highway. The river shallowed out about twenty feet upstream of the bridge, where layers of limestone and shale led to the water from a minor bluff just an easy jump from the road.

Haines had scouted the place on horseback and knew to watch for goat shit but had forgotten to warn Moss. Shaking his fists, his friend cursed as he eased down the slanted rock to wash his boot in the stream.

"Picked up some talk about you," Moss said while he cleaned off the shit. "Watch your ass."

Haines was mildly surprised. "Do you know who?"

The men squatted by the stream in a native style of relaxed conspiring.

"Can't tell yet. Chatter in all directions, official or not, is still burning up with JFK and Dallas, but stirred in there yesterday was an agent they'd found dead in New York, name of Underhill."

The stubble on Haines' scalp rose.

"Seemed to be the same thread as the one your name was dropped on," Moss said. "You know him?"

Haines took a cigarette from a pack in his shirt pocket. "Yeah." His hands had the slightest tremble.

Underhill was the first known casualty among Company men that Haines himself could tie back to Dallas. He knew the dead agent from Guatemala in 1960, but Tucker had put Underhill on the list of guns they'd spotted in Dallas that week, before it all came down.

"How did he go?" Haines asked.

"Single bullet to the temple. Ruled a suicide by the locals."

The men could see each other in the pale moonlight and exchanged a glance.

"Watch your ass, too," Haines warned. "Things are different now."

They continued to chat for a while, talking of two men from New Orleans who died in a small plane crash recently. Again, both of the deceased were obscurely linked to the assassination. One of them was the mayor of New Orleans, the other ex-CIA, and both had been questioned about alleged connections to Oswald and Dallas.

Haines stood and dug a lighter from his pocket before flaring the cigarette tip. A sudden splash of headlights and sound of tires on the gravel sent the cigarette arcing into the stream, and both men scrambled into darkness. The car moved inordinately slowly, then stopped a few yards beyond the bridge and sat there idling.

Stark still for a count of ten, the men exchanged hand signals and split up without a pebble displaced. Haines watched Moss slip into the blackness of cedar and live oak. Both men had plausible stories if caught. No human sounds had come from the car though, so Haines eased his head above the end abutment to get a look. The sight was a little creepy, a big sedan backlit by headlamps just idling in the dark, road dust settling around it.

It was a mid-fifties Pontiac four-door, with two figures inside, the driver holding a map to the light.

People lost in the night, that's all.

He retraced his path back to the bunkhouse, and had just rounded the barn when the very same lost Pontiac came rumbling around the bend onto the property. From the shadows, he watched as the dark sedan rolled toward the main porch steps and a hand brake engaged just as an adolescent girl hopped out. She quickly fetched a suitcase from the back. The driver, a man Haines didn't recognize, got out and stretched, then walked with the girl to the door. Evidently Joanne Massey expected them because the man stayed a brief ten minutes, then came back out and drove away. Alone.

EIGHT

Tucker

Philadelphia, Mississippi

A neon sign outside the travel court flashed "Cool inside," and the window air conditioner made the racket to prove it. But Mississippi humidity rendered the damn thing useless. Tucker kicked off the flimsy bed sheet, breathing hard and fighting his brain to settle down. He should have just surrendered to taking a sleep aid hours ago.

He sat up. A sense of helplessness made him short of breath, and he sucked in the dank, moist air as if the room might run out of it.

"You'd better come through for me, Vincent," he said to no one.

Calling on his brother was a desperate act at first, but it seemed brilliant. Vincent and Carla had a history, and she would respond to him, answer the door if he knocked. Tucker needed Vincent so he could focus on the task at hand for LBJ.

The heat—and his nerves—were causing sweat to bead up in his thick hair and make his scalp itch. He tiptoed barefoot across the gritty linoleum floor to grab a hand towel from the john, then rubbed his head to the point of pain.

Silently, he damned his brother if he didn't find Carla, and damned Carla if she went to the ranch. Joanne might shoot her.

Nah. His mouth turned up, but he didn't exactly feel amused.

He reset his jaw, determined. Given the vitriol flung around Carla's apartment the other day, he felt like the proverbial rat cornered by a terrier. The woman wouldn't back down.

She knows she can't keep this baby. I'm no good at being a daddy.

That he might have to quit his lover of nine years didn't go down easy, either, but with the pregnancy, the fucking investigators, and her stupid diaries, he just didn't know if he could afford her anymore. Pulling on his shoes, sockless, he cast thought of Carla aside and fished in his bag for the roll of Tums and collapsible plastic glass he always kept handy.

Tucker felt in his bones that this mission in Mississippi was high on the White House agenda. Maybe it meant a chance to prove something to his father's goddamned ghost and to his own overly ambitious wife. At least, he hoped it did.

Thurman W. Massey, *the old man*, had been an early speculator in north Texas oil and real estate, and a legendary shaper of Dallas-Fort Worth, now called "the metroplex." He'd met LBJ in 1932, when Thurman's classmate at Tulane introduced them during a card game. While not clear yet as to the nature of any genuine debt between President Johnson and his father, Tucker, like Joanne, felt he'd inherited special consideration from the man.

But in the dark, as he chewed Tums tablets like candy, he admitted his doubts. Did he really want to chase a career in intelligence or security, even at the national level? Tucker was pretty sure his old man had planned for him to *occupy* the White House, not just turn occasional tricks for it. He thought more along the lines of the State Department or Diplomatic Services, but he'd yet to speak with LBJ directly since he took office.

Not even when the old man died.

Tucker's father had died in Dallas the same weekend as Kennedy and Oswald. His memorial had been a sloppy, rainy affair. Hardly a blip on the newsroom radar, considering. Lady Bird had telegrammed, and sent a tasteful spray of carnations, but Tucker never received any form of direct communiqué from the Oval Office. Not even a nod. It bugged him. At the time, Tucker told himself they had their own burials going on.

The fact that Johnson's underground crew continued to call with assignments made him think a position was being arranged for him somewhere, but the silent treatment was disconcerting.

Lying back down, his feet hung off the end of the bed. He counted backwards from twenty, started over twice, then sat up again, slid back into his shoes, and dragged the room's only chair in front of the air conditioner. Standing there in his boxers, he didn't like the look of the chair's ripe upholstery so he yanked the top sheet off the bed and draped it over the questionable fabric before sitting down. He reached for his rumpled pack of Lucky Strikes, and his lighter on the bedside table, and lit one. Taking a deep drag, he blew into the manufactured, tepid wind of the AC. At least that familiar smell overtook the mildew stink.

He'd been sent to Mississippi on a private jet from Dallas to Key Field in Meridian. There, he'd met the case officer, Philips, and another three men, all strangers but with the same ex-military look and demeanor. They'd climbed into a rented sedan and thirty minutes later pulled into the drive of the lovely motor court outside Philadelphia, MS. Tucker had sneered at the irony. Philadelphia, PA was known as "the city of brotherly love." Mississippi, Tucker knew, was the South's State of Hatred. Newspapers called Dallas the City of Hatred now, owing to its loud-mouthed far right fanatics and the death of a president, but Mississippi hid true menace, worse than the infamous Ku Klux Klan.

He remembered the day, as a young boy of ten, when he'd first discovered his father rode with the KKK. "Racial cleansing" had been a term he'd just learned of in World History class, and he instinctively disapproved, perceiving Thurman as out-of-date. How terrified Tucker had been to decline his own membership in the local chapter years later. But old Thurman had surprised him and allowed Tucker to pass up involvement in that club. Actually, throughout his life, the old man had allowed Tucker to develop his own political ideals while schooling him on how the world actually worked.

Texas had racial tension—there was no doubt about that—but when Tucker had deplaned in Mississippi, he'd sensed visceral conflict in the very air. This particular hellhole was an American pressure cooker waiting to blow. Racial equality was getting a foothold in more sophisticated areas of the country and Mississippi wanted no part of it. Their army de resistance was the Klan.

The Klan was just another label for Nazism or Fascism to Tucker, and to think of his countrymen as the enemy made his stomach turn sour. He took another drag of his cigarette and forced his mind back to reviewing his current mission.

According to Philips, national Klan membership had quadrupled in the past ninety days. Mississippians up and down the food chain in state government, local government, and law enforcement sheltered a secret club of extremists who made the ordinary Ku Klux Klan and their version of threat look like Elmer Fudd. Tucker and his teammates' mission was to penetrate that incendiary faction. Tucker knew how Johnson worked and suspected they were part of his backroom maneuvering, a primo spot to be while legitimate agency operatives were tending to race riots and sit-ins.

Tucker allowed the internal question to ring through his mind again: Did he really want to be a contract operative for Lyndon Johnson now that his old man was gone? For the last eight months, any time Washington called he'd dropped everything, completely cleared the decks of his law practice within an hour of summons. He'd followed every order to a T, asking no questions; nothing but the mission mattered. And even though he could die a hero, no one would know because they'd have to cover up his involvement. If he got busted, would his father's crony have his back? Tucker suspected not, that he was fooling himself. He lit another cigarette.

Truth be told, Joanne had made their ranch so damned alluring that his current dream job was as a horse breeder and cattle rancher at Dahl House. With his old buddy Haines on board as foreman, his valuable knowledge finally came into play, and all that bountiful land was just waiting for the two of them to make something of it.

Resting his head against the back of the chair, Tucker closed his eyes and tried filling his mind with relaxing thoughts of central Texas. He pictured rolling pastures of wild grass and clover…saw himself atop an overlook on Paul Mountain… And of course, there was his private swimming hole.

A favorite image of Carla's backside, naked in the river, flashed before him. Slowing his breath, he conjured up a hill-country breeze so real he felt the sensation and heard the water tumbling past. Their hidden nook was the reason Carla ever agreed to go to Dahl House.

River sex, she called it. Not the easiest thing to manage, but the simultaneous thrill of a hot, wet orgasm in rushing cool water made for phenomenal, blow-your-socks-off pleasure.

When he'd first invited her to the ranch for skinny-dipping, Carla surprised him with coy desire to play naughty in the wild. Forget the brand new swimming pool. Tucker had scouted the riverbanks with a hard-on and a very clear idea in mind. The Leon River wasn't known to be swimmer friendly, but it had been a rainy year and he'd found a sweet spot just below a bend in the river's path, an easy cooler-carry walk from the house.

A natural pool had encouraged dense growth of elm and cypress trees, forming an arbor that inspired frolicking, privacy assured. Tucker replayed that first day in his mind…

His sex kitten had been impressed with his prowess in discovering and preparing a get-nasty place for them. The pool was ten feet by twelve feet, shaped something like a grand piano, and mildly swift. On the far side of the pool, the roots of a stooped old cypress reached into the current and hooked under. Conveniently adjacent to that natural anchor was a two-yard river rock that probably chunked off last century and now slanted partially in and out of the water. Perfect for his mistress's kinks. Carla liked to be tied. She liked to be chased and taken. He'd chosen brown cotton bootlaces.

Carla entered the pool naked, her nipples as hard as his cock, and sunk low so the water covered her breasts. Tucker had started with small talk, like school chums, while contemplating the art of surprise. Then they'd tussled and he took her under, where unintentional brushes with flesh felt amazing, and his raging hard member sensed the thrills in wait. His hand found the folds of her hot center, and she'd moaned with sudden pleasure.

Tucker lifted her to the rock with authority, both of them breathing fast, and she'd wormed away again, but he trapped her under him. Hefting her into position again, he lashed her wrists above her head. Under his weight, her breasts ballooned against the smooth rock, filling with her breaths. She'd smelled sweetly of creek water. Grabbing the cypress lash, he'd tied her right ankle as she thrashed, her left foot slamming into his head. He'd grabbed that foot and widened the vee of her legs, then shocked her with rapid finger insertion. She sharply gasped, then moaned and surrendered, again.

When Carla Summers's world-class pleasuring kicked in, Tucker always wanted one foot free for the most spectacular grinding and build up his dick had ever known. The talented girl's energetic thrashing, and very vocal orgasms, made him crazy.

Fireball ejaculation in a swift, cool river.

The sensation had redefined kinky.

Tucker closed his eyes, drinking in the memories. Her breasts had been a little scuffed up after, but she'd never complained, and they learned to take a beach towel. Dragging on a fresh Lucky, he wondered if Carla ever talked about the size of his tool to her friends, and exhaled real slow.

She cannot show up at the ranch this weekend.

All hope for a peaceful future at Dahl House would be history if Joanne found out Carla had ever been there. Years ago, his wife had confronted their affair, and he'd sworn to give Carla up. Joanne was tolerant of an occasional dalliance, and masterful at ignoring gossip about harmless flirtations, but she'd warned him once, speaking very clearly, "Don't bring your whores home."

NINE

Ivy Jean

<u>Dahl House</u>

Ivy's brain registered a sharp noise and her eyes flew open. It took a moment to remember why she slept in a large room with two beds where everything matched, so unlike her own room in Prosperity. A plaid chair in the corner was covered in the same fabric as the bedcovers and the rectangle thing across both window tops. The closet was the same size as her whole bedroom.

Remembering where she was, Ivy Jean's confounded feelings over Vincent leaving her with strangers hit hard. Joanne, who'd asked her to drop the "Aunt" title, wasn't anything like Aunt Bee, but she seemed alright. Very blonde and smart. Ivy's redheaded cousin Debra, on the other hand, proved to be a stinker who would require special handling.

Pale and gauzy sheers hung behind the plaid-border of the window above Ivy's head, lifting and falling with a contrary breeze that felt surprisingly cool for June. It carried the scent of hay into the room. The darkness outside had just shifted to gray—the day was barely getting started. A surge of anticipation made her smile. *This is an adventure, alright. In the style of Richie Rich, Esq.*

She wandered out to the luxury bathroom shared with Miss Priss, who slumbered next door. Ivy had trouble grasping all the fanciness, but during last night's mini tour she'd counted at least three bathrooms—and that was just downstairs. At least the bathroom they shared came with two basins, and Ivy had her own space for her toothpaste and hairbrush. Decorated in bold, striped wallpaper, softened by a set of seashore pictures, the bathroom had too much pink for Ivy's taste. But it was less nauseating than Debra's disgusting room where everything, *everything,* was some version of pink, top to bottom. It truly made Ivy want to puke, like she'd had too much cotton candy at the county fair.

Debra had personality problems beyond spoiled rotten or red-headed temper, Ivy thought. She had never witnessed such outright hatefulness to a parent as what her cousin dished out to her aunt.

PSYCHO CHILD GETS AWAY WITH MURDER

Joanne made a sharp contrast to the little monster with her aura of serenity. She exuded an almost eerie calm, though tension seemed to be tolerated in her house.

As Ivy looked around, the house still seemed to be asleep. On her way back to bed she took a look out the window, eager to see the grounds in daylight. Her room overlooked the back of the house—west, judging from the direction of the sun coming up. Directly below her window, the brown-shingled porch roof sloped to the deck area where she could see the outer edges of the swimming pool.

Shade trees covered half the yard and probably served to break winter winds coming off the hills to the north. Just beyond the manicured portion of the yard was a slight downward slope of patchy grass leading to an airy arrangement of white pipe. In the gray light it appeared to be illuminated from the inside. That had to be the new corral Joanne mentioned because on the other side sat a neat rectangular building with large, shuttered openings that must be the stable, which was also new, according to her aunt. Ivy squinted so her eyelids almost touched and pretended for a moment that the dewy pasture at the foot of the hills was an iced-over pond. So far, Dahl House promised several avenues of entertainment.

A pair of horses appeared then, one brown and one yellow, and headed toward the glistening pasture. Behind them, a man came from the stable, leading a pair of orange-and-white cows with short horns and enormous heads. He whistled and hit them on their rumps.

That would be the ranch foreman. *Mr. Haney did Joanne say?*

He looked small against the horses. She narrowed her eyes again to see him more clearly. *Maybe he used to be an actor on TV,* she thought, *because something about that man is familiar.*

• • •

A few hours later, she sat on the edge of the neatly made plaid bed, fully clothed, including sneakers but no socks, eager to get on with the day. The gray skies of dawn had progressed into a rich, deep blue that gave Ivy the feeling heaven was closer to the ground. Wondering when she'd see signs of life, she tried to be patient. Struck suddenly by the obvious, she dug her swimsuit out and stripped again, carefully refolding the shorts and shirt and stacking them on top of her folded underpants. She tugged on the threadbare, olive-colored tank-style suit, wishing she could stretch the shoulders to fit better, but she really didn't care that much. Where she came from, kids swam in the creek or the stock pond and, so long as private parts were covered, nobody noticed what you wore.

Triple-stepping down the back stairs, she fully intended to disobey the strict rule to never, ever swim alone, but when she barreled out the patio door she found surly Debra just settling onto a chaise with a wide straw hat over her face. Ivy pulled up, just shy of jumping in the pool, not bothering to hide her presence or her disappointment.

The memory of Debra standing in the bathroom doorway the night before, with her arms crossed, glaring at Ivy brushing her teeth, assaulted Ivy.

"You're not wanted here," she'd said, just like that.

Ivy had sunk inside with a whole bunch of complicated feelings, shock at the top of the pile, but she only had a second to react, and she spat a mouthful of foamy toothpaste in the sink.

"Buzz off," she'd said. Then holding Debra's gaze in the mirror, she spit again.

Her moody cousin had then tossed her red hair and suddenly got all friendly.

"Do you like girl bands?" Like a pressure valve between them was shut off somewhere, she'd started acting human and puttered around gathering stuff to show off.

"Girls at school make up dance skits and mime the records. Come on, I'll show you."

So before she went to bed last night, Ivy had a whole new understanding of girl bands and rock and roll and woke thinking maybe she could withstand the stinker in Debra long enough to experience the adventure and thrills this place, and this wild girl, seemed to offer.

Standing by the pool, Ivy hung around a few minutes, admiring Debra's bikini and trying to sense her mood—and was ignored, as though she didn't even exist. The foreman, working near the house at an outside water faucet, started for the corral with a toolbox. Just as he passed the pool area, Debra stood up, tossed her hat on the chaise, and pranced toward the diving board, real dramatic, and pretended to stub her toe. She started hopping around on one foot, jiggling her boobs so much they almost sprung out of her skimpy top.

Disgusted, Ivy concluded the air around Debra was tainted with a kind of poisonous gas or something. *This isn't worth it.*

Ivy trudged back upstairs and changed back into her cutoffs, sneakers, and her favorite T-shirt. No one at Dahl House needed to know Mrs. Polk just happened to buy it at a thrift store. "Treasure Island Florida," it read in pink, raised-up lettering beside a palm tree. Because of that shirt, Ivy dreamed of going to Florida. She imagined treasure chests full of pirate booty and full-figured women serving exotic beverages in coconuts.

Get her daydreaming and Ivy Jean Pritchard conjured up all kind of plans for worldly experience, far beyond Prosperity, Texas. Far beyond Texas, even.

Maybe the moon.

Dour Debra could have the pool for now. It wasn't going anywhere.

The private library beckoned downstairs and led Ivy to the front of the house again. Joanne had been holding a magnifying glass when Ivy and her father arrived last night, and later explained that she'd gotten hooked on the history of Dahl House while making a scrapbook of her renovations. Stacks of pictures and papers, several boxes of different shapes, and used-up spiral notebooks littered a massive wooden table situated between the floor-to-ceiling windows. Her aunt's talk of old family secrets and hidden graves infected Ivy's curiosity, but good. Now, with the house so quiet, it was a perfect chance to look around.

The windows flanking the project faced south toward a sprawling barn structure. Ivy pulled a chair over and had just taken a seat when tires crunched against the gravel outside and a flash of sunlight glanced off chrome. *Daddy?*

She hurried toward the foyer. A dainty knock confirmed that it wasn't her dad, but before she reached the door it opened, and a pretty woman dressed in a shapely summer suit stepped into the house. She jumped on seeing Ivy.

She must be a fashion model or an actress. Tucker and Joanne must know tons of famous people. Ivy tucked her bangs behind her ears, feeling shy.

"Hello. I'm Ivy." She thought she saw an eyebrow arch behind the woman's sunglasses. "A relative, visiting," she clarified, noticing it felt good to say.

The lady smiled and the perfection of a hundred toothpaste ads came to mind.

Ivy felt a sort of soothing energy from that smile and flashed her own teeth back.

"I'm Carla Summers," the lady said. "Where is Mr. Massey?" Holding a stylish plaid overnight bag in one hand, she tucked a mass of hair behind her ear with the other. Luxurious glossy waves fell around her face like a Halo Shampoo girl. Ivy's own stringy hair was usually in a ponytail, for good reason, and even the ponytail was skinny. She coveted thick, pretty hair.

CELEBRITY ADOPTS MOTHERLESS GIRL

"Uncle Tucker isn't here," she said, and then offered to get her aunt.

Miss Summers snapped the plaid bag away as Ivy reached out to help. "Do you know where he is?"

Ivy shook her head and noticed a Corvette in the driveway behind the woman. Ivy was just about to gush when Joanne stepped onto the porch, her footfall seeming extra heavy on the wood. Both women froze at the same moment, and a hot breeze shot across the threshold. Ivy picked up the scent of two fragrances, as separate and distinct as the wearer's very dark and very light heads of hair.

Miss Summers spoke first. "Hello, Joanne." She took off her sunglasses and revealed swollen eyes and no makeup. Gray pupils seemed pale, and lost in the jet-black frame of all that hair.

"Dear God," Joanne said. "What are you doing here?" She cleared her throat.

Ivy sensed a difference in her aunt's regal posture and thought her striking porcelain skin had just paled whiter. Joanne replaced a fallen strand of hair in her up-do, clearly displeased.

"Ivy, go find a book to read or something." Her aunt spoke to the air over Ivy's head and led Carla Summers by the elbow to a small room on the other side of the grand staircase.

"Very nice to see you, Ivy Jean," Miss Summers spoke over her shoulder with a wide, friendly smile.

Joanne closed the door and Ivy studied the painted wood, confusion wrinkling her forehead. Had she told the woman her middle name? Or did her aunt? She liked the way Miss Summers said "Ivy Jean," like one word, like something special or familiar, but she didn't think she'd mentioned it. She made a move to listen through the door. The lady had asked for *Mr.* Massey.

According to Debra, who liked to exaggerate, her father wasn't at the ranch that weekend because "the White House called him away on assignment." But Vincent had told Ivy that Tucker practiced law in Dallas. Debra claimed he did, but that *sometimes* he did special work for the President of the United States, Lyndon Baines Johnson, who was an "old family friend." Ivy was impressed, all right. Having a Texan as the boss of all of America was a big deal. It made her wonder about what kinds of "special work" her uncle did, and if her father might be helping President Johnson too. *Maybe that's why he left me here.*

Ivy changed her mind about eavesdropping and turned to close the double front doors, still wide open. The Corvette's shiny tan color was muted by a chalky coat of caliche dust, reminding her of her dad's creamed coffee. Ivy also knew the ride was a brand-new 1964 coupe since the back glass was plainly all one piece. Wade read car magazines and left them lying around everywhere, so she browsed them sometimes when she got really bored.

What if I sped away and escaped from Dahl House in that?

Ivy imagined the gearshifts and pedals.

```
RUNAWAY TEEN DIES IN RUNAWAY SPORTS COUPE
```

The annoying *tap, tap* of Debra's high-heeled sandals announced her presence, and Ivy sighed. Her cousin came prancing up the hall from the back of the house, still wearing the hat and bikini and bringing a chlorine smell mixed with coconut oil with her. Pool water dripped on the floor.

"Who's here?" she demanded.

Ivy raised her pert nose. "I'm not your damned servant." Debra and her mother had sniped at each other, cussing and name calling almost constantly since she'd gotten there. Ivy could get to like saying what she felt like in a place without rules.

"Oh, God," Debra said, fixing her eyes on the car. She took off the hat and her copper curls fell loosely around her shoulders. "Where's Mother?"

Suddenly "crazy bitch" had become "Mother," and it sounded foreign on Debra's lips. Ivy just pointed to the closed parlor door. Both girls had stepped in that direction when the door flew open and Joanne, white as a bed sheet, motioned them closer. The girls gasped in their tracks upon seeing Miss Summers in a heap of bright green linen on the floor.

Panic closed Ivy's throat. She could see something serious had happened plain as day on her aunt's face. Did Joanne kill the lady looking for her husband? Ivy tried to remember hearing a muffled gunshot.

"Get cool water, Debra," Joanne ordered. "And washcloths. Bring my pills." She spoke with a calmness Ivy didn't see in her eyes. "And get Haines." She looked straight at Ivy, stern but clear. "Don't panic," she said. "She's only fainted. Hurry!"

Maybe her mother's order made Debra feel needed or something because Ivy didn't see her make a face or even argue. She didn't even stomp up the stairs as they raced to the second floor.

The door to Joanne's room had always been closed before but Debra entered with authority and started making a racket, shaking pill bottles, and slamming drawers. The sounds echoed off the mint green tiles covering every surface of the bathroom. Ivy hung back, taking in the royal space. A giant bed—she guessed it was one of those California Kings—seemed doll-sized in the room, covered in quilted golden luxury and surrounded by massive, deeply carved wood furniture. Museum-like paintings of mansions and horses in the countryside hung in thick frames at a downward angle so they seemed to lord over the darkened space. Ivy smiled noticing a pair of high-backed, dark-red chairs arranged around a fireplace—in the bedroom! *Wow.*

"Hey! Close the door." Debra spoke sharply from the hall behind her, and Ivy snapped out of it. Somehow her cousin had done a quick change from bikini to cotton shift and was heading back downstairs, barefoot. The air she wore of being in charge both annoyed and comforted Ivy Jean as she followed.

Reaching the kitchen, Debra stepped out the back door and issued two short, loud yips—like a wrangler on a cattle drive. The maturity of the feat surprised Ivy and she gaped with shameless admiration.

"Where'd you learn to do that?"

Debra shoved a jug of water and washcloth at Ivy to carry. "At the club." She sneered. "Where do you think?"

Rich people have a club for everything.

The girls hurried back to Joanne and, with great relief, Ivy could see past her enough to confirm Miss Summers was alive. She was still on the floor but propped against the couch, shaking. Pale hands covered her face.

Ivy had never seen a person who'd fainted before.

Joanne spoke in a harsh whisper. "I told you to fetch Haines." In one motion, she took the pill bottle from Debra and slid it in her bra.

"He's coming," Debra said, and her mother nodded.

"Get lunch started, girls. Make extra." She took the cloths and water next.

Both girls just stood there frozen, staring at the fallen woman when the foreman shoved past. Without any effort at all, he picked

Miss Summers off the floor and settled her onto a blue tweed divan. He seemed to recognize the stranger, concern on his face.

"Go on, now," Joanne said, shutting the door in their faces.

Ivy followed Debra down the hall to the kitchen, all the while wondering if Joanne happened to notice that her nasty-tempered teenager had just turned and marched, as told. Twice in a row.

Back in charge, Debra scrounged around in a walk-in pantry and brought out cans of tuna. Working the can opener, her face wrinkled into a frown like she was diffusing a bomb.

"Paper plates and chips are in the pantry," she said.

Ivy found scissors in a drawer and opened a bag of Ruffles first. "Do you know who she is?"

After a beat, Debra stopped mixing tuna and faced her. "Yes, I do," she lifted her determined chin. "She is my father's whore."

TEN

Tucker

PHILADELPHIA, MISSISSIPPI

Tucker paused outside the door of his unit in the motor court and finished a cigarette before heading to Philips's cabin for briefing. The Mississippi dawn cast an edgy orange hue around, and raw nerves made him feel hung over from lack of sleep. A train bleated in the distance, and he imagined hitching a ride out of there before it was too late. Taking one last deep drag, he dropped the butt in the dirt and ground it out with his shoe.

The door of the case officer's unit stood open, and the air conditioner in the window whined in overdrive. Guys in white button-downs and loosened narrow ties clamored around a coffee urn and plate of donuts on the bureau. Tucker waited for an opening in the crowd then helped himself to a paper cup of black coffee. The unmade bed had been pushed into a corner and some metal folding chairs were opened up in a row. Tucker sat on one by the door and moved his legs off to the side. The small space felt crowded and tense and smelled of clashing aftershaves.

Barely hot, the coffee was hard not to gulp, but its caffeine helped Tucker acquire some life and tune in to the intriguing events. Two more fellows showed up and Philips cleared his throat to draw the crew's attention. Short-necked, his large head sat on his shoulders like a pumpkin. He wore a short-sleeved shirt, snugly fit to muscle-laden arms and a broad chest.

With the verbal flourish of a southern gentleman, he spoke in a distinct, educated drawl. "Gentlemen, war is brewing on this soil, and we are here to nip that bad boy in the bud."

A breeze came in and lifted the mood a tad, papers rustled in a stack under a stone beside Philips, who squinted at the arrival of the sun and shut the door.

"You might have seen or heard news reports of civil violence around here."

Tucker was unsure whether to be amused. Only the most rural—or the comatose—could deny knowledge of the civil rights conflict in America. But unlike the average guy, Tucker understood the threat it posed, having the country's vulnerability broadcast around the globe every day.

"All of you know," Philips went on, "that President Johnson has a distinct, private style of persuasion that contrasts his eloquent, public manner."

Tucker certainly did, but he wondered if the other guys really knew him as well. The senator's legendary chameleon-like smoothness had inspired politicking as sport for Tucker when he was young and impressionable. Seamless and imperceptible, Johnson's entire physical presence could molt in a heartbeat, from a hard-ass charging an opponent about to piss his pants, to a genteel communicator with a heart as big as Texas.

"We're the private effort this time," Philips said.

Tucker was pleased. His favorite Johnson persona was the badass.

"Mississippi government insists their way of life suits them just fine," Philips went on. "And according to them, the same goes for their colored population. Everybody is fine, and state offices in Jackson don't want interference from Washington in Mississippi affairs. They've threatened Secession."

Southern racists dividing the nation again over Negroes. Great.

Images of warring states stole Tucker's breath, and he sat up straighter to give his solar plexus room to expand. Such endangerment to the nation could not be allowed.

"Klan membership in this region has grown by more than fifty thousand in sixty days," Philips stated.

The numbers tripped through Tucker's head and little grunts of reaction went around the room. The Klan was a bunch of lawless, cowardly rednecks hiding behind bedclothes and bonfires. But fifty thousand of them represented a massive increase in righteous, reckless manpower.

A chord locked deep away in Tucker reacted. *Every bit the threat of Nazis.*

"A particularly violent and highly specialized club of operatives is harbored here," Philips emphasized. "Deep within the bowels of their empire, they cover the 'White Knights.'"

The irony of the name brought a few sneers. Philips didn't seem to notice.

"Klan MO is downright flamboyant when calling attention to themselves and their activities. But not all the local bubbas with guns are loud and stupid. These White Knights are a covert element of well-trained and impressively skilled operatives."

He raised a finger. "At no time be without a partner." Everybody got a direct look from him.

"Feds are already here. They are for the cameras. Avoid 'em like the clap."

Philips took a sip of coffee while the chuckles died. Tucker liked the man's style.

"Just to make things interesting, a *non*-violent and largely white challenge to the disturbing world of Jim Crow has converged here in bus loads, too. Affluent college students, it seems, are invading the heart of racism where it lives."

Poetic words.

"These kids are passionately altruistic," Philips stressed. "They are well organized and have a name: Freedom Riders. In their minds, and deeds, their black brothers and sisters in this wasteland deserve the same chance at opportunity and freedom that they enjoy—it's as simple as that."

Tucker knew about the idealism of youth, how quickly passion ignites and action is inspired. The feelings of a concerned father stirred in him—Debra was showing all the signs of hotheaded passion.

"Two weapons are employed by Freedom Riders," Philips continued. "Rote memory and news cameras."

Tucker responded to the murmurs around him this time. "Newsmen following *non*-violence around will be nice for a change."

Philips explained that the student workers were trained and organized by professional activists. "This is what they are calling Freedom Summer. Young volunteers from places like Ohio and California, and I'd say most are left-leaning innocents truly desiring to make a difference. Peacefully."

Tucker took a final sip of his coffee.

"Their peaceful approach, however, incites the sickest violence. After dark."

Tucker knew the tactics of the Jim Crow contingents, the racist Mississippi politicians. They were the almighty and untouchable voice of Mississippi and did not like cameras in their business. He restrained a thrill; this settled the assignment's importance. *Mr. President is paying close attention.*

"Okay, so these optimistic volunteers land here to save the world and get paired up with media folks toting cameras. Teams are deployed into counties and fan out in impressive numbers. They knock on doors where people live who have never ridden in a car, much less taken part in an election." He looked around, wanting that to sink in. "Such a colorful snapshot of oppression is Mississippi," he said. "This is where a secession uprising will launch, if it does, gentlemen. The President and the Pentagon simply cannot allow that."

Philips picked up the stack of papers and sent the stone to the floor. It rolled close to Tucker's foot and he swept it out of the way.

"President Johnson must prevent a bloodbath from being replayed on television—in either camp, gentlemen. We need to get him re-elected."

. . .

The briefing concluded outside where Tucker got paired up with a guy named Chess.

"Like the game," the carrot-topped beanpole said as he extended his hand, an "aw shucks" grin on his face. His coloring made Tucker think of Debra.

"Jack," Tucker offered, returning the smile. Real names were not used but, like most intelligence operatives, he found his middle name easiest to respond to. They shook hands. Chess had a strong, honest shake and his smile disarmed. He didn't actually look like Deb at all, of course. His curls were close-cropped and wiry for one thing, but the fairness of his complexion and his confident manner brought her to mind anyway. Except that she didn't smile much anymore.

"It's good you're both southern men. You need to fit in." Philips handed Tucker a blue duffel. A piece of paper folded into the handle had one word on it: Carthage.

"It's likely you'll run across some of J. Edgar Hoover's men, so a minor disguise will be employed." He pointed to the bag, then explained their part in the plan.

They were to drive to a neighboring county to see a judge, an elder who'd offered inside knowledge about the White Knights to President Johnson. Current chatter had the group blowing up churches, businesses and the homes of Negroes and liberal-minded whites all over the South. Supposedly the judge would confirm responsibility and give up names of the White Knight's leadership.

"Take no action," Philips said. "Strictly intel today."

Pulling a U-ring of keys from his pocket, he uncapped an end, gave Tucker a key, and pointed to a rusted-out Chevy pickup.

Tucker and Chess split up to change into their Mississippi attire. Tucker donned the dungarees and tan work shirt in his room. He wondered where and who the costume people were, thinking there must be elves in a workshop producing and packaging props and passports. They'd even included a secondhand Sears & Roebuck belt in the supplies.

Back outside, he waited for Chess by the truck and lit a smoke, thinking surely by now Vincent had reached Carla in Dallas. It'd been over twelve hours since he'd begged his brother for help.

Thoughts of home got tossed in the dirt with a cigarette butt, though, as Chess returned to the truck and they boarded the Chevy. Tucker's heart beat in a warrior's anticipation for the thrill of a hunt. He needed to focus. Every man there had experience with terror, and Tucker knew, under whatever administration, terror tactics on American soil must be decisively rendered impotent.

ELEVEN

Ivy Jean

<u>Dahl House</u>

"No kidding." Ivy didn't want to react with the shock Debra expected. "Does your mother know who she is?"

Her cousin's angry green eyes widened. "You really are clueless, aren't you?"

Ivy blushed but ignored it. "So you're not worried about your mother?"

A big, fake smile spread across Debra's face. "Oh, no. Never a worry about Miss Calm-and-Collected," she said. Then she sneered again. "As long as the bitch has her pills, we'll be okay."

Her small, freckled face scrunched into a frown as she stirred the tuna concoction faster. Then she stopped all action, looked at Ivy straight on, speaking like a teacher simplifying rocket science.

"It's part of being an important man. You have a wife and family on the one hand. The little family serves as public relations for business and church and society in general. On the other hand, for the private, sexual needs important men have, you have another woman, or women." She slammed bread into the toaster then faced Ivy again, crossing her arms. "Commonplace."

"I know about men having wives and mistresses," Ivy snapped.

Debra snorted, forcing Ivy to notice how un-pretty her cousin's face could get.

If the girl despised her mother so much, then what was the slobbering obedience about earlier? "I didn't know anyone could hate their mother so much."

"Yeah? Well, just be glad you don't have one."

That struck below the belt, and Debra knew it. Ivy tried not to react and squeezed her brain for a clever and equally hurtful comeback. She felt foolish for thinking Debra might've had a good side.

"My brother calls that a sucker punch," Ivy said. "Bad form." She put her hands on her hips. "Do y'all get away with that shit at your fancy clubs?"

Astonishment proved Ivy had trumped, or at least stumped, her cousin. Debra threw her head back with a dramatic groan, turned abruptly, and pounded up the back stairs. Ivy felt victorious for a moment, but then noticed that Joanne had come into the room.

It felt like a giant vacuum had sucked all the air out. A door slammed upstairs, and the pressure was felt in the kitchen.

Joanne had her head in the refrigerator. "Gee, I wonder what could be wrong with the poor creature now?"

Feeling like she'd landed in a foreign place and didn't know the language, Ivy didn't know what to say. "She made a good lunch."

Joanne poured milk into a short glass she took from the freezer. It looked frosty and tasty, like a milkshake, and Ivy made a mental note to try it. But right then she could only imagine the stuff going through her aunt's head and wondered if what Debra said about the whore and the pills was true.

"Is Miss Summers going to be okay?"

Joanne shot her a look and pointed eyebrow. "How did you know her name?"

Ivy's entire body tensed. "She introduced herself to me before you came in the house."

"Oh. Yes, she's fine."

Joanne took a paper plate and stacked sandwich quarters on it, then stood behind the bar and faced the hills to eat, exactly as Debra had earlier. She drew a deep breath and talked with food in her mouth.

"There's been some kind of mix-up with Tucker's schedule. God only knows what made her faint."

Ivy followed her aunt's gaze to the hills. "Did she leave?"

"No, not yet."

The view seemed to have a soothing effect, inspiring calm on Joanne's Swedish-milkmaid features. Or maybe it was the pills she'd stored in her bra.

Ivy slipped away and left her aunt alone, suddenly even more curious about Carla Summers. The foyer seemed hushed and peaceful, and Ivy listened for signs of human life, but all she heard was a cow lowing in the distance. She stood in the library and checked the east windows. Across the front porch she saw the Corvette still sitting by the steps, looking thirsty and hot. Beyond the driveway, the river created a wooded stretch past the barn and beyond. *More adventure awaits.*

The oversized, south-facing windows offered pleasing views of the property, too. Ivy liked all the windows in the library, separated by neatly shelved rows of leather-bound books. The room sat squarely beneath Joanne's suite, but the space felt much lighter, more airy than its upstairs counterpart. Painted glossy white, the bookshelves and all those colorful spines drew Ivy in, and the subtle, leather-scented greeting the place offered was soothing. Heavy, masculine chairs covered in cowhide were grouped with more delicate pieces, striking an artful, balanced appeal. It seemed to Ivy that her aunt had strived to achieve a mood of brightness throughout Dahl House.

It seemed eons since Miss Summers had knocked on the front door, Ivy realized as she moved around the room. The scrapbook table appeared exactly the same, not a paper out of place. In the center, peeping from under musty-scented maps, Ivy spied a thick book, scuffed and chocolate colored. She scooted the chair in and sat, drew the brown book nearer. The worn, stained leather promised a treasure of pioneer-life stories.

Movement outside the window caught her eye and she stopped to watch Mr. Haines put the Corvette in the barn. *I guess Miss Summers isn't going home anytime soon.*

TWELVE

Vincent

<u>Dallas, Texas</u>

Vincent rested the back of his head against the wall. He sat in a booth at a diner in Oak Lawn, a district near north Dallas. He'd taken a table set for four, and the waitress, who wore too much eye makeup, kept staring and making him uncomfortable. Maybe his unshaven face and slept-in shirt made her think he would skip the check. Just being in Dallas—especially on a flawless, sunny Friday—made him irritable, but he softened his scowl for her benefit. No doubt he looked the part of the vagrant.

Taking a comb from his back pocket, he pressed short, wiry tangles into place again. He took out his wallet, pretended to find something, and cast a shy smile in her direction.

Anger at Tucker roiled in his stomach again. According to his brother, who was now unreachable, Carla was supposed to be hiding at home and not answering her telephone, but it wasn't so. And

Vincent wasn't an investigator or missing person's detective. He felt like a flopping fish out of water trying to track her down.

His food arrived and he dove into the meatloaf and onion gravy with gusto. Out the window, he tried to ignore signs of aging and decay. He'd been away from the city a long time and a lot had changed. Leaning and twisting, he tried to stretch his back. Sleeping in the car hadn't helped his mood, or his pains. He might as well have been kicked in the kidneys. And he'd left his daughter with virtual strangers. With horses and swimming to keep her entertained, Ivy Jean hadn't given it a second thought, he reminded himself.

He tried to savor his greasy lunch, which smothered the roiling stomach acid, when an image of Wade in a foxhole somewhere eating canned rations made his food taste flat. Military recruiters were genius at making the business of war attractive. Why hadn't he prepared his son better? Vincent bet they didn't serve up battlefield food during the romance phase of their promises. The threat of losing his son felt almost unbearable. It definitely felt sickening.

He pushed the plate away and asked for more coffee.

Two refills later, his mind pinged at rocket speed from one source of irritation and failure to another—Carla.

He couldn't just sit there and think anymore, so he left a buck for the waitress and paid at the register, then decided to take advantage of the clean pay phone by the door to call the ranch. While fishing in his pockets for coins, he pondered how to find out if a certain brunette had shown up unannounced—depending on who answered the phone, of course. Fourteen times the telephone buzzed in his ear before he gave up. He glanced at his wristwatch. They were probably all out enjoying the swimming pool.

Back in the Pontiac, he picked up a yellow writing pad and stared at the next name on the list, but it was too bright to focus so he lit a cigarette and reviewed things.

He'd agreed to help Tucker, and had come to Dallas, hoping for a chance to restore Carla's affections. He hadn't meant to hurt her with his response to her proposal and desperately wanted to atone for it. Her friendship mattered, a lot. And whether Tucker's distress was real or not, his call last night was alarming enough that here Vincent was, driving all over Dallas acting like Dick fucking Tracy for some misguided familial fence-mending. A slug of milk of magnesia from the bottle in the glove box helped bring forth a low, growling belch. Trying to force his car into traffic, he almost rear-ended a sedan covered with tissue mums and white shoe-polish lettering: *Just Married …*

Perfect.

A rush of embarrassment heated his face with disbelief, dishonor and shame all at once, remembering that, for a few moments, he had actually entertained the idea of marrying a woman who was carrying his brother's child.

Good God. Caffeine taunted him in his head, laughing at him, while he stuck to streets he knew to reach his next target of inquiry.

The word "love" hadn't even come up during Carla's proposal. For Vincent it was simple: Carla's world was too tightly wound around his despicable half brother for him to get involved. A scandalous, mixed-up mess *created by Tucker* wasn't a smart reason to marry, even if Ivy Jean did need a mother.

Hitting the brakes of the Pontiac, Vincent pulled a sharp left and rolled into a strip-center parking lot. The beauty shop listed in Carla's address book was a three-chair place and surprisingly dingy. Finding the phone directory in her apartment last night had felt like a bonus, but so far it hadn't helped a bit.

A petite, gaunt beautician stepped away from a dye job to speak to him once he'd introduced himself at the door. "Mister, I am worried." Her brassy, blonde hair was cut Moe-Howard style with straight bangs an inch above her painted eyebrows. He leaned in because she mumbled.

"She didn't show up for an appointment yesterday." A lacquered fingernail raised and pointed, for emphasis. "Those raven locks are not a hundred percent, if you get my drift."

Vincent nodded and thanked her for her time.

In the car again, perspiration made his shirt stick to the seat. A missed beauty appointment. *Not a good sign, Detective.*

Still, it was something, he told himself, *a recent indication she was not in the city, though had meant to be.*

When he'd arrived in Dallas the night before, after dropping off Ivy, it was past midnight. He'd gone to Carla's apartment first. She wasn't there so he'd found the door key exactly where Tucker had described and went inside for a look. He'd found some things in disarray, but nothing had alarmed him. Cosmetics were strewn around the vanity, empty clothes hangers tossed on the bed. The AC had been turned off. All signs of leaving for a trip in a hurry.

The only thing he'd found of possible use was the address book in a desk drawer in the bedroom. Vincent had felt odd about sleeping in her home having struck out finding her, thinking if Carla came home she'd freak out. So he had slept in her parking lot instead, but he wouldn't make that mistake again.

First thing that morning, he'd used her phone to dial people listed in her book with just a phone number. People with an address, he'd decided to stop by and quiz in person.

Vincent drove to both Parkland and Medical City hospitals—and the morgue—all resulting in nada. Although relieved he hadn't found her in those places, frustration simmered. And all the driving around gave him too much time to think.

Where are you, Carlita?

Remembering Gwen's pet name for their friend brought a wistful smile.

In the weeks after his wife died, Vincent had checked-out too, like he'd gone over a cliff. It took confronting his selfish, righteous, gin-soaked stupidity before he could see that being numb and without his kids sucked worse than the grief. Wade had been nine, Ivy Jean barely three. Just babies. They'd needed him. So from the edge of darkness he'd come back and stood up to the judgmental, meddlesome relatives who'd whispered about his parental fitness.

One day, anything not bundled in the Pontiac got left behind.

His mother had met with attorneys behind his back, about the welfare of his children, and he was so shocked and insulted that he took his children away from the violent city forever, without favor to anyone. They weren't *suitable* influences for Wade and Ivy anymore. He didn't have Gwen to buffer anymore, so every tie to family, friend, or foe was severed like snipped phone wires. Gone, just like Gwen.

His obsession over appropriate influences naturally altered Wade and Ivy Jean's concept of family, which was another one of the constant sore topics on his mind since the boy left. Just like *he'd* left, Vincent thought. He'd turned his back on everything they knew.

Children truly repay us our sins.

At least this Dick-Tracy action engaged his mind and gave him something to think about besides Wade William and the war in Vietnam. The vast geography between Texas and Southeast Asia was what had him reconsidering old rifts to begin with. That distance, and the immeasurable emptiness it represented, gave him fresh perspective on aspects of family he'd previously rejected. Having a safety net, a sense of belonging—all things *not* including Tucker himself—were things Vincent wished he could bottle and mail to Wade.

Maybe this favor for his brother would please the gods and keep his boy safe.

The Dallas streets endured a constant stream of pedestrian and vehicle traffic going in all directions at once as Vincent moved along. There were snarls every way he turned. Exhaust haze lingered in smelly layers and filtered the summer light so it seemed brown. He'd only been back to the city once since Gwen died. From the shadow of an oak tree, he'd paid dutiful respects at his mother's burial in 1960, but that was his only return. All the city represented, to him, was death.

It hadn't surprised Vincent one bit when JFK was murdered there.

So far, he'd avoided the street where they had lived as the happy Pritchard family, the old neighborhood. Vincent held a deeply secreted fear that should he return to Tremont Street, he'd be lost forever. His children, their life together as a family, their need of him, would cease to matter.

THIRTEEN

Haines

<u>Dahl House</u>

Haines enjoyed the low rumble of the Corvette coming to life. Bucket seats, competition steering wheel and cockpit gadgetry made for a tight, low-to-the-ground pilot experience as he jetted along the fifty yards at five mph. Backing into the barn, he thought about Miss Summers's pale and ghostly coloring. She'd barely reached the toilet to vomit, twice, before finally accepting that she couldn't drive home. Hearing her claim it must be the flu, Haines thought the coincidence of that was bizarre. And when a case set off alarms in his head like this, exit procedure automatically engaged. But this wasn't a case, and he wasn't going anywhere. Tucker was in a jam.

Haines lowered the power windows of the 'Vette, then sat looking back at Dahl House. He never would have guessed another dwelling stood inside there, and mapped in his head the floor plan elements hiding it.

"Stairs aren't wise in her woozy state," Joanne had said as he carried a lifeless Carla bride-style, across the foyer to an oddly small doorway he'd never noticed before. It looked like storage, but Joanne had ducked slightly and disappeared, so he maneuvered and stressed his knees to follow her.

"These rooms are to be maid's quarters eventually. Right now it's storage," she'd explained. A freshly made double bed with crisp sheets, a blanket and a spread had been neatly turned down. Joanne motioned to put Carla there. By the wall, a stack of boxes was covered with some fabric and a lamp placed on top, which didn't brighten the space much but made it cozy. While he drew the covers over Carla, she'd opened her eyes and held his, imploring and glassy. Looking over at Tucker's wife drawing towels from a cabinet, then back to him, she'd closed them again. Resigned to staying put, he thought.

Haines knew this woman had been a part of Tucker's life for a while. He'd met her in Dallas years ago, briefly. While he didn't know her well personally, he'd observed them together over the last months whenever they'd come for a weekend at the ranch. Tucker was playful and buoyant around her. She had a contagious, cheerful spirit.

Haines looked around, trying to make sense of the tucked-away space instead of the apparent miscommunication between Tucker and his other woman.

"It's the remains of the original rock dwelling my ancestors built when they settled here," Joanne said, setting a small wastebasket on the floor near Carla's head. "Made of fieldstone harvested on the property."

The contractors had plumbed a toilet and shower and installed laundry machines, but she paused on finishing the rooms until she was ready for live-in help. Half the space was bare drywall, taped and bedded. Unvarnished, louvered doors served to separate appliances and fixtures. It reminded him of the secret rooms in European castles.

"A generation or so later," Joanne continued, "Another of my ancestors cocooned the original farmhouse and crafted the massive structure of today's Dahl House around it."

The air in the space felt cool and moist. No windows, he'd noticed, except near the top of one wall, which faced east toward the river, where there were two narrow, perpendicular slits.

"For a pair of eyes and gun barrel and nothing else," she'd followed his gaze. "Arrows can't get at you."

Haines wondered if Joanne knew about Carla. She had acted very graciously to her uninvited guest. But he was more in awe of this secret, inner Dahl House. The idea of a family occupying one spot of land for generations appealed to his baser, and heretofore neglected, need to belong. Evidence of a bloodline seeping into ancestral land held a powerful draw on his imagination, and he decided to ask for a look at Joanne's history project in the library later. He'd noticed it when readying the house but felt uneasy taking a peek. The family's personal items were just that, and off limits.

After getting Carla settled, Joanne had said to move her car out of the sun, and then find Tucker. *Inform him the ranch isn't functioning so smoothly.*

He'd rather drink goddamn cyanide.

Haines had allowed a dream to take shape around the quiet peacefulness of Dahl House ranch and, oddly, around this family. A surprise visitor didn't warrant alarm.

He entered the bunkhouse, flipped on the air conditioner and vowed to do right by Tucker. He'd make some calls at least, to appease the boss's wife. He got down on the planked floor by his bunk and strained to retrieve his bag, taking a palm size book out of a secret fold. Holding a lifetime of coded information and contacts, it was the only physical clue of his whole career in intelligence.

Sitting down at the table in the kitchenette, he lit a cigarette, frowning at its stale taste. The pack must've been months old. He stubbed it out in an ashtray and dragged the phone across the table. Moving his face closer to the book, he squinted to read the page. When he nodded in understanding, he dialed a number in Virginia.

FOURTEEN

Tucker

PHILADELPHIA, MISSISSIPPI

Transformed into local characters—complete with dungarees and a pickup—Tucker and Chess prepared to set out for their assignment in Carthage. A serape covered the truck's cracked Naugahyde seat, and Tucker put the colorful blanket in the truck bed to keep a set of garden tools from sliding around. The plan called for them to act as landscapers at the home of a retired federal judge, the honorable Ely Cummings.

Philips said the old judge sent word two days ago to his longtime political ally, President Johnson, saying he'd rat on the White Knights; they needed taking down. But certain operatives in the organization had sensed his drastic change in loyalty. He was being watched, and he suspected that his home and office were bugged.

Tucker volunteered to drive, and they spun gravel out of the driveway as they headed west. Their pickup came equipped with a gun rack and two twelve-gauge rifles, as well as a pair of handguns that were nestled in the dash with boxes of shells. The cab smelled like hot plastic and gun oil. Open windows and slick pavement made the ride noisy most of the way, but the men still got acquainted.

"I'm from Florida." Chess spoke loudly, not quite a shout. "You?"

"Dallas," Tucker said.

"Yeah? This your normal outfit?"

Tucker shook his head. "Contract."

"Retired CIA, here." Chess nodded. "Keeping my toe wet, as they say."

"You don't look old enough to retire," Tucker said, impressed. He rolled his window up a bit to reduce the noise.

Chess shrugged and rolled his side up too, smiling like they were old friends. "I signed up young. Part of a Marine intelligence outfit in France, but my stint didn't end with V-J Day, so I knocked on the door of the OSS."

America's various military intelligence divisions had combined to make the peacetime Office of Strategic Services, now the CIA. Tucker's friend and foreman, Haines, had traveled that path, too.

"The work is hard on family," Chess said.

Tucker nodded, reflecting on his own complications around absence and deceit.

Chess said, "What's your day job?"

Tucker was surprised at the man's chattiness, but he seemed earnest. "I practice law—corporate litigation."

"In Dallas? Were you downtown when Kennedy was taken out?"

Tucker was asked about the assassination everywhere he went the moment people knew where he was from. At least Chess wasn't hostile. More than once, Tucker had encountered fanatical opinions of Dallas's fanatical elements.

Tucker stuck to the story. "No. I was having lunch somewhere else."

"I've heard inside chatter about Company involvement. Disturbing idea. You know anything of that?"

"You mean like Oswald was CIA?" Tucker had heard that was so.

"More like Company men bagging Company men…or Company assets."

Tucker was stunned by the statement and suddenly unsure whether his partner was baiting him, pumping him, or just chatty and felt safe talking off-the-record.

"That kind of talk doesn't make it into mainstream news circles in Dallas. The city's public position is that the assassin was caught and killed. But a deeper grapevine carries gossip of what you say."

"A Company agent I knew—a guy named Gary Underhill—died with a bullet in his brain last month. Suicide is not uncommon in our business, but Gary told people he was marked because he knew things about Dallas."

Tucker hid his surprise. He knew Underhill too, vaguely, and he'd seen him in Dallas the week Kennedy was taken out. An uneasy feeling overtook him. "Maybe it put him over the edge," he said.

"It's just talk. So much went down in the hours after Dealey Plaza."

Tucker tried to focus on driving—being apprehensive now wouldn't help him any. Woods hugged both sides of the narrow highway for a stretch, and only an occasional vehicle passed in the other direction. Rain showers had swept through the area and seemed to take the humidity down a notch. The truck's tires hissed on the slickness of the pavement.

Chess changed the subject. "You experienced with the Klan?"

"I'm not," Tucker said, keeping his father out of the conversation. "I know all about the slime balls. They're afraid of black people who can read. It might be funny if it wasn't so fucking inhuman—and real."

Tucker smirked. "Is it true that the Klan is backed by millions?"

Chess nodded. "They are heavily backed by every resource in Mississippi. White Knight operatives are more skilled than Hoover's FBI. President Johnson's dream of a 'Great Society' will never happen if he can't get things under control in Mississippi."

This mission was all about Lyndon. He couldn't forget that. "I smell war," he said, jesting. Chess got the gun-oil reference and both men smiled, continuing the trip in silence.

• • •

Thirty minutes later, they reached the township of Carthage, seat of Leake County. A tired, mildewed-looking courthouse dominated the square and silvery moss dripped from the oak trees like the beards of old men. Every structure around the square bent and tilted with age and neglect. There were so few people around that it might as well have been Sunday instead of Friday.

The state of hopeless, dismal poverty was what had struck Tucker most about Mississippi so far. Signs for WHITES ONLY or COLORED ENTRANCE didn't surprise him; segregation was practiced everywhere in the south and Texas was no exception. It was the utter absence of dignity on the faces of Mississippians, black or white, that jarred him.

Moving through the obviously depressed central business district, Tucker turned to make a highway connection, and they entered a small neighborhood of residences that typified Middle America of the past. Homes sat close to the street, now with only patches of dirt around the steps and sidewalk. Once-nice porches offered saggy seating in one junked-up form or another. Tucker stopped at an intersection and a white woman holding the hands of two small girls waited for him to pass, all of them barefoot and very blonde, like his wife, Joanne. *Jo wanted towheaded babies.* Too bad Debra inherited his Irish looks so completely.

They turned again onto an oil-paved farm road that took them straight through a neighborhood of tarpaper shanties bunched around a clapboard church.

"A bright summer day and no children at play," Chess said, putting voice to Tucker's thoughts.

Two miles later, they reached a dirt road that had been smoothed recently, a shady avenue canopied by massive walnut trees. Around a slight curve they faced an imposing antebellum mansion a hundred yards off the Pearl River. Everything freshly whitewashed, the place oozed a romantic aura of the Deep South. Here was the wealth. Thick and leafy vines wrapped around neo-Greco columns, lazy and meandering. Azaleas of every color bloomed in a hundred bunches on impossibly green grounds and, of course, Spanish moss literally dripped from the abundant shade of two-hundred-year-old oaks.

Tucker downshifted and parked before entering the circle drive. "Impressive," he said.

Ten yards away, a miniature cast iron plantation servant stood in a circular bed of ivy. Dressed in enameled livery, the figure seemed to point visitors toward the grand porch.

"Straight out of Hollywood," Chess said.

Dahl House could be this grand.

Per their orders, they each took a shovel from the bed of the pickup and walked down a footpath leading away from the road, parallel to the river. They were Mississippi workmen now and nothing else. The woeful call of a loon encouraged both men to scan the shadows, making a discreet sweep. Even minor intelligence could turn deadly if breached.

"Philips said the death of the judge's grandson was why he reached out to Johnson." Chess spoke in low tones.

Tucker felt wary about speaking even a word about LBJ here, but he nodded curtly anyway.

As they moved along, they encountered a string of urns with caldrons marking the ends, all overflowing with fragrant herbs, serving as borders for rows of hearty vegetation behind them. A tall but stooped-over white man, with pale, watery eyes, came around a hedge across the path. He wore a short-sleeved dress shirt. Philips told them Judge Cummings's identity had to be confirmed before they could trust any information, and he discreetly lifted his right sleeve to reveal a birthmark just inside his sagging bicep. They'd been warned it was an unpleasant sight, looking roughly like the state of Texas with a greenish, hairy hill in the middle, and if it didn't appear faked, he was their true target. Tucker wondered why the judge didn't get the hideous thing removed.

Without discussion, Judge Cummings led them toward a grove of pecan trees and showed them a cluster of saplings still in burlap root sacks. He pointed to indicate where he wanted the new trees set and stepped aside. Tree frogs carried on a lively conversation while Tucker and Chess started chunking soil, without talking at first. Tucker's coarse hair fell over his eyes and allowed him to watch the judge's face.

The old man's voice drawled raspy and at low volume then. "I am betraying my people." Then louder, "They're mean bastards! I have grandchildren."

Tucker and Chess exchanged a confused look. *Was that code for something?* The judge seemed fit enough for a man in his seventies and plenty steady on his feet, but his gaze was daunting. Like he could see through all your lies and expose your guilt.

Their orders were only to listen. They kept to a tight circle while Tucker and Chess performed the hired-help charade and the judge talked, gradually making sense. Meanwhile, four saplings were moved twice.

"Ever since their leader, Edgars, was assassinated, the colored folks have been gathering in secret, in every county, *conspiring* to take over Mississippi," he said, agitated.

He scowled for a moment then rattled on. "Up north Negroes and their MFDP and their NAACP and their CORE... Jesus Christ Almighty. They are crawling everywhere and stirring our locals into frenzied bloodlust. White Knights!"

Tucker and Chess kept digging.

"White Knights!" the judge barked again, and the men flinched. "That's who is behind the *intolerable* violence."

Tucker leaned on a spade and stared at the ground, hoping they could expect more revelation than that.

"Sam Bowers, a businessman from Laurel, is their leader," the judge added.

Payday. Tucker looked at Chess and mentally recorded the name.

"Bowers is a fervent speaker, a cunning subversive who employs scare tactics and violence. And not all his targets are colored." The judge had the speaking style of an orator, the way he hit the modifiers and employed pause.

"Adolf Hitler is his hero." The judge looked Chess in the eye, seeming to know he was addressing a veteran. "There are probably twenty-thousand fools in these surrounding counties alone who have sworn to the purpose of preserving white supremacy in Mississippi at all costs. They are *galvanized* by the oath of secrecy."

Chess opened his mouth to speak, but the judge cut him off.

"Tell Lyndon that the coloreds are being dangerously *non-violent*," he warned, "getting the attention of the national news, subjecting themselves to humiliation to prove they are not violent, saying all they want is basic human consideration." The judge had his hand in the air, like Moses. "Using the television was a stroke of genius!" His voice took on a cautionary tone. "But in the end, it just stirs up the yahoos, makes 'em meaner and slicker."

Tucker reset a spindly tree again; tamping dirt at the base like it was going to stay there. He tried to stay with the old man, even though he knew everything the judge was saying. Tucker hoped he'd give them more names, more new intel. Chess kept at it too, letting the elder have his say.

"The Klan is night moving. They are *unchecked* and impervious to local law." The judge paused. "Outside press is their biggest threat. Damn foreign reporters won't be observing their activities until it's too late."

The judge finally got around to stuff they didn't know. "Sam Bowers is the ring leader and he must be stopped. And one other guy, Shayne DuPree; stop those two and you have a chance of ebbing this infectious, violent fervor."

The judge's eyebrows met. "The worst perpetrators are the young men who follow them."

"Do you know where to find Bowers and DuPree?" Chess asked.

"Bowers runs Sambo Amusements, out of Laurel; jukeboxes, party props and such crap. Shayne DuPree is a school teacher down in Meridian." He glanced up to gauge their reaction.

Ready access to youth under sanctioned disguise. God almighty.

The information touched a fearful place in Tucker. Children being raised in a climate of racial hatred evoked memories of the ethnic cleansing he'd witnessed in Germany and Italy. Those thoughts stoked a patriotic fire that literally churned his gut and made him want to ride off after the yahoos right then in that pickup full of guns. Malleable, oppressed white children of the South were becoming an army of hate mongers.

"There's a school," the judge said. "Go see why my loyalties are different now."

Tucker listened to the Judge's directions and had his mind made up before they even returned to their truck.

Grinding the gears, Tucker drove away from all that peaceful wealth, secreted off the road on Pearl River.

"Philips said Judge Cummings's grandson was riding in a car full of white boys speeding away from a Negro church they'd set on fire," Chess said. "The car hit an abutment, flew over a bridge and fell fifty feet onto the dry riverbed. Four boys burned up."

Tucker didn't hide the skepticism he felt. "And that's how Cummings's eyes were opened to the evil ways of Klan?" He smelled Lyndon Baines Johnson's arm-twisting at work.

"I can see how it might affect a man's politics," Chess added.

For them to detour by "the school" on the way back to camp would mean ten or fifteen extra miles. Without really discussing it but getting no questions from Chess, Tucker headed in the direction the judge outlined. They had completed today's assignment and would make debriefing with time to spare, so Tucker skirted Carthage and took back roads to the north.

At a crossroad stop sign, a billboard appeared to be freshly painted with professional lettering: Don't Let the Sun Go Down on Your Nigger Ass in This Town.

Tucker wasn't sure if "this town" meant Carthage or not, but a half-mile farther up the road they came upon a prosperous white settlement.

Seeded lawns and young trees separated rows of neat, fairly new homes—most of them brick. Whirly-bird sprinklers spread water over the yards like the gospel of Jim Crow pitched on thirsty youth. Tucker scanned the area. A brand-new elementary school and playground took up the block next to a brick church. HEIGHTS BAPTIST, the sign read. Youngsters were playing softball in the side yard, all of them white. The kids seemed happy enough, and the men looked at each other.

"That can't be the school the judge meant," Tucker said, driving on.

They entered farm country next, turning onto a narrow, unpaved road almost hidden by the stalks of sweet corn that reached the pickup's roof. A kid flew out of the crop, directly in their path, and Tucker jammed his foot to the brake pedal. Clouds of dirt swirled up around the truck.

A young Negro girl in a cotton dress, her legs and arms harmonizing at top speed and perfect form, had disappeared again before the dust settled. She never even looked at them.

They were close to where Judge Cummings said a school had showed him the light. Tucker wasn't sure now what to expect. He stayed in low gear until Chess motioned him to stop again, as two black-skinned boys blew out of the corn and abruptly stopped.

Their eyes, wide with naked fear, locked on the pickup's gun rack.

FIFTEEN

Ivy Jean

Dahl House

Ivy Jean tried to lose herself in the Dahl House relics and papers on Joanne's project table, but her mind kept drifting back to current events unfolding under their roof. Soft voices and distant noises kept her looking over her shoulder. She got up to check. The entry to Dahl House was spacious and airy, with tall, double front doors surrounded by windows.

"Helloo?" She smiled at her own voice when it echoed in the space.

The main staircase halved the foyer with wide, carpeted risers that narrowed to a small landing where a short second flight led to the upstairs hall. Black, hardwood banisters lined the lower portion of the stairs and a chandelier made of a zillion crystals seemed suspended in midair. It wasn't lit now, and not as dazzling as it had been last night.

Ivy swept her gaze around and landed on a door, slightly ajar, where she'd never noticed one before. Positioned to blend into shadows under the staircase and painted the same buttery yellow as the walls, of course she'd missed it.

Vincent's ranch selling point of "adventure" popped into her head. Glancing around the foyer one more time to make sure she was alone, Ivy slipped inside the open door and pulled it snug real fast. When her eyes adjusted to the dimness, she saw that, straight ahead, a small lamp outlined an empty bed. Covers were tossed aside and pillows were piled against the wall.

Holy cow, this must be where they put Miss Summers.

A toilet flushed, and Ivy froze. There wasn't time to get out. Light spilled into the narrow hall and, sure enough, Miss Summers came out another door. Stooped over, she moved slowly to the bed.

Ivy didn't want to be discovered snooping. She also didn't want to frighten the lady so she cleared her throat and Miss Summers turned, her face instantly breaking out in a bright smile.

"Hi, there, Ivy Jean." Her voice was weak. "I'm glad you came to see me."

Ivy had wondered a hundred times how Uncle Tucker's mistress knew her middle name. She was pretty sure Tucker himself didn't even know she was called Ivy, let alone Ivy Jean. The lady's warmth made her feel welcome, however, and her worry disappeared.

"Do you need help?" she offered, pushing her stringy hair out of her eyes.

Miss Summers shook her head no. Her glorious black hair looked faded, and pulled back from her face with a headband, it didn't seem as glamorous anymore. She signaled Ivy to follow her through the clutter to the bed. It felt odd and crowded, but as a makeshift rest area, it was cozy enough—in a camp-like kind of way. Miss Summers sat down and plumped the pillows. Her small feet slid under the covers and she patted the mattress beside her.

"Sit."

Ivy sat; pleased for a chance to ask some questions, even though the lady was tired and ill. She settled her long-limbed self to stay awhile, not a tad self-conscious or shy.

"Sure was a shocker to find you here," Miss Summers said. "Where's Vincent?"

Ivy sucked in some air. "You know my father?"

"I do."

Ivy couldn't hide her immediate delight at this surprise. It took a moment to get un-flabbergasted, and she sputtered. Vincent's phone call with Tucker came to mind.

"Are you the 'she' Daddy mentioned to Tucker?"

"I don't know," she said, reaching out gently for Ivy Jean. "Probably. I'll need more information to know for sure, though."

Something about Miss Summers made Ivy want to curl up like a child and just be held. Ivy scooted closer and offered her hands. Softness and warmth telegraphed friendliness and safety. Remembering what Debra said earlier made Ivy wonder what her uncle's lover had to do with her dad, but at least it explained, in a way, how she knew her middle name.

"Do you know where Daddy is?"

"No, but let's back up and see if we can figure this out." She put her head against the wall but kept her eyes on Ivy. "You are the spitting image of your mother."

That did it. Meeting someone who knew her mother had never happened before, and Ivy Jean's eyes shot wide open, her astonished brain flat, unable to grasp the news.

"You knew my *mother*?"

Miss Summers gave her a lopsided grin. "She was my best friend in the whole world."

Thrill mixed with a wary realization that Vincent must have more secrets locked away, but Ivy pushed those thoughts off into a corner when Miss Summers opened her arms for a hug. Leaning into the lady's embrace, she hoped they could be best friends too. She'd never really had one before. Maybe someday Miss Summers might even show Ivy how to get her own limp hair to have glamorous shine and poufy waves.

"I've never met a friend of my mother's," she said, sitting back to look at Miss Summers. "Do you know my brother, too?"

"Of course I know Wade. I bet you miss him. Your father is beside himself with worry."

Warmed by the familiarity, Ivy nodded. "I know. When was the last time you saw Daddy?"

"A few weeks ago. I stopped in to see him at the bank in Prosperity."

Could it be that her dad was having a secret romance, with his brother's secret lover? That line of thinking got uncomfortable fast and Ivy shook it off. She looked around the small space instead and noticed the green dress that sat folded on top of the plaid suitcase, recalling the sight of Miss Summers out cold in Joanne's parlor. "Are you feeling okay?"

"Oh, sure. Don't worry about me."

"Did you faint?"

"Yes. That's all it was. It felt weird, like someone dropped a heavy blanket on me." She uttered a small laugh. "It's never happened before. Probably just the heat."

Ivy wondered if heat made you puke, too. She felt pretty sure she had heard retching before Miss Summers emerged from the toilet. "How can I help?" she asked again.

"By keeping me company." Miss Summers took Ivy's hand. "I promised your aunt that I wouldn't drive just yet, but I'll have to get back soon."

Ivy noticed the manicured hand that held hers was pale and felt extra warm. "Do you live in Dallas?"

"Uh huh. Not far from where you were born."

They shared another smile. To think of Miss Summers in terms of her mom shook Ivy's sense of what was real. Her mother was a legend to her and her brother, which was bound to happen with the subject of her being as hushed as it was.

"Tell me why you're here at the ranch," Miss Summers said. "Is your father coming also? I would love to see Vincent walk through that door."

"Everything happened so fast… Daddy just suddenly told me I was invited to come stay at my uncle's ranch. I only even know Tucker existed because Wade told me. That's how much Daddy talks about his brother."

Miss Summers smiled, sympathetic. "I know. Vincent doesn't talk much about anything." She leaned back against the pillows. "Do you know where your uncle is? Have you met him yet?"

"No. Joanne and Debra are both mad because he didn't show up. They fight all the time, you know. It's really uncomfortable." She couldn't help but add a little gossip. "Debra got expelled from school and that's why they're here instead of Dallas, I think. Joanne gripes because she needs a housekeeper and Debra just seems pissed off all the time."

Her thoughts came back around to her father. She just couldn't quite grasp his involvement, or why Miss Summers *and* her apparent uncle were kept from her.

"How come I never knew about you?"

"After your mama died and y'all moved to Prosperity, your dad and I lost touch."

"Huh. You and everybody else. He acted like our life with mama was just a bad dream."

"He hurt a lot when your mama died, Ivy Jean."

Ivy Jean's face went bright red, but Miss Summers patted her leg, she was safe speaking her mind.

"I respect your father and honored his decisions for a long time. It doesn't mean I stopped caring. When I heard about Wade going into the Army… Well, I needed to check on y'all."

Music started all of a sudden from somewhere in the house, muffled because of where they were but loud enough that they had to speak a little louder. Debra's record player cranked to top volume. Ivy knew what that meant. *She's pissed at her mother and letting the whole county know about it.*

"Debra says you're her father's mistress," Ivy blurted, careful not to use Debra's word, *whore*. She felt instantly ashamed at the admission and immature, despite the adult nature of the statement.

Having said it, though, she desperately wanted Miss Summers to deny Deb's claim and Ivy strained to keep her expression under control, prepared for the answer either way.

Miss Summers looked at her lap, then brought her chin up, tilted her head and spoke in a wistful way. "Poor Debra. She's like a wounded bear cub." Then she added, "But yes, it's true."

Miss Summers's honesty struck her as courageous. They were strangers, but she'd spoken like they were old friends. She didn't appear disappointed by Ivy's directness or her savvy about the topic, either.

"Being a teenager sucks," Miss Summers said, matter of fact. "I wish Debra could see how important she is to Tucker. He does a terrible job showing her, mind you, but he would die for her in a heartbeat." Then she closed her eyes and, in a dreamy way, added, "That's what parents do."

Seeing Miss Summers drift, Ivy realized the lady needed rest and started to stand up. But warm fingers found her small wrist and Miss Summers looked at her then with sharp eyes.

"Not so fast, cutie pie," she said. "You kind of dropped a bomb with that M-word."

Then, all of a sudden, Miss Summers sat straight up with a stricken look on her face. She shoved Ivy aside and scrambled to get out of the bedcovers. Ivy Jean stood frozen, watching Miss Summers stumble to the toilet and heard her heave twice before she understood the crisis. Wretched, empty sounds trailed off to agonizing moans, made louder by the commode.

"Shit," Ivy said, without thinking. "What can I do?"

She scanned the room for washcloths—that's what Joanne had sent them for earlier.

"I'm okay," came Miss Summers's soft voice, barely audible. She hunched at the basin as Ivy Jean stood in the doorway and, with a backward shove of her foot, Miss Summers tapped the toilet door shut, just as Ivy caught sight of blood on her pajamas.

Another "I'm okay" barely got out before she retched and gagged again.

"You don't sound okay," Ivy said. She began to pace and wring her hands and then her body froze when she noticed a huge bloodstain soaked the bed where Miss Summers had sat.

Ivy Jean had to get her aunt, and had turned to go, when, like magic, the small door to the foyer opened and backlit Joanne's slender figure. As if she'd been caught breaking the law, Ivy nearly ducked to the floor.

Joanne paused. "Ivy Jean, is that you?"

Ivy decided Miss Summers should explain things and tugged covers over the stain. "Yes, ma'am," she answered too cheerfully.

Hands clammy, she watched Joanne approach, her disapproving face growing clearer. Before she spoke, Miss Summers called out, breathless and weak.

"Ivy Jean, did I hear Mrs. Massey come in?"

The toilet flushed and the sound hid Ivy's answer—and her honest sigh of relief. Miss Summers emerged and saw Joanne, color rising to her sallow cheeks.

"Oh, hi, Joanne. I'm glad to see you." Coal smudges circled sunken eyes as she attempted pleasantry. "Ivy just came to check on me and I was about to send her for you." She gripped a blue bath towel around her waist. Ivy could see the pajama bottoms on the floor behind her but the blood was no longer visible.

Joanne's gaze stayed on Ivy. "Is everything okay?"

"Sure, it is." Miss Summers drew Joanne's eyes to her. "Can we talk?"

Then to Ivy, like she'd just arrived a minute ago, she said, "You're a nice girl and I'm glad you stopped by. Run along now and enjoy this summer day, okay? I'll see you again before I leave. I promise."

Ivy was thrilled to pick up Miss Summers's signal. *We have a secret now, too.*

She wondered if her aunt knew that Miss Summers knew both of Ivy's parents. Picking up tension in the air, she remembered the complicated relationship between Joanne and Miss Summers, her father and her uncle. So, with a half-smile at Miss Summers, Ivy Jean left the odd little guest quarters.

HEIRESS SEALS MISTRESS IN MANSION'S SECRET CHAMBER

SIXTEEN

Tucker

LEAKE COUNTY, MISSISSIPPI

The boys stood frozen in the middle of the road and forced Tucker to brake so hard the truck swerved toward a ditch. Tall summer corn blocked their immediate view but both young blacks took a look behind them and shot in the opposite direction. Dark and oily plumes crept into view behind the cornfield at the same time an acrid odor reached the truck.

"Shit," Chess said. "Something's on fire."

Tucker ground into gear and whipped the pickup out of the ditch and straight into the cornfield. Bumping and crashing, they barreled toward the smoke. Tucker slid to a stop and leapt from the truck once the flames were in sight. He ran in the direction of screams, away from the blazing house to his right. It was too late to save the structure. Chess triaged the yard and hurried to the side of an elderly female on the ground who had smoke seeping from a gray mass on her head. Ten or so young adult Negroes, male and female, wandered around, some crying, one puking behind a shrub.

The inferno appeared to have engulfed a residence, not a school like the judge said would be there. As Tucker neared, the screams began to stop and a sick feeling set in just as a white male in a checkered shirt flew from the field ahead of him, stumbling for his footing as he tried to refasten his jeans. Fighting the urge to chase the boy, Tucker hurried in the direction from where he'd come first, toward the screams he'd heard.

In the trampled stalks, a young white woman mumbled through wet sobs, clambering to cover her pale, freckled skin with torn and bloody clothes. She screeched when she saw Tucker, terrified. He knelt a distance from her, showing he meant no harm, but she scuttled sideways and tried to run. A gash on her head pulsed blood and, unable to see, she stumbled. Fine, red hair matted in clumps around her face, but Tucker could see her lips were fattened and cut. She was young—maybe twenty. She made him think of Debra and he felt a surprising rush of parental fury.

The girl gasped for air then curled up and wailed. "How do we…strength to…work in the face of hatred?"

Words were coming out singsong, like recitation, not like she expected answers.

"Chess!" he shouted. "Over here!" Then he said to the girl, "I'll be right back. Someone is going to come take care of you." He had to catch the monster that did this.

The wind had changed and carried dense soot across Tucker's path, blinding him. He squinted and tried to hunker down below the smoke, running in the same direction the checkered-shirted man had gone, praying no plows were in his path.

The fire made a deafening roar and Tucker sifted through the din to catch an engine rev, just as he ran out of the smoke and sucked in breath. Fishtailing away, a flatbed truck threw dirt and stones—a checkered shirt in the black cab. Tucker set chase with everything he had.

The driver spotted him in the rearview and floored it. Tucker leapt after it, straining to reach the tailgate. His thick chest thudded to the ground first and cushioned his forward velocity some, but his chin met the hard road with a sharp burst of pain.

"That fucking hurt," he groaned, glad to sense no broken bones but feeling foolish and old. He rolled over and climbed to his feet, spitting Mississippi real estate out of his mouth. Tucker hurried, limping slightly, back toward the girl, pissed that he'd left her to begin with when he had nothing to show for it. His feet tangled with a rag in the dirt and caused him to stumble but he recovered. He looked down. He'd tripped over a white sheet with holes cut out. And the girl was gone.

The orange, angry tongues of destruction lessened as the timber frame of the nearby blazing house succumbed. Ashier smoke hovered in the air now and made it nearly impossible to breathe. Wood crackled and fell, punctuated by sobs, and a crow cawed from the woods not far off. It was otherwise eerily quiet.

Chess had the red-haired girl in his arms, at least, moving toward the truck, and Tucker let out a sigh of relief.

"She needs a doctor," Chess strained to speak.

Adolescents and teens huddled in groups, dazed, clearly wary of the white men trying to help. Most wore stunned looks of horror, a few of them defiant or channeling pure anger. The elderly woman's hair no longer smoldered and she sat by the tree, speaking to a slender Negro man crouched beside her. She held a cloth and wiped sooty tears from her face. The man stood and came toward Tucker and Chess.

"I'm Desmond Carter," he said, extending a hand. The porch roof fell and Tucker didn't hear the rest.

"What was that?" he asked when the collapse was complete. "Snick, you said?"

"SNCC—Student Non-Violent Coordinating Committee," the man repeated. "We sponsor this school." He looked back at the wreckage. "Or did. They threw Molotovs."

The crispy, oozing scrapes on his face had once been eyebrows.

"What other injuries do you have?" Chess asked. "Any casualties?"

"She's the worst, I think," Desmond said, indicating the girl. He nodded toward the woman by the tree. "Mrs. Whitehouse is banged up and agitated, but she's not critical. The kids are mostly scared."

Chess set the girl down in the middle of the truck cab and barely got in himself before the vehicle lurched. Tucker had already climbed behind the wheel and started with the gear and clutch.

"Where's the nearest hospital?" Chess asked, slamming the door.

"Carthage. Leake County General," the man answered.

"We'll send help," Tucker shouted as he started to drive away.

Chess noticed the tall man's half-smile and leaned out of the window. "What's her name?"

"Julia!" Desmond called back. "Julia McPherson, from Connecticut!"

Tucker glanced over, realizing Chess could be the girl's father, their coloring was so close and their ages were about right. He took it slower through the cornfield this time as he retraced the road back to Carthage.

"Two white males sped away in a Ford flatbed," Tucker announced. "What did you learn?"

"It's a Freedom School," Chess said. "She's a college student who came here to teach blacks how to vote."

Tucker barreled through the pure-white settlement, passing Heights Baptist Church at a faster speed this direction, but he still scanned the streets and driveways for a black Ford truck. The streetlights had just come on and all the tidy homes were lit, their children safe and cozy inside.

Tucker glanced back at the girl, this Julia McPherson. Her breathing came more evenly now, which was a good sign, but the sight of her face made him cringe. Both eyes were swollen to slits and darkly bruised, same as her misshaped, bloodied nose. Someone had put a shirt around her bare shoulders where her ripped blouse hung in shreds. He hoped her injuries looked worse than they were. They'd checked for broken bones and it appeared her face had taken most of the blows. The nasty cut at her hairline was crusting but still seeped red blood. Chess dabbed at it regularly with a handkerchief from his pocket.

"She seemed to be asking questions when I found her," Tucker said. "Or listing things, reciting."

"Probably both. Memorization and rote recitation is basic to their method."

Chess told him what he knew about SNCC and the Freedom Schools. The organization's technique included memorizing a series of human rights questions and that sounded like what Tucker might have heard young Julia uttering.

"Kids teaching kids," Tucker noted.

"Yeah, about human dignity and, in theory at least, that it's okay to *non-violently* assert their rights."

"There's nothing non-violent about any of this."

"That is correct, my man. Julia McPherson was raped and brutalized as a symbolic message from the Klan: Here's what you can do with your nonviolence, Outsiders."

"How do you think her father will feel about that?" Tucker looked at the girl. Freckled knees swayed with the movement of the truck. *Basic human rights had been violated, all right.*

Ropes of sticky hair had fallen back over her face and Tucker imagined Debra again with another surge of outrage. He rarely thought of Debra as needing protection, though, because she never seemed vulnerable. And while he'd seen her get plenty impassioned, he could not see her sacrificing civilized life like these kids. But then, he didn't really know her, beyond the fact that she'd arrived at womanhood in a nasty mood. Her mother said she was violent and angry and he supposed he should try to figure out why. *Don't all young women go through a violent and angry phase?*

The words "womanhood" and "Debra" didn't go together for Tucker. Call it denial, but he didn't even try to grasp the idea of his spunky daughter being a sexual creature.

His father's offhanded lessons about women came few and far between, but it seemed what he said had stuck.

"Useful creatures," old Thurman had called them. "Keep the darlings feeling useful and in their place. And don't even try to figure them out."

Tucker had found it simple advice as a young man. His father had several "useful creatures"—one to bear his name, one or two more to suck his dick, then two or three especially pretty ones standing by to adorn his arm. He even had creatures to teach his sons the finer pleasures.

Tucker squirmed, considering what *usefulness* Debra might provide a man. Right then Tucker wanted to hunt down the fucker in the checkered shirt and apply a father's *unchecked* anger to the racist scumbag's slimy hide.

"SNCC, and organizations like it, are on their last gasp," Chess said as they entered the dismal town square of Carthage for a second time. "They've combined every one of their resources for a valiant, final effort to do this peacefully."

Tucker spotted an arrowed sign that said HOSPITAL and turned. "You'd think the yahoos, if they're all that intelligent, would realize an *army* of militants is waiting to send the peacemakers home and fight cracker violence properly."

"With black power," Chess added, raising his fist in the manner of those who disagree with the peaceful approach.

Leake County General looked busy from the parking lot. Plastered on the glass of the emergency entrance, large lettering spoke plainly: WHITES ONLY.

"Well, well," said Chess. "Lucky for us she's not purple."

SEVENTEEN

Vincent

<u>Dallas, Texas</u>

Vincent had had enough of driving around Dallas for one day. His mission to find Carla was a big, fat failure. He'd run out of clues, had no new leads, and couldn't think of another possible trail. Jolted to the decision as if from a trance, he jerked the Pontiac out of a turn onto Tremont Street—their old neighborhood. Sitting up straighter, he resumed purposeful direction after two U-turns and picked up Lemon Avenue, which would take him all the way to Carla's place in Oak Lawn.

At the apartment he could at least have a shower and use the phone, maybe even sleep if he had to stay over again. No more sweaty nights in the Pontiac, he promised himself with a glimmer of hope that Carla would be home this time. His heart raced at the possibility and he sped through a yellow light to keep a breeze in the car.

Owing to one-way streets, getting to the parking lot of her apartment complex required a couple of zigzags. If Carla still wasn't home, he'd try to call the ranch again. He wanted to check on Ivy Jean anyway and, while he didn't want to give up yet, he craved to hear that Carla was safe. Tucker said they'd had an ugly fight. Vincent knew she must be wounded—and being pregnant sure wouldn't have helped matters. He tried to convince himself that maybe she'd borrowed a friend's lake cabin or took a getaway to give herself space. But all day a sense of something overlooked had nagged at him.

A crew of pavers had portions of the parking lot cordoned off, so he drove around her building to a different stairwell. The blast of cooking asphalt that mugged his nostrils also stung his eyes as he climbed the stairs. From the railing, he scanned the parking lot on both ends. No tan Corvette, no 'Vette at all.

He decided to knock on a neighbor's door first, an easy lead he'd nearly forgotten. The neighbor hadn't been home when he'd gone by earlier, but the beautician he'd spoken to had said she was Carla's "spiritual guide." Exactly what that meant Vincent wasn't sure, but lilting music and a woody fragrance coming from inside seemed to fit.

A woman with long, graying tresses appeared at the door as soon as he knocked. She wore a gauzy, dark purple pantsuit and a beaded leather strip tied around her forehead like an Indian princess, sans feather. The fashion looked very Californian.

"I'm glad someone from family is here," she said, and Vincent didn't correct her. Her English was clipped and thick, suggesting Russian or maybe Polish heritage. "Please, come."

She ushered him inside and shut the door. The floor plan mirrored Carla's, and she invited him to sit in a chair near the picture window overlooking the pool. He declined her offer of a beverage.

Following his gaze across to Carla's balcony, she said, "Her place has been dark since Wednesday."

Tucker had said he'd tried to reach her all day yesterday—Thursday.

"The poor girl was miserable. More angry than downhearted, I think, but I worried." The woman sipped from a teacup. "Nothing I said or did calmed her. I could see her pacing, speaking on the phone for long time. Lights on very late. Unusual. Except for that man, she is peaceful woman."

Vincent didn't pursue what he felt sure was a reference to Tucker yet. "Do you know why she was so upset?"

She eyed him carefully and he shifted in the chair.

"How much do you know about Carla?" she asked.

"We've been good friends for a long time, since college." Vincent hoped that would be enough but added, "Maybe she mentioned going to Prosperity recently?"

The lady visibly relaxed and then the floodgates opened. In no time, he knew more about Carla's adult religious and spiritual views than he'd ever hoped to, but it felt good to hear her friend report Carla was still in awe of life. He'd have thought Tucker sucked all of that out of her.

The arrangement between his brother and Carla sounded like a whirlwind, a veritable tornado of parties—make that orgies—flowing with booze and all flavors of decadence—of Caligulan proportions. It disgusted him.

"Poor girl is conflicted," the neighbor said, bringing Vincent back. "Man has his talons deep and demands she remain same stupid girl stuck in same pathetic life. Too bad she loves him. These days woman is not required to love lover."

She held his gaze. Vincent could imagine this old sage casting a spell on him right there and then.

"I think Carla is close to leaving him, at last! She is trying. You have helped her, Vincent. It is good you accept her back. You are Tucker's brother, but she forgives that."

It seemed Carla had told the woman a lot.

"Did you know she was pregnant?" he said.

The question unleashed another elaborate and detailed story of Carla's soul quest. She gestured constantly and multiple silver bracelets seemed a form of emphasis.

"Everything about him and his evil seed causes Carla agony," she said, summing up. Then she leaned in and whispered, "I offer to help find someone to abort fetus." Her gaze didn't waver. "She took risks last time. Got lucky."

The gypsy sat back and dusted her hands together. "Your brother is no help. A doctor friend of mine can lead us this time."

"Is that what she's decided? Abortion?" Vince dreaded the answer.

"The whole spectrum, I tell you. She threatened many solutions. Suicide, too." Noticing Vincent's reaction, she added, "Indirect though and mostly when she wept. But you see why I worry."

Suicide didn't fit Carla. She was a tough lady, still excited about life, her spiritual guide said.

She's safe somewhere avoiding Tucker. Vince didn't let himself think worse than that. He settled instead on the warmth and relief he'd feel again when she surfaced.

"One more question before I go," he said. "A lady I spoke with mentioned Carla had a friend at the newspaper? She didn't know a name, said it just came out when Carla was angry at Tucker and scheming revenge. Do you know who that is?"

Vincent was pretty sure a reporter hanging around acting chummy with his mistress would make Tucker skittish. It pleased him that he'd remembered to ask. Like a real investigator.

The neighbor didn't know anything about Carla's friend in the press, but Vincent left for Carla's apartment in a lighter mood, feeling like he'd been with an old friend somehow. It dissolved as soon as he unlocked the door, though, because something smelled awful. Not powerful like decomposing flesh, thank God, but distinct and unpleasant. The AC was still off, he noted, and he followed his nose, turning on lights as he went.

This apartment is so much like her. He took in the color scheme, the modern lines and sparkling appliances, whimsical touches here and there, like a tortoise figure peeking from behind the recliner, watching the door.

In the powder room, off the kitchen, he located the smelly source in a wire basket behind the toilet. A heavily soaked menstrual pad had leaked and gelled in a malodorous pool on the floor.

His head snapped back on finding it. "Ugh!"

He emptied the basket into a pail from under the kitchen sink, where the brown-paper grocery bag lining was all but empty.

On a closer inspection of the powder room, he discovered smears on the linoleum where blood had been wiped at but not cleaned. He raised the toilet seat to a dried, red-brown blotch staining the porcelain and he silently declared his first mystery solved, the sources of stench identified.

Excessive bleeding and/or careless disposal. Brilliant deduction, he thought wryly.

But sloppy hygiene didn't fit Carla. Vincent walked around the apartment inspecting the floor.

Did she miscarry?

Unless she'd lied about being pregnant, wouldn't that be the only explanation?

Vincent wanted very much to keep his thinking positive. He cleaned up the bloodstains, then took the paper bag from the pail in the kitchen and gathered up all remaining trash in the apartment. There was very little waste, underscoring that she'd planned to be away, but she must have left in a hurry. He carried the bag outside and down the stairs to a dumpster in the parking lot. While he was there, he grabbed his valise from the trunk of the Pontiac.

Carla's small apartment was fresh again in no time with raised windows and the air conditioner fan on. The asphalt stink from outside tinged things a little bit, but he didn't mind. Vincent sat down in the kitchen and looked at the phone on the plate-glass table, exactly where he'd left it the night before.

It felt like he'd traveled a million miles since he'd left Ivy at the ranch. In the context of exhaustive, consecutive hours focused on one thing, he couldn't remember the last time he'd invested this much of himself, not even in his kids.

Find Carla and go home.

He reached for the phone and, willing her to be there, dialed the number for the ranch. It could be thorny if she was actually there and Joanne answered, though Ivy Jean would have juicy news for a letter to her brother, at least.

Still, no one answered the phone.

Where are they?

Vincent lit a cigarette and thought about what to do next.

EIGHTEEN

Ivy Jean

D<small>AHL</small> H<small>OUSE</small>

Ivy made her way back to the kitchen, still worried about Miss Summers after seeing all that blood. *All women menstruate,* she reminded herself. Some were just more frail and sickly with it than others. It was rotten luck for Miss Summers to have the flu and her period at the same time.

Sipping on a bottle of Coke she'd taken from the fridge, Ivy gazed out the windows over the pool and noticed Mr. Haines down by the corral. He looked to be attacking a pyramid of hay bales with a pitchfork. In the pasture behind him, the farther one that rose and blended in the foothills, one of the horses had started toward him, nodding its huge head up and down.

Surely a horseback ride would take her mind off Miss Summers. Ivy set the Coke bottle on the bar and hurried out, deciding that sliding patio doors are not for people in a hurry as she pulled and tugged on the handle. Once out, she half skipped around the pool and across the yard. Maybe she could help Haines feed the animals, too. The smell of fresh hay wafted past her nose, mixed with the scent of lilac, and gave her happy feet that inspired more skips. Closer to the feed trough, other smells of summer reminded her she was on a western adventure. *Focus on having fun, Ivy*, she scolded herself. *It's summertime!*

She slowed and walked up to the foreman, breathing hard and smiling. Mr. Haines worked a broad pitchfork deep in the straw, back and forth, loosening the tight cluster. Muscles strained the seams of his khaki shirt. Shy all of a sudden, Ivy watched him through a veil of bangs.

"Can I help?" she asked, eyes wide.

He laughed. "I don't think I've ever seen a person approach chores with that much enthusiasm before."

Handing over the pitchfork, he nodded respectfully and hooked his thumbs in his jeans pockets, watching her. Acting like she had experience, she tried to copy his method, best she'd observed, and, grunting with gusto, she was amazed at how much work it took to move a single hunk of hay on a pitchfork from the bale to the trough. She could probably do a much quicker job of it with her bare hands, but she wasn't going to say so.

"There's an extra pair of Wellies in the stable by the back door. Recommend you wear 'em," Mr. Haines said and walked in that direction.

Maybe Wellies made it easier. Ivy followed him. "What're Wellies?"

"Boots," he said, pointing at a neat row of tall rubber work boots just inside the stable, lined up like soldiers at attention. "Made for people who walk around in muck all day. They're named for the Earl who invented them in England, where it's often wet and mucky."

Ivy figured *muck* meant the same thing as *mud* but wondered now at her ignorance. She glanced outside at the dry ground and sunshine and thought it silly that she needed boots. Except Mr. Haines had on a pair. His worn-out cowboy boots stood propped against each other at the end of the row.

Ivy shed her sneakers with a single yank per foot and pulled on the smallest-looking Wellies, then strutted around in a circle. She felt *equipped*. She squared up her sneakers in line next to the foreman's cowboy boots then headed back outside to the job at hand.

Mr. Haines stopped her at the door with "*Ahem.*"

He stirred a tangled pile of leather straps on a workbench in the corner. Astride old whiskey barrels opposite the bench sat a pair of elaborately tooled saddles. Their leather fragrance dominated Ivy's senses, just like in the library. It layered the air in familiarity. Mr. Haines tossed a pair of canvas gloves at her with a flash of dimples so friendly she couldn't help but smile back. She wondered if her dimples looked that attractive as she scrambled to catch the toss.

"To avoid blisters," he said, gesturing at them.

• • •

Ivy got lost in the strenuous work, realizing that if she worked this hard every day her muscles would show like Mr. Haines's. She wouldn't mind that. After moving a few more forkfuls of hay from the bale to the trough, she followed him around, eager-puppy-style, learning that cattle and horses each had their own feeding area in the yard. "Pasture grass is the best food for both animals," Haines said, but alfalfa hay was like vitamins. Secured behind their stall doors, she fed the horses oats from her hand.

They didn't mess with the cattle much and Ivy was glad for the distance. They looked like almighty beasts up close, recalling Old West stampedes, not the least bit tame like the ones she'd seen in pictures of dairy farms.

"Do you think you'll ever get milk cows?" she asked.

"Not if I have a say," he said, laughing again. "Hold on," he added. "You need one more thing."

Mr. Haines returned from the stable with a bandana. He shook it out of a neatly folded square and handed it to her. She wiped her brow like she'd seen him do, then twisted the kerchief lengthwise to sweep her sweaty hair up in a loose ponytail. At least wet bangs stayed behind her ears better.

"Milk cows are too much damn work," Haines answered finally.

Ivy laughed at the irony. "Like this ain't damned hard work," she said, and ignored his surprise. Having exchanged cuss words with him relaxed her even more. It was nice to feel welcome as a helper and not a nuisance, like when her brother Wade let her help raise his chickens in 4H, and later on let her help with his prize-winning vegetable garden.

Mr. Haines fitted the enchanting palomino with a bit and reins, leading her out of the stall to the bricked aisle. She looked just like Dale Evans's horse, Buttercup. He motioned Ivy over and told her to always move toward an unfamiliar horse at the shoulder.

"When you approach, notice how she reaches out her muzzle to sniff you. With the back of your hand extended, she can take in your personal scent and determine that you're not a predator."

Ivy followed his lead and stroked the horse's long, soft nose. "What's her name?"

"Bella. It's Spanish for 'beauty.'"

Ivy nearly snorted, wondering if Mr. Haines realized his Spanish beauty was a blonde. But she sure admired his gentle authority with the animals.

"A mare of good quality," he'd called the palomino.

The bigger horse was a male named Blade. He was a brown color that Mr. Haines called chestnut. He led Blade to the horse trough, then showed her how to brush Bella.

Shoulders, back, then rump. Keeping wary and respectful, especially around the hindquarters. They examined all four legs and Ivy mimicked his confidence with the animal, tried using his soothing manner of speaking as she combed Bella's shiny mane, which she realized was the same platinum color as Joanne's hair.

"I like the way the stable smells."

Mr. Haines looked at her like she spoke Martian.

"Fresh-cut lumber?" She shrugged. "The hay and leather. It's not bad."

He laughed. "I promise the smell around here will be *eau de horseshit* soon enough." They both burst out laughing.

Ivy Jean quickly developed a soft spot for the foreman. He didn't mind her questions and he liked talking about ranch life, she could tell by the way he remembered his days growing up on a horse farm in Kentucky. Mr. Haines seemed trustworthy and there was something familiar about him that she couldn't put her finger on.

"Do you wear that gun in case one of the animals gets out of hand?" she asked, noticing the pistol on his waist. Mr. Haines shot her a look, not pleased, but the gun's carved handle showed under his shirttail and had been hard to miss a couple of times when he bent over. It had to be for something.

"Not to shoot a horse," she said quickly with a laugh. "But to get their attention?" She hoped to assure him she didn't see anything odd about his having a gun. "Don't all cowboys carry guns?"

"Not your concern," he said with a sternness that stung.

It got quieter between them after that. Ivy followed his lead and didn't ask so many questions. When he told her they were done for the day, she returned the gloves to the workbench, the Wellies to the row, and put her sneakers back on. She thought with that stable full of exotic horses they'd have to hire help someday.

"How old do you have to be to work on a ranch?" she asked.

Mr. Haines stood near the door in the shadows. "It's not age, so much as ability, strength. You're pretty good," he said tipping his head.

Ivy nearly hugged him but restrained herself. "Really?"

Those dazzling dimples appeared and he said, "Come see me next summer."

Dusk fast approached and June bugs and locusts chorused around them in stereo, familiar for a summer evening.

"See ya," she said.

He nodded and put a cigarette to his lips.

When he lit it, gooseflesh zipped across Ivy's scalp and she remembered an image of the same lined face, lit in the dark. Her mind searched while she walked up the slope toward the main house... almost smack dab into Princess Debra near the swimming pool.

"Yesterday morning," Debra said, "I was out here minding my own business." Her arms were loosely crossed and she stared intently at where Ivy just came from. "I heard something over by the stables. Nothing scary, just a noise that made me look. After a few seconds I could make them out in the shadows."

"Who?" Ivy had to admit she liked the way her cousin told stories.

"Mother and the ranch foreman." Debra glanced over to check Ivy's reaction. "Sick, huh?"

Ivy knew the girl didn't really want an answer. "Shit," was all she said.

"It was like she was kissing him goodbye after a night of torrid passion, not wanting to go but needing to return before her innocent child woke up."

"Huh," Ivy said. Debra's mix of sarcasm and drama sounded like one of those ten-cent romance novels. "Your mother is having sex with Mr. Haines? You sure?"

"Yes, of course, I'm sure. And I can't bear what it will do to my father."

Ivy tried not to react and watched as the late afternoon light played off the swimming pool's surface.

"Want to put on our suits and go in?" Ivy thought a dip sounded divine; she'd been working hard.

Debra said no but took off her shoes anyway and sat by the edge of the pool. Ivy did the same. The cool liquid felt delicious and she leaned to swirl her arms around and splashed her face. Debra was angled back, leaning on her palms, looking up toward the hills.

"I like Mr. Haines," said Ivy. "He's nice to the animals, talks to them kindly, like Dr. Kildare. He showed me how to come at a horse and how to brush them."

Debra swirled her feet around. "He's hiding out, you know. They call it 'being burned' in spy language." She acted perfectly serious. "I'm not even sure Haines is his real name. My father gave him this job at our ranch because it's in the middle of nowhere."

The tale spinner had Ivy going again. It didn't matter if she told lies because Ivy went along willingly. Thinking of Mr. Haines hiding in the shadows jolted her memory. She remembered why she'd recognized him.

The night that she and Vincent drove out to the ranch, it'd been pitch black. Vincent had taken a hundred turns on roads with deep ditches and kept stopping to peer at a useless map. This one time, as the car slowed, Ivy had hoped he'd given up and was turning back home. But before they'd stopped all the way and the dome light came on, she'd been straining to see into the dark outside. Mr. Haines's face appeared off the side of the road, just for a second, like the flash of a cigarette lighter. She'd assumed it was an illusion, like when she saw faces in the wallpaper, and had forgotten the whole thing. Most likely Mr. Haines didn't remember that night either.

Big hairy deal.

Maybe he was meeting a lady friend. Ivy smiled to herself and imagined a cowgirl from a neighboring ranch.

Debra kept on about the spy business. "I overheard my father discussing it on the phone," she said. "Daddy didn't know I was around the corner of his study—I'd been sent to the library to do my homework. But Haines is a secret agent, a government *spy*." They looked at each other. "Really, it's true. He's a hired assassin or something."

Ivy was curious but doubtful. "What exactly did you hear?"

Debra came up off her locked elbows and swished her hands in the water, then leaned back on them again. "There are some men calling themselves investigators, asking where both Daddy and Haines were when President Kennedy was shot. And something about an outfit scrubbing or a scrubbing outfit."

Ivy didn't know what to say.

Debra seemed to drift for a moment. "My mother is so stupid," she mumbled. "She's going to ruin it for all of us."

Daytime TV wasn't half as twisted as things around there. Debra wasn't even making sense. What did her mother have to do with Mr. Haines being a spy?

Then Carla's face flashed in Ivy's mind. "Because your dad has a mistress?"

"Can you blame him?" Debra's voice rose. "Affairs happen all the time anyway. Now there's a birth control pill and we all just better watch out because most people are sex crazy. My mother is a hag. Always, *always* nagging my father." She scrunched up her face and added a drawl. "What will people think, Tucker? What do I say to so and so, Tucker? You need to do this then that so we can have more, more, more, Tucker." Her shoulders drooped. "It's disgusting to watch. She wants to be first lady so bad it's like poison in her."

Ivy's eyes widened. "You mean there's a chance she could be first lady?"

"Shh!" Debra shushed as she jumped to her feet, fixing her gaze on the hills. "Did you see that?" She walked around the corner of the pool gazing intently at the hills. "I think somebody's up there watching us."

Ivy scrambled to join her as Debra pointed to a spot where two hills seemed to intersect. Ivy could just make out a piece of guardrail showing.

"To the right. There's a car stopped. You can barely see the sunset reflecting on the windshield. He must have opened a door—that's what caught my eye."

"So what?" Ivy shaded her eyes and strained to see what the heck Debra saw. "Maybe it's my father coming back, getting lost again. Could be anybody who's lost."

Debra shrugged and returned to the pool. She sat down at the shallow end on the steps, drew her knees up and studied her toes. "They're looking for Haines."

A twinge of fear mixed with a thrill and Ivy itched to talk about secret agents again. "Who are 'they,' and how come they want Mr. Haines? How do you know anyway?"

"Listen, Bubblehead, I told you. He's a covert agent. I heard my father talking about it."

Ivy liked the word *covert*. It sounded more official than secret.

NINETEEN

Haines

DAHL HOUSE

Later that evening, Haines sat at the table in the bunkhouse with the telephone and a libation placed in front of him. It was Friday after all. He leaned back in his chair and swept both hands over his stubby scalp, eying the drink. Early on in his residence at the ranch—at Tucker's insistence—he'd helped himself to a lead-crystal highball out of a lesser collection in the library at Dahl House. Now, watching an ice cube shrink under the stress of fine whiskey, he raised the short, heavy glass and sipped.

Outside, the ranch seemed peaceful enough. That's what he needed—normal and calm. Having the little girl, Ivy Jean, around that afternoon, so eager with the horses, made him forget Tucker's crisis for a while—his secret girlfriend lying ill in the house. The girls' screeching by the pool before dark got his attention, though, jerking him out of the serenity. Tucker's girl had acted like someone was in the hills, so he'd watched where she pointed. Not wanting to affirm their suspicions, he'd waited until they lost interest, then took a ride up there. There weren't any vehicles he could find, but his instincts were aroused.

Haines set his glass down and stood to check the locks on both of the bunkhouse doors, suddenly feeling paranoid. He slid the desk in the living area away from the wall. Pulling on a loose piece of paneling, he set it aside and removed a rectangular metal case from between the wall studs. He carried the case back to the table where there was decent light. As he took out the weapon's hardware and began to disassemble, he let his mind work while he cleaned.

Know your way out going in. It was ancient but timely advice.

Recalling lessons from his grandfather served as grounding when Haines handled weaponry. Granddad Luke, or Lucas Davies Haines, had raised his only child's illegitimate son from infancy. Through the years he'd transferred valuable knowledge to his grandson, much more than the obvious love of horses and guns. Every evening after chores, impassioned storytelling commenced, carrying right through supper to lights out. Young Gabe would sit cross-legged and eager on the floor by Luke's pine rocker, captivated by his vivid tales of triumph. In the context of these stories, Luke had also shown him ancient Zulu traditions of his maternal ancestry.

"Bush baby—*Isinkwe*," Luke had impressed upon the boy. "*Isinkwe* is nocturnal and can *see* with all senses. He sees with his ears, with his nose. *Isinkwe* is constantly tuned in to what surrounds him."

The telephone rang and jolted Haines back to the bunkhouse. He listened as the contact in Virginia he'd called earlier updated him without pleasantries or emotion.

"I left word for my guy in Baltimore," the caller said. "He's the only chance of helping you locate your guy, Massey. If I find anything else out, I'll let you know."

Tucker was way off the grid. It surprised and aggravated Haines that neither of them thought to plan for emergency contact—they had no contingency in place for any kind of unforeseen crisis, like the mistress showing up at home. *We are old fucking men getting sloppy.*

Thoughts of Tucker getting pulled out of commission for something personal, and most likely trivial, made him uneasy. The ire in the man's blood might not be quick to forgive on the matter. Haines sighed. In his mind, Tucker didn't really have to know yet. He might show up here tomorrow on his own, and Carla was ill, true, but if it was the flu, it'd surely pass. However, orders were orders and Joanne was in charge.

Haines would tend to matters at hand the best he could. He owed Tucker that much. The lieutenant had saved his life twice during the war and had used his family contacts unselfishly to further Haines's career—not to mention this chance at a peaceful existence on his ranch.

One thing Haines was sure of was Tucker hadn't *known* Carla Summers would show up. He'd have warned him otherwise. Of course, there might have been some missed phone calls, Haines supposed. If Tucker couldn't reach him by phone, what was he going to do, send a messenger?

This is one holy mess.

TWENTY

Tucker

CARTHAGE, MISSISSIPPI

In the Leake County General emergency room, Tucker and Chess managed to hand off young Julia McPherson without too many questions. As they wheeled her away, Tucker remembered the county cruiser in the parking lot and found the driver in the hospital cafeteria. A deputy uniform barely fit the overweight, pimpled kid with dark, close-set eyes and a hostile glare. At hearing "school fire," the kid got a serious look on his face and, leaving the bag of donut holes on the table, motioned Tucker and Chess to follow him. But when Tucker described the fire's location and told him what they'd seen, the deputy stopped in his tracks and, clearly annoyed, snapped open a notebook from his shirt pocket and rolled his eyes.

"Who's the white girl? Did y'all get her name?"

Tucker's voice rose. "Haven't you been listening?"

Deputy held Tucker's glare. "Where'd ya say y'er from?"

Tucker moved toward him, but Chess stepped between them and led the prick outside, talking friendlier. Tucker hung back and watched his partner work the boy another way, and eventually, the deputy reached in the cruiser's open window and radioed the station for backup.

"Base, you copy?" The radio made a scratchy, empty sound, then an ear-piercing squeal, before a voice spoke hesitantly. "Ahem. Everybody's code ten. They're all—"

"—I got ya." The deputy cut him off, then hit the mic key again. "Over and out." He reset the mic, turned and shrugged. "It's the dinner hour."

Tucker reentered the hospital just as a stone-faced doctor came out of the double doors marked STAFF ONLY. The man looked around, his expression blank. Tucker tried to speak, but the doctor addressed him before he got the words out.

"Are you Mr. McPherson?"

"No, but I brought the girl—"

"—Get me kin," he said with a curt nod and left.

Tucker looked around for a friendlier face. He stepped to the nurse's station where the pretty brunette who'd quizzed them at the girl's intake sat behind a stack of files. He peered over them. Her uniform showed off nice, pert breasts.

"Miss," he said, meeting her eyes. "I've got to get out of here, but I'm worried about that girl we just carried in."

The nurse stopped writing and waited. Tucker felt compelled to hurry.

"A man named Desmond Carter said she's here in Mississippi with the SNCC, sometimes called Snick. Do you know what that means?"

She shook her head, but her eyes shifted back to her paperwork, suggesting she might actually mean *yes*. "Do you know if she's regained consciousness yet?"

Another shake. "Here's the thing, Belinda," he said, reading her nametag. "I don't know who the girl's family or friends are, other than Mr. Carter, the snicker guy." He flashed his usually irresistible smile, but she didn't react. "We can't stay, but I need you to locate Mr. Carter so he can put you in touch with her family. They're in Connecticut."

The nurse closed her eyes for a beat and looked around before giving Tucker the slightest nod.

That had to be enough. This was not why he was called to Mississippi.

• • •

By the time they left the hospital, nighttime had arrived and the truck's cab swarmed with mosquitoes. Tucker took the wheel again and headed toward Philadelphia a second time. More bugs swarmed the headlights but, soon enough, a fifty-mph cricket song blew past and the noisy biters split.

Chess kept quiet for most of the ride and Tucker was grateful for the time to think. The damp air seemed to require shallow breathing so he rolled up his window. As the pickup topped a rise, they met a rapid series of headlights coming at them. Tucker didn't brake but took his foot off the juice, pressed the clutch and shifted to neutral. Five vehicles traveling close together at high speed streamed past, their headlamps blinding Tucker and forcing him to focus on the road's center stripes. Chess had turned to watch behind them and Tucker resumed third gear to keep the truck moving.

"They're all turning off the highway a mile or so back," Chess reported, "disappearing into the trees to the east."

They just couldn't seem to get out of Leake County.

Tucker noted the odometer and slowed. Three minutes after the first convoy, another stream of cars approached, caravan-style, not in such as hurry as the earlier group but clearly together. This time, Tucker could make out two cars and two pickups filled with men. Chess noted rifles in racks and in arms. When their taillights disappeared from the rearview, Tuck pulled over to the shoulder and cut the lights.

"I don't like this," he said.

"Me neither." Chess waited a beat. "Should we—"

Before he could finish, Tucker reversed direction and backtracked, lights on. When they came to a dirt road near the point where the first line of cars and trucks had disappeared, Tucker switched to parking lamps and followed the deep tire ruts through a barren field toward a dark tree line. Fifty yards or so into the foliage he stopped and wound backward through a thicket before cutting the engine. Whoops and laughter drifted past.

"Sounds like a rally," Chess said. An engine gunned. Night critters of the woods tried to get a melody going but firecrackers or gunshots kept stunning them silent. "Celebrating."

The Klan gathering to celebrate, maybe? Tucker felt uneasy. Was this even his business?

Joanne had declared once that he'd become an addict of "war-game adrenaline." Only these weren't games and he was starting to think he might not care enough to fight another war for his country.

He righted himself in his seat and took a deep breath. Reliable intelligence had to get through to Washington. President Johnson must be frantically seeking calm in the country, desperate to focus on November elections, so maybe this did concern Tucker. He could imagine the president operating behind a mound of phones on his desk, calling shots from the Oval Office like he did from the Senate building for a dozen years—barking orders into one telephone and pouring honey-coated words into another, manipulating gears and greasing wheels and whatever it took just to keep things moving his direction. Both sides of the civil rights controversy were forcing their position, constantly in his face and damning to hell all other matters of government. Without question, the president needed to keep himself publicly distant from anything sounding like civil rights *forces*. Deployment of any stripe would require supreme delicacy.

But Lyndon might just let the military settle it, and he needs intelligence from the ground.

The rally noise seemed to originate a few tics northeast of where Tucker and Chess were parked. They watched, undetectable from their position, as another group of cars bumped past. Tucker estimated a dozen vehicles so far, maybe fifty men.

"Let's go in for a look," he suggested, finally committed to performing recon. This kind of thing was everybody's business.

He geared up with ammo and two of the weapons from the truck. Chess followed suit, and they quietly slipped into the trees. Not even the frogs noticed their movement. Keeping to the dense backwoods, they circled a swampy meadow and moved within sight of the gathering but far enough away not to be noticed. Tucker wished he'd brought binoculars.

White men of all shapes and sizes moved around in smaller groups, laughing and shaking hands, bumping beers like they were congratulating one another. *It is a celebration.* Two guys were shooting at beer bottles lined up on the trunk of a fallen tree. Grayish-white piles of Klan disguises lay in heaps on cable spools and truck beds. The men looked dirty, but they could have been regular old hunting buddies gearing up to raise hell.

Only their prey was other citizens.

Tucker wondered if they were celebrating the school fire. He didn't want to imagine another reason for their cheering.

The vehicles were parked in a rough circle around the clearing, at least a handful of them black Ford trucks. Tucker looked for a checkered shirt, but it was hard to make out that kind of detail. A bonfire crackled and roared, casting long shadows on the scene. It looked like armed point men watched the perimeter.

Tucker and Chess ducked abruptly when headlights swept across their hiding spot and more cars arrived. Law cruisers, this time—three of them. Tucker couldn't confirm the insignia painted on the cars, but one of them looked like that of the hospital deputy. The other two might be city cops. From Carthage, he supposed. Six uniformed occupants in all got out.

Of course lawmen are Klan. Racial cleansing, SS style.

"Do you think this group is the White Knights?" Tucker whispered.

"Hard to tell," said Chess. "They seem a little overt to me."

The bonfire blazed like the schoolhouse and heat blurred the air. Tucker and Chess didn't detect any signal, but suddenly the crowd noise dimmed and Klansmen came together near the fire. Tucker made out a central figure addressing the group from a higher point, as if he stood on a pedestal. It was impossible to decipher his words but he apparently called the mob to prayer because their heads bowed in unison.

"A fucking prayer meeting." Tucker couldn't believe it.

"The Klan is righteous. Devout believers," said Chess.

Applause and shouted approvals came next and the speaker stepped off the crate or otherwise disappeared. Tucker felt in his gut that the celebration had something to do with the Freedom School and the violent rape of that college girl. Now every third shirt he could see looked checkered. He didn't know what he'd do if he saw the bastard again. Tear into the campfire mob with guns blazing like some kind of cowboy?

He needed to ID those lawmen.

TWENTY-ONE

Ivy Jean

Dahl House

Ivy slid her aunt's meal tray onto the makeshift table by the bed where Miss Summers rested. The little lamp threatened to topple, but she caught it in time. Miss Summers seemed to be asleep, so Ivy whispered her name as a question. It was a great relief when she saw an arm lift and reach out. Ivy took her hand, startled that it felt like the heating pad her father used on his back, always set on high. Miss Summers tried to sit up and Ivy helped ease her into position on the bed to take some food.

She slicked her hair back with pale hands and took a deep breath. Her pupils looked starkly bigger in her pale-gray eyes than before, but she showed interest in the chicken soup and, encouraged, Ivy lifted the bowl to help her.

"You'll feel better after eating."

Hearing herself made Ivy think of her brother—Wade knew how to be tender.

The bowl was too heavy for Miss Summers, so Ivy started feeding her with the spoon. Knowing what to do, how to care for her friend, felt natural, even though she'd never done it before. She hoped the horse and pool smells on her didn't offend the patient's appetite.

Miss Summers watched her face. "Did you get some sun?"

She sounded tired. Ivy buttered a saltine and nodded.

The older woman spread her hands over her body. "Ain't this a kick in the butt?" Meaning her illness, Ivy guessed. She cast a sympathetic smile and fed Miss Summers soup until she didn't want any more and eased back under the covers.

Her head had dropped more than once like her chin was too heavy. Maybe Joanne or Debra gave her a pill or something.

MOTHER-DAUGHTER DUO CONSPIRE TO DRUG MISTRESS

"When Vincent gets here, tell him I'm sorry," Miss Summers said softly.

Ivy's pulse quickened. "Sorry for what?"

"It sounded good at the time," she said as she closed her eyes.

That didn't make sense. Her pretty grey eyes looked so dopey. Could that really be the flu? There was surely more going on than heavy menstruation.

"What sounded good?" Ivy watched her mother's friend and tried to decipher if she was hallucinating.

"Ivy Jean, I'm your godmother." Miss Summer's dull eyes implored hers, seeking approval.

Ivy didn't know what a godmother was but the word contained both "mother" and "God," so it excited her to know she had one. And just like that, so much changed.

She hid her astonishment at this new secret and beamed. "Gosh, Miss Summers, I wish I had known that before."

"Call me Carla, dear," she said. "We're nearly family." She paused a beat. "I have to get home."

The normal-sounding statement brought Ivy's focus back to the problem at hand. "I'll help you, but don't you think we should get a doctor?"

"Not here," Carla said, straightening her legs. "I'll see a doctor in Dallas. I'll be okay."

Her words and the way she spoke them didn't exactly inspire confidence in Ivy, and sure enough, Carla closed her eyes and went still for a slow count of five. Then, without warning, she began to talk again.

"It's just ssssilly," she slurred, eyes closed. "But it's *my* business."

Carla shook her head and drew away, like something unwelcome was after her. Ivy didn't know what to do. She tried to reach out to pat Carla's arm, hoping to calm her, but she pulled away again.

"Everybody!"

Ivy startled, set off kilter by the strength of Carla's emphasis and volume of her shout.

"Everybody wants them, but how do they know?" She softly begged for answers, turning back toward the wall. "How do they all know?"

Alarms clanged in Ivy's head.

"I'm sorry," Carla wailed, and she sat upright again. Her eyes darted around, not seeing Ivy. She had gone somewhere Ivy couldn't follow. Carla moved, shoving the covers aside, her eyes searching for something on the floor at the end of the bed.

Hands shaking, Ivy reached for a saltine and tried to bring Carla's focus back to the food. But Carla looked at the cracker like it was a hand grenade.

"He's dead."

Ivy felt dumbfounded and barely heard her godmother whisper again.

"Dead…"

"Who's dead?" Gooseflesh traced down from the crown of Ivy's head to the tips of her fingers. She had said she was sorry first… *Did she… No.*

Natural panic at the thought of her father or Wade William made Ivy reach out and touch her shoulder. "Carla, you're scaring me."

Ivy had turned to run for help when Carla spoke normally again.

"Oh, Ivy Jean." She rolled over and faced her. "I didn't mean to scare you, baby. My mind's not right."

"I know." Relief washed over Ivy and hope sprung back in her heart.

"It's the baby, honey. I'm not pregnant anymore."

Before Ivy could respond, the door opened. She nearly jumped out of her skin and ducked behind the wall when a call rang out. "Hello there!"

Ivy relaxed on hearing the voice. "Mr. Haines, you surprised me," she said, showing herself. "I'm helping Miss Summers with her food."

Carla seemed to rally. "Haines!" she said with surprising exuberance. Mr. Haines gave her a hand as she tried to sit up.

Ivy was glad they knew each other.

"How are you?" he quizzed the patient. His dimples creased while he looked over her, but he wasn't smiling. "I'd say you're not a hundred percent."

Carla shushed him and pulled her hair off her face again, holding it there a moment with a soft smile on her lips. She pointed to the corner of the bed where Ivy Jean had been earlier, inviting him to sit.

Ivy sunk inside a little but saw Carla wink in her direction and the quick index finger to her lips.

"Would you excuse us, doll? Come back in a little while?" she said.

Ivy got the code and nodded. "See y'all later," she said, leaving them.

"I have to go home," Carla pled with Mr. Haines the second Ivy turned to leave. "Please drive me to Dallas."

Ivy opened and shut the small door leading out to the foyer, but she'd only pretended go through it. Slightly ashamed at her urge to eavesdrop on Mr. Haines and Carla, she still squeezed herself in the corner shadow and melted against the door hinges. She thought her aunt might not be pleased with this meeting, so she'd be the doorstop, just in case Joanne dropped in.

She could see part of Mr. Haines's body in the dim light at the edge of the bed. The lamp table and dinner tray hid Carla's head and shoulders and she was the hardest to hear from where Ivy stood. But she didn't dare move closer with the lamp's circle of light only inches away.

"It's late now, but in the morning I will get you home," Mr. Haines assured Ivy's godmother. "You're feverish." He sounded surprised. "I think we need to get a doctor out here."

There was sudden movement and Carla's head appeared by the lampshade. "No! Don't bring a doctor here. Promise me, Haines. Tucker is going to shoot me as it is."

Mr. Haines shushed her and mumbled a hurried assurance. Ivy bet he'd promise anything to calm her.

Carla spoke about books, emphasizing *her* books, saying she'd brought them for Tucker, not anybody else. It seemed to fit some of her confusing jabber earlier—people wanting something of hers. Ivy heard the word "investigator" and flashed back to Deb's story by the pool, about men hounding Tucker and Mr. Haines. Something about President Kennedy, or was it President Johnson?

"Are the books here?" asked Mr. Haines.

Ivy heard only murmuring, and then a few clear words. "Don't let anyone have them." She paused. "There's more," Carla said louder, getting heated again. Ivy couldn't hear it all. "Two other guys, not…types, more like thugs, came to my house…where Tucker was when Kennedy got shot, being pushy…"

Ivy's eyes flew open and her hand covered a gasp at the part about President Kennedy. It was the same thing Debra had said.

"Punks with attitude. And accents," Ivy heard.

"What kind of accents?"

Carla mumbled an answer to Mr. Haines that Ivy couldn't hear and, after a few moments of quiet, Mr. Haines stood up. "We'll talk about this on the drive to Dallas in the morning. Maybe they're hanging around your place and I can get a look."

Ivy was so relieved to hear Mr. Haines promise to take her newly found-out godmother home and to a doctor that she'd heard enough, it felt more like she was intruding now. So when he leaned over to smooth the bedcovers, rattling the dinner tray, Ivy took the chance to slip through the door. She wasn't used to judging people's trustworthiness, at least not in a thoughtful way, but something inside her lightened at knowing Mr. Haines was both her friend and Carla's, and she forgave herself for spying.

I'm going with them to Dallas, she decided.

Ivy hurried up the main staircase so Haines wouldn't catch her around, Carla's words still ringing in her ears: "I'm not pregnant anymore."

She didn't know her godmother was expecting a baby to begin with, so she didn't feel surprise, per se. In fact, she'd barely recognized the earlier comment. She didn't have experience with heartbreak, either, but she could see it plain as day on Carla's face. Girls at school had called it a "miscarriage" when a classmate's mama lost her baby. Like the stork just dropped it on the way. Ivy thought the words "lost a baby" implied so much—mostly sadness and grief—but it also meant bleeding. And everybody knew pregnant women puked. It all started to make sense. A wash of sorrow messed with understanding, and it all felt heavy on her shoulders. But there was nothing she could do now. She just had to trust Mr. Haines would take good care of Carla.

Upstairs, Dahl House seemed abandoned, quiet except for the drone of the central air conditioning. Following an urge to talk about lighter stuff, Ivy knocked on her cousin's closed bedroom door. Not hearing an answer, she opened it to total darkness. She could detect Debra's form on the farthest bed and didn't apologize for disturbing her. She just waited.

"Where have *you* been?" Debra's voice sounded hoarse and sleepy. Ivy had concluded Deb's habit of demanding answers came from being mollycoddled. Entitled—*as in, owner of slaves*. For someone so twentieth-century, Debra needed to get with the program.

RICH TEEN CAUGHT WHIPPING SERVANTS

"I just left Miss Summers," Ivy told her. She was about to share the news of her godmother and the lost baby when she caught herself. Her head filled with conflict again over the tangled relationships at work inside Dahl House, but she could appreciate Debra had different feelings about Tucker's mistress.

"She's sleeping," Ivy said. She heard Debra sniffle in the dark and asked, "Is everything okay?"

Debra flopped over to slam her face in the pillow. She wore the same shorts and sleeveless top from earlier, exposing densely freckled shoulders. Her voice was muffled when she finally spoke. "No, everything is *not* okay, and surely to God you have figured that out."

They must have a smart-ass class at those fancy schools.

Ivy decided to dodge the bratty remark. "Well, are *you* alright?"

Her shoulders relaxed and Ivy saw hint of an opportunity to turn her cousin into an ally. Ivy just needed to act like Debra was at the center of everything. She shut the door to the hallway and switched on the lamp made of pink knobby glass by Debra's head.

"What's going on?" She crossed her ankles and lowered herself into the pink shag cloud in one slick move. "Are you afraid of something?"

"No, stupid. I'm not afraid. I just need to think!" She still had her face in the pillow.

Ivy noticed the room smelled like wax crayons being melted or something.

"Come on," she urged. "I'm not your enemy."

"Are you crazy?" Debra turned her head and glared at Ivy sideways, kind of upside down, through glossy, untidy red curls. "You're just a pesky kid."

Rejection delivered with venom.

Yeah, well, you're a shithead is what Ivy wanted to say. Instead, she plowed ahead.

"Well, maybe, but I'm smart. And I bet I'm the closest thing you've got to a friend right now."

Behind a mask of a cocky smile, Ivy was horrified. *I'm smart? How stupid.*

Debra didn't answer anyway, but Ivy noticed she'd flinched at the word "friend." Maybe she was gaining the girl's trust.

She eased her argumentative tone. "I never knew I had a cousin, you know," she said. "Until you guys invited me to visit… Do you have more cousins?"

The pile of red hair didn't move; the princess continued to pout. Ivy surveyed the knickknacks and other feminine touches around the room that seemed left over from a little girl. She pressed on.

"Seems to me you live the life of a princess."

Debra sat up and glared at Ivy, then flopped down again, this time on her back, but she pulled a heart shaped, pink pillow over her face. "Oh, why do you care? My life is a wreck! It'll never be the same!"

She probably meant since she got expelled and her father's mistress showed up. Ivy watched her cousin lift the pillow for air. She sobbed to the wall but her wailing sounded fake.

"Are you upset about Miss Summers?"

Debra sat up in bed again, and this time hung her feet over the side like she planned to stay upright. She didn't seem quite so vexed.

"She is such a stupid, stupid cunt!"

More tears came after that. The girl had considerable acting talent if she was faking it this time. Crying people caused frantic urgency in Ivy Jean, sometimes a sense of impatience or helplessness, depending.

"There, there," she said, feeling an urge to comfort her cousin—and herself, so she didn't have a panic attack.

"Do you like that word? "Cunt"? It feels funny to say." Ivy tried to change the topic. "You don't even see people who curse in books use that word."

"It's just the vilest thing I can think of," Debra said. "You see it in filth magazines, but then, you're little Miss Innocent."

Ivy scowled, and Debra slickly glossed over the jab. "The point is *she* hates the word." She mimicked her mother's accent. "Cursing is unladylike, Debra, and sooo unbecoming."

Then she shot off the bed wearing a kind of smile, stomped around Ivy as she sat on the floor, and disappeared into her cavernous closet. She came out holding something close to her chest—a pencil pouch or something—and went to the window. With practiced motion, she lifted the framed glass, unlatched the wooden screen and, taking a slight leap, disappeared, feet last. The wind sucked the pink sheers through the opening, and they waved lazily to the night behind her.

Ivy went over and stuck her head out. The window's bottom ledge was slightly higher than her waist. "Hey, where you going?"

Debra had the pouch thing in her mouth and crab-crawled along the roof. Ivy realized she sounded like a "pesky kid" and withheld further questions, instead joining the redhead in something Vincent might call "daring behavior." Debra stopped halfway to the dark window of Ivy's room, sitting with her back against the outer wall. She concentrated on the items in her lap and didn't seem to notice Ivy scoot up beside her.

They faced westward to deepening starlight, the barest hints of orange backlighting against the dark hills. A vapor-light pole standing between the corral and the stables at the bottom of the slope flickered and cast a wide, if weak, alien glow.

The contents of Debra's bag were being lined up on the shingles between them. A rectangular bottle made of chrome or silver, with a screw cap that looked like a giant thimble had come out first, and Debra looked up with a grin.

Liquor? "Is this some kind of ritual?" Ivy said, intrigued.

Debra produced a cigarette lighter—silver again—and a hand-rolled cigarette. Ivy didn't know she smoked, but that's what grown-ups did, right? Only, store bought ones usually. A school friend's grandfather hand rolled his cigarettes with fragrant, sweet smelling tobacco from a pouch, but that's the only time she'd seen anything like it. He had let them observe his cigarette assembly, but they couldn't ask any questions. And his didn't have twisted ends like that.

TWENTY-TWO

Vincent

DALLAS, TEXAS

Happy to discover some bottles of beer in the refrigerator at Carla's apartment, Vincent sat down to telephone the hospitals again with a cold one in his free hand. New admissions had no record of a Carla Leah Summers, neither did the city morgue, and there were no "Jane Does" reported anywhere. Her seeming disappearance was making him more nervous by the minute and he wanted to reach someone at the ranch. That he kept getting no answer there concerned him, especially if Carla had shown up.

A leaded cut-glass ashtray sat on a colorful cloth in the middle of the kitchen table. He pulled the whole thing over, took a cigarette out and lit it. A coughing spasm caught him by surprise, but he cured it with a swig of beer.

The room had a modern air, the table made of glass, but Vincent thought it unappetizing to look down at scuffed boots under your food. Two slick metal chairs with curved backs had been made more comfortable with yellow fabric stretched over the seats, and the color drew his eyes to the yellow-framed clock on the wall; even the flowery blue curtains tied back by the balcony door were flecked with bits of yellow that matched the fabric square on the table. *Definitely a woman's touch.* It felt cozy and inviting and, for the most part, Vincent ignored mental glimpses of Tucker there.

Would Carla go home? He wondered whether to call her parents in Longview.

Serious, ages old friction had existed between Carla and her father for as long as Vincent had known her. Probably still did. And she did not have siblings. There was a lot about Carla that Vincent didn't know, of course, and during college he'd assumed everyone despised their father. But he remembered how naked anguish would settle on Carla's pretty face if you asked too many questions.

More than once he heard her fake a thick east Texas accent and a booming preacher's voice. "This family's dignity, the family's future, rests upon your shoulders!" Then she'd crack wise. "That impossible shit would buckle Charles Atlas."

Vincent could relate to a father who didn't even *try* to hide his disappointment in you. It was more than that for Carla, though. A kind of wistful resentment came through her descriptions. Vincent didn't know her parents, but he'd gathered her mother was old school tolerant, the submissive good wife, her father squarely righteous on the moral landscape.

"But *she* loves me," Carla would say about her mother. "She's never turned her back."

Even if it was a long shot, Vincent had to try. He fetched Carla's address book, knowing he had to rule out a retreat home. He paused a moment before dialing to plan what to say. He didn't want to distress her folks or give them reason to worry.

The number in Longview began to ring and his hands began to sweat. He was immensely relieved when a female voice answered.

"Mrs. Summers?" he assumed. "My name is Vincent Pritchard and I'm an old friend of your daughter Carla's." He wiped a hand on his pants.

"Why, yes! I remember. You're Gwen's husband, correct?"

That surprised him and everything he'd planned to say flew right out of his head. "Y-yes, ma'am, that is correct."

He switched the phone to his other ear and wiped the other palm on his leg.

"We are so sorry for your loss." She said this as if Vincent had buried his wife just the week before. "Is everything okay?"

"Yes, yes, everything is okay." He collected himself. "Thank you, Mrs. Summers. I was just passing through Longview on my way back from a business trip over in Shreveport, and I know Carla likes to visit y'all. By chance is she there?"

"Why, no dear. To my knowledge she isn't expected either. Did she tell you she might be on her way to Longview?"

Vincent covered his tracks. "No, ma'am, nothing like that. I was just giving it a shot in the dark," he said calmly, in rhythm with the lie now. "I stopped off the highway for supper and thought to myself, 'Wouldn't it be nice if Carla were visiting her parents and could join me for a bite?'"

He had to backpedal then, of course, when Mrs. Summers offered to feed him.

• • •

Later, huddled in the corner of a burger joint on Lemon Avenue, he stared at a plate of onion rings, feeling morose. It was a familiar place if his mind was left to dwell on certain things.

An errant bullet. Vincent's face twisted, just thinking of the phrase used to explain his wife's death. The newspaper's description had sent him agonizing inward for weeks during the aftermath. He'd functioned somehow despite it, showed up and nodded yes and no, squeezed his children, and begged God for what it took to comfort them. But his soul went somewhere else. Vincent understood he suffered a form of shell shock, but knowing didn't help any. That state of mindless functioning went on for a while. Various prompts became excuses to *excuse* himself from the world—and his children. To spare them his pain, he'd rationalized. He had stayed away long enough the last time for his mother and Gwen's Aunt Janelle to take his children away. *Gwen's babies.*

The TV newsman had called it "a tragic case of dreadful timing." An artful way to say that in a split second Gwendolyn Pritchard ceased to be a living, breathing woman. Vincent inhaled deeply and let himself get it out. Sadness stole him from the diner and ensconced him in the memories.

Tremont Street…their small, perfect piece of the world. The memory of their house was as sharp and clear as if he'd just come from there. "A bungalow," the realtor had called it. Wade had walked to school, Ivy Jean had napped on the porch, and Gwen had made the place home. The five tree-lined blocks to the bank where he worked made it almost foolish to own a car.

What would happen if I went there? Just for a drive through the neighborhood...

Gwen had always spent time outside the house every day, regardless of the weather and usually with the children. On laundry day she'd played games with them under a clothesline of drying bed sheets magically transformed into clouds. She'd sweated over the flowerbeds and made sure the children had a green, sticker-free lawn where the neighborhood kids liked to play. Vincent had always felt so lucky when Gwen spent her precious outdoor time with him.

One cloudless, spring day she'd packed a picnic lunch for them to share. Ivy Jean was next door at the neighbors' house, and Wade was in school. Catty-corner from the bank sat a small city park with huge oaks and benches where the old timers fed pigeons. It also offered picnic tables in the shade. Gwen had stopped to fetch him, and at the exact instant her hand had reached for the door handle a single .38-caliber bullet pierced her forehead and sailed through her brain like a warm pellet through butter. A pair of slick migrating bandits had made off with six thousand dollars—and his wife's soul.

Police had later confirmed the bullet that killed her had come from the security guard's gun. He'd been an employee of the bank, a cheerful, lawful man who had become their friend over the years. Gwen's death almost killed him.

It had almost killed Carla, too.

Oh, God.

Remembering got to be too much, and Vincent forced himself out of the reverie, digging for his wallet to pay the check. He didn't notice a stranger walk up to his table until the guy slid into his booth and faced him. A well-fed man in wrinkled shirtsleeves covered up the red-tufted vinyl, and with his belly pressing the table, he cast an apologetic smile.

"A moment?"

He flopped a wallet badge open with one hand and swiped a handkerchief across his brow with the other. Vincent glanced at the ID then back at the man's face, unable to speak. He'd seen plenty of Fed credentials after the bank robbery and this guy showing up now was an uncomfortable coincidence. He mentally shook his head clear so he could speak.

"Sure," he said, noting the man's unkempt style.

The waitress appeared and reached into her apron for a ticket book. Before she spoke, the man said, "Black coffee, then bring him the check." He extended a fleshy hand across the table, the girl clearly dismissed. Gordon Sims."

"Vincent Pritchard," he said, shaking the man's hand. "How can I help you?"

"I saw you come and go from an apartment leased by…" He consulted a spiral from his shirt pocket. "Carla L. Summers." He shut the spiral but left it on the table. "A couple of times, actually. But she doesn't seem to be there."

Vincent kept his expression neutral. "That's right. You guys think I'm a vagrant or something, breaking and entering?"

He didn't know whether the man could detect his sarcasm. Feds don't monitor vagrants.

"Let's just say I've been asked to interview Miss Summers." A friendly smile effectively disarmed Vincent.

"About?" Mindful of body language, he placed both hands on the table and loosely coupled them. He had nothing to hide.

Sims opened the spiral again. "You are Vincent Pritchard, a resident of Prosperity, Texas, correct?"

The Pontiac plates of course. But he wondered, near panicked, what his brother Tucker was getting him into.

"I already told you who I was. What is it you want?"

"Why are you here?"

"Why do you care?" Vince discreetly wiped his palms.

"What if I said she might be in danger?"

Vincent got hold of his good sense. "Alright now; enough with the cloak-and-dagger business. I am Carla's friend from college, and I'm checking on her while I'm in Dallas on a family matter. I don't know where she is. Do you?"

"You're Tucker Massey's kin, correct?"

Hearing his brother's name threw Vincent's guard straight up. He *knew* Tucker was behind this.

Sims could tell that had gotten to him and pressed. "Where were you during the ambush?"

What? His whole body tightened, feeling accused. "Do you mean the attack on President Kennedy?"

Sims tilted his head and shot him a look like Vincent was playing games.

"First Cattlemen's Bank of Prosperity. I was at work when it happened."

"Where was your brother?"

Vincent realized, with a mental groan, that the only lawyer he knew was Tucker. A freight train raced through his head, crowded his thinking. As smoothly as he could, Vincent turned out of the booth and stood up. "What do you mean Miss Summers might be in danger?"

Sims shrugged thick shoulders. "She's being watched by unsavory types, for one thing."

More unsavory than you? Vincent had had enough. "Excuse me, but I'm done with your questions tonight, Mr. Sims."

The plainclothes agent tore off a piece of paper from his notepad, scribbled down a number, and pushed it at Vincent

"Ask for Merle and your call goes straight to the top."

Vincent left a five dollar bill at the register and hurried out of the diner.

Who the fuck is Merle?

Vincent walked back to Carla's place, thinking he'd rather be in Prosperity worried over Wade and Ivy Jean growing up. He massaged his left shoulder and paused to look around on the street, nonchalant, wanting to confirm that the sense of a million eyes on him was imagined.

Once back inside, he opened another beer and tried not to pace, yet he made regular trips to the kitchen sink—and the only window that faced the parking lot. Thinking TV might settle his mind, he wondered whether Carla's fancy console set had a color picture.

When the doorbell buzzed, he instantly thought, *Hide!* But he regained composure and skulked to the peephole, expecting Sims or worse. The pea-sized glass was filthy, and he couldn't be sure, but it looked like a woman on the other side. He opened the door to find a tallish brunette. Her eyes widened, surprised.

"Is—uh, is Carla here?" She smiled easily and stood on her toes to see over his shoulder.

"Who are you?" Vincent asked, all sorts of internal guards engaging.

"I'm her friend, Cassidy. Who're you?" Commanding hazel eyes met his.

"I'm Vincent. Carla's not here." He decided to go for it. "Do you know where she is?"

"I'm in front of you because I thought she was *here*."

"She's not. When was the last time you saw her?" He didn't mean to interrogate but he was about to snap.

She took a pleading posture. "Can I come in? I didn't expect the third degree."

Vincent's face flushed over his crappy manners, and he stepped aside. Mid-thirties, he guessed she was, wearing trousers and a silky gray shirt tucked in, kind of manly in her sense of fashion, but she didn't seem masculine, or federal-issued. His guard settled a bit. She might be a cop, though.

"How long has Carla been missing?" The tall woman crossed into the living room like she knew the place, plopped on the white leather chair and nodded for Vincent to sit too.

He stayed standing. "Who said she's missing? And how do you even know Carla?"

"How do I know you're not an intruder?" she challenged. "You could be a serial killer."

They exchanged reluctant grins. Vincent sat down in the middle of the sofa, facing her. This would get them nowhere fast.

"I'm here because a family friend has been trying to reach Carla," he said, hoping this woman would be able to shed some light on the situation. "Wednesday was the last time anyone saw her. Late evening, around ten. Have you seen her since then?"

"No. We had lunch last week and I haven't spoken to her since."

He didn't hide his disappointment. "Did you have plans with her tonight?"

"I only stopped by because the lights were on."

He sensed her answer was not entirely truthful. "How is it you two are friends?"

Prominent cheekbones suggested American Indian somewhere in her lineage. "We met at a fund-raiser last year. Clicked right away, you know? A natural friendship just blossomed. Don't you think she might be somewhere with her boyfriend? I mean, it's only Friday, so we're talking about a couple of days here."

"What boyfriend?"

Her eyebrow arched, doubtful. "You have a key to her apartment but don't know about Tucker?"

He looked away and changed the subject. "Where do you work, Cassidy?"

"The *Dallas Times Herald*," she said.

Her friend in the press? He stayed calm and fibbed. "I don't remember Carla mentioning a newspaper friend."

"Probably because she's afraid of Tucker finding out. He's paranoid, you know. And mean."

"You seem to know a lot."

"Did she tell you about the goons who showed up to interrogate her?"

Vincent's scalp prickled. "Yeah," he lied. "Do you think she might be with them?"

"No. Not willingly." Cassidy leaned forward. "One guy really pissed her off. Scared her would be more like it, I think."

Carla had mentioned people investigating Tucker. She had seemed annoyed though, not afraid. "Evidently you're not worried," he said, using an eyebrow arch that rivaled the one she'd been tossing his way, only bushier. "Anyway, I know she's not with Tucker."

Cassidy frowned.

Vincent considered whether this "friend" knew about the pregnancy. Carla felt great tenderness toward Tucker's baby growing inside her, and Vincent felt sure very few people knew. But if Cassidy knew about the baby—or even the row with Tucker—he might be able to trust that she's an actual friend and not just a reporter working a story.

"Who have you talked to?" Cassidy asked.

"Her beautician. Her parents. The morgue attendant."

"The nutty neighbor?"

He smiled at her description. "Yeah, she's been worried."

"Have you talked to the law?"

She smells a story.

He chose not to mention Sims and the other implied surveillance. *Unsavory types.* "I don't have any reason to expect foul play, so no, I haven't involved the police yet. What, exactly, do you do for the *Herald*? Are you a reporter?"

"I am. Is that a problem for you?"

"Kind of."

"Well, I might be able to help, you know."

"Okay, so, tell me what you know."

"I meant I could help you investigate. Leg work, you know, run down the facts. That's what reporters do."

The Doubting Thomas in Vincent made the decision for him. "Leave me your number. I'll call you if I need help."

"Do you know where Tucker Massey is?" She pressured him like a pro. "And what about his wife?"

Tiny hairs stood up on Vincent's neck. What was really going on in Carla's world?

TWENTY-THREE

Ivy Jean

DAHL HOUSE

Treetops brushed over the end of the porch roof and made a rustling noise in the breeze. A lopsided three-quarter moon had risen and gazed down on Ivy Jean and Debra. Ivy sniffed the air, wondering if a skunk was in the yard, and felt a slight chill as she studied the odd collection from her cousin's pouch.

"Did you make that cigarette?"

Her cousin had strange skills for a rich girl. She didn't respond, but her lips turned up in a smile as she focused on pouring liquid from the bottle into the oversized thimble. It did hold liquid, like a canteen, and she brought the cap to her lips, tossed her head back, and downed the stuff.

"Argh!" Her teeth were bared but she wasn't smiling. Ivy had seen movie cowboys do the exact same thing in a hundred saloons.

After a few more sound effects, a softer, friendlier Debra spoke. "Grandmother Natalie says a thimble of vodka steadies the nerves." She smiled and shuddered. "Takes the chill away."

Ivy wondered if the grandmother used a giant thimble too.

"I've never tasted vodka," she said, admiring the sophisticated pinky-out manner in which Debra held the little cup. Ivy had never tasted any alcohol, actually, except for a sip of Vincent's beer one time when they went fishing, and that had tasted utterly putrid.

"Two or three of these little pick-me-ups do the trick every time," Deb said. "Small doses only." She wagged a finger. "Keep you from getting stupid." She suppressed a hiccup. "Then, like magic, the Cunt becomes *almost* bearable."

This time she fully belched, then giggled and poured another dose, spilling some. She handed the fresh "pick-me-up" to Ivy Jean.

"Go on." She looked at Ivy from under pale curls that reflected the moonlight. "Who's going to know? More importantly, who is going to care?"

Her eyes didn't waver. Ivy had just been dared.

The good girl in Ivy told her to go to bed and let this redhead whine to the moon about her horrible life. But the aspiring teen inside wanted to keep her cousin talking, to feel mature and liked. Maybe vodka helps rich, troubled people cope. Ivy had been left there at the ranch, after all, to experience the ways of this part of her "family." Who *is* going to care? It was a good question. She took the thimble and tossed it back the same way as Debra.

A fireball hit the back of her throat first, then hit her brain.

"Man." She sputtered and coughed, wanting very much to seem cool and experienced. But with the stomach churn and the fire searing her throat, for a second she thought she might puke. Instead, she just aimed a pained grin at her cousin.

Debra insisted on another, but Ivy waved her off with a hearty belch, and they both laughed. The burst of noise echoed in the night and, after a while, Ivy's stomach settled down, so she braved another thimbleful. She wasn't thinking about getting in trouble anymore; she was thinking about bragging to her friends. Or making some.

Ivy Jean Pritchard has a bona fide secret.

Ivy crept toward the edge of the roof and peeked over to see two moons, one in the swimming pool and one in the sky. She tilted her head, trying to see both of them at once and got dizzy. She moved herself back to her spot next to Debra. Trees near the house dappled moon shade around and lulled Ivy to a sense of calm with their familiar *swooshing* in the breeze. She remembered the supposed watcher in the hills that Debra had spotted earlier, and Ivy peered and pointed that direction.

"Any signs of the car you saw earlier?"

Debra glanced over and shook her head.

Lying back, Ivy marveled at the Milky Way as it spread a vivid pathway to the whole universe before them, as sharp and clear as a photograph in the encyclopedia. Ivy thought of her brother and wished on the brightest star for his safety. Certain that he was somewhere looking at the same moon, she lifted her hand and waved at the orb.

Sometimes her father spent time gazing at the night sky, usually from the hood of the Pontiac in the driveway. He'd throw a shop towel across the bugs on the glass and sit propped against the windshield. This had happened more often since Wade left. Ivy joined him when she knew he was out there. She liked the feel of the warm engine but hated the sound of crunching bugs when she leaned back. Most of the time, she and Vincent stayed quiet, making it feel like church. One time, he had stared at the sky for such a long time that Ivy imagined he was composing messages to Wade William and telegraphing them through the stars. Later that same night, he'd spoken to her about the importance of them all looking out for each other, of being a close family—no matter how far apart they got.

Ivy decided not to think about her dad and brother anymore just as Debra's voice brought her back to the roof.

"Do you know what's going on here, kiddo?" she said. "How old are you?"

Ivy snickered at the wise-elder tone her cousin used. "I'm twelve and a half. And no, I don't know what in hellisss going on here." *Did I just slur?* "Aren't we getting drunk?"

"Yeah, you're old enough," Debra said. "I was fucked when I was barely older than you." She paused to let her blurted, random words register, and Ivy felt adequately stunned, it felt so out of left field. Somehow, what had started feeling pretty good was going another direction.

"What?" she asked, but she honestly wasn't sure she wanted to hear more.

Debra's sneering grin made her look like a hungry spider about to pounce. It gave Ivy the uneasy feeling that an ugly truth was about to come out of that pretty mouth; then she sat back with a little laugh, and the air lightened with another breeze.

"Vodka doesn't smell on your breath." She leaned close and blew in Ivy's face. It smelled a little like medicine. "Mother hasn't noticed a single time."

Ivy doubted that, but was relieved her cousin had veered off the sex subject, even though at least twenty questions had already formed in her head.

Debra picked up the hand-rolled cigarette and flipped open the cover of her lighter.

"My brother smokes since he joined the army," Ivy said, before realizing the cigarette in Debra's hand was also the source of skunk smell.

Debra lit the end. It flared, and the twisted part burned away and disappeared. She sucked in until the tip glowed. Then she sort of burped out, "Yeah? Well, I promise you he's smoking some of this shit wherever he's at, probably this very minute. Hell, I got this from a soldier." She exhaled vigorously, passing the cigarette to Ivy.

Ivy waved it away, "No, thank you. I don't smoke."

She'd heard someone say that once and thought it sounded well mannered.

Debra made a gurgling sound through her nose and said, "Child, this is a joint. Pot. Weed?"

"No shit?" Ivy thought it a reasonable question, which also hid her ignorance.

"No shit," Debra said. "It's pretty good stuff. Here," she offered the thing to Ivy again, who leaned away. "Haven't you *ever* smoked before?"

Ivy shook her head. "Joint" was a funny word for a cigarette. Pot was curious. She'd read a few things about kids smoking pot and parents going freaky over it, calling it dope. It came from a plant, but they said it can ruin your life like all drugs ruin lives.

"Did you learn about pot in private school?"

Whenever the evils of drugs were talked about in Ivy's school it was usually with high school kids. Prosperity's parents and preachers seemed to want all drugs to be illegal. Vincent said once that he thought such laws would turn out worse than in the old days when illegal liquor spawned gangsters like Al Capone.

Debra flared the lighter again and sucked the joint. It hissed and popped as she inhaled. Ivy noticed the same melting-crayon smell from her cousin's bedroom earlier.

"If my mother only knew the truth about the stupid schools she so carefully picked and cultivated since I was in diapers, she'd really freak out. They're nothing but an extravagant front for sexual deviants. They hide things, including mind-boggling wealth, and the nighttime faculties at in-residence schools treat their charges like slaves. I had sex before I even turned thirteen. Ha! That news might shock your average mother, but mine just complained that I fucked a minor priest and not the goddamned Bishop."

Ivy's stupefied look clearly pleased the storyteller. "If I smoke that cigarette will I have a fit or strip naked or something?" Embarrassment warmed her cheeks when Debra's eyes rolled.

"That is such a load of crap. I know tons of people who smoke weed, several of them young, prissy Catholic schoolgirls. It just makes you mellow."

Ivy watched Debra puff, the tip going from orange to red, its sloppy ash scattering. From a corner of her liquor-infused brain, the thirst for experience won out.

"What do you mean, mellow?"

"You don't give a shit. Guys call it laid-back. I promise it won't make you dance naked, but it might make you laugh," she said, extending the thing. "This place could use some laughter."

Ivy reached for the cigarette, picturing the look on Vincent's face if he learned about this daring behavior. She didn't really want her father mad, but he should have thought about that before keeping her godmother a secret all those years.

Debra relit the joint. "Suck on it like a straw, holding it between your thumb and finger like this." She demonstrated. "Then hold your breath and keep the smoke in your lungs for a few seconds before you let it out."

"What if we get caught?" Ivy Jean asked. "Is it against the law?"

"You are such a baby."

"I'm not a baby!" Though that was kind of a babyish reaction, she realized.

Ivy followed Deb's instructions and promptly gagged, choking on the smoke until she almost threw up. Debra shushed her and patted her back until Ivy could sit still and take ragged breaths. Debra held out a thimble of vodka and, without a second of hesitation, Ivy downed it. The liquid strangely soothed that time and, with practice, she puffed on the piece of cigarette without coughing. They each had a turn pouring vodka into the thimble, huddled close, smoking pot and giggling.

Ivy imagined Joanne and Mr. Haines chasing them around with paddles if they got caught. She described the imagery to Debra who looked shocked but then laughed out loud and Ivy went on about her mother running after them across the yard, promising a whipping. Ivy wiped hysteric tears off her face and couldn't remember ever having such infectious fun.

Kids back home will never believe this.

Somehow, both girls came to lay on their backs, side by side, breathing hard after another round of silliness. Ivy's head was on the downward slope of the roof, which made blood rush to her brain. She wished they had a blanket or towels to lie on but the roof shingles were better than dirt and rocks.

Debra abruptly sat up. "Let's steal the whore's car!"

Ivy twirled around on her butt to face her cousin, who was stuffing the goods in the pouch. "You're crazy," she said, almost toppling with a dizzy rush.

Debra gathered all evidence of their crimes, and Ivy was reminded of a bumper sticker on the Methodist minister's car in Prosperity: *If You Drink and Drive, Drink Milk and Stay Alive.*

She knew she wasn't supposed to drink and drive—or even drive sober—and adding that to her big list of crimes tonight brought Vincent squarely to mind with a shiver.

But Debra was already sliding through the window back to her pink kingdom. And Ivy would not be left behind.

TWENTY-FOUR

Haines

DAHL HOUSE

Haines reassembled his freshly oiled rifle parts while listening to country music on the bunkhouse radio. That somebody could be staking out the ranch plagued his thoughts. It recalled the odd conversations he'd had with Moss and made him nervous. He'd promised Carla Summers a ride to Dallas in the morning, but if somebody had staked out the ranch, immediate measures had to be taken. He wondered if the "punks with accents" Carla had described might be connected to goons watching the ranch.

Did they know he was there? Were they after Tucker? Carla?

After frying a pork chop and washing up, he slipped out the back door of the bunkhouse with a small, powerful flashlight in his pocket. The perimeter of the homestead needed scouring for signs of hunters—and not the licensed seasonal variety.

The ranch was bedded down, and darkness offered him cover. Various spots along the property fence offered coverage that Haines might use if he were the observer. He scanned each one carefully with his flashlight, finding them all vacant and undisturbed. Making his way to the switchback in the hills where the girls had pointed again, he found a nesting site five yards off the road where most of Dahl House's roof and a corner of the pool were visible. The stables and corral had wide-open sightlines. Haines estimated 300 yards, an easy sniping range even with gravity and wind factors. There, he found the evidence he didn't want.

A scrunched up piece of trash blew in the wind. Haines picked it up and held the light in his teeth to unfold the stray paper enough. "Hoyo Monterrey," he thought it said, and under that, in smeared gold letters, "Habana."

Hoyo Monterrey was a hugely popular brand of Cuban cigar, made illegal in the U.S. by the trade embargo but, thanks to the gangster element, regularly available in the back room at the Swinging K Lounge in Ybor City, Florida. Company men smoked them every chance they got. *And all the other south Floridians who enjoyed fine tobacco.* Not exactly a narrow list of suspects.

Coincidence? Maybe.

Haines found two more potential nest sites accessible from the road but no recent evidence of humans.

A possible Florida connection on his trail tripped alarms in his mind. The agent found dead in New York recently, Underhill—who Tucker had seen the week of Kennedy's ambush in Dallas—had been part of an assignment in the Keys once. Haines hadn't known Underhill then, but they knew each other in Guatemala. He remembered their talks about Alpha 66, the compound where

American agents trained Cuban revolutionaries in the Florida Everglades.

Cuba was being linked a lot with the Kennedy assassination. He'd read newspaper articles theorizing about a conspiracy "triangle" between Cuba, Dallas and the CIA. If there was an effort underway to douse that speculation, he could understand them wanting to talk to him—assuming they knew he'd been in Dallas, on November 22nd—which brought him back to Horace Ortiz, the Cuban exile who poked him "hello" in Dealey Plaza.

Deep concern came over Haines. If dangerous people had tracked him to the ranch, he needed to draw them far away from there. Having Tucker's family in the crosshairs could not happen on his watch.

Following the river, he made his way back to the barn and considered whether it was safe to drive Carla out of there tomorrow. Riding off on an errand to the city wasn't a bad maneuver—he might draw them after him—but it would risk Miss Summers's safety.

The sight of Dahl House when he emerged from the river path brought on an undeniable ache for more sunrises there. Just reading the paper on that splendid porch was an activity he would sorely miss. A few lights burned behind the windows, and the porch was dimmed to just small bulbs at the corners and steps. He took a veritable snapshot in his mind of the peacefulness.

Company protocol, if he were on assignment, dictated immediate abort. Coincidence does not exist on a mission. But, he reminded himself again, this was not an assignment. Tucker depended on him as a friend and employee now. Confronting the matter head on would be best.

Sitting on the floor by his bunk, he pulled his road-weary duffel out from under his bed, mentally checking off items required to hit the road again, just in case.

TWENTY-FIVE

Tucker

Philadelphia, Mississippi

As the rusty pickup rolled to a stop in the motor court parking lot, Tucker and Chess were discussing the pros and cons of an open flame barbecue. The scintillating smell of it seemed to be everywhere in Mississippi, and they were almost two hours past briefing and way past supper.

Light shined in several windows of the motel units and cabins.

"I wonder what time the café closes," Tucker said. The shabby roadside place in the next lot had one lonely sedan parked outside, but all the lights were on. "All that talk about barbecued meat was cruel."

Their work boots crunched gravel as they crossed the quiet parking lot to report in. The door to Philips's rented room was propped open with a brick, and Chess tapped the frame. The rest of the guys in the room sat on folding chairs talking quietly, baseball being called on a pocket transistor. Philips sat at his makeshift card-table desk, smoking a cigar and scribbling on a yellow pad.

He acknowledged the pair with a nod and dismissed the other agents. "Shut the door."

After closing it, Tucker stood by the bureau. He tried to filter his breath carefully—it was not a cheap cigar Philips smoked but the heavy puffs would overwhelm the small space in a hurry. Chess turned off the ballgame and sat down on a folding chair.

"Sorry for the late hour, sir." Tucker took the lead. "Judge Cummings gave up the names of White Knight leadership, Bowers and DuPree—a businessman with teenage customers and a fucking schoolteacher, respectively."

Philips waited.

Chess chimed in. "The judge advised us to drive by a rural school for proof of why his loyalties had shifted. It wasn't far out of our way, but when we got there it was blazing out of control from a Molotov bomb."

"One of the teachers, a white girl, was in the process of being violently raped," Tucker added. "She was the worst injury, and we took her to the hospital in Carthage. We were told she came there with SNCC. Do you know the group?"

Philips looked at his wristwatch. "What time was that?"

"It was dark when we left the hospital," Tucker said. "There's more, though. On the road back from Carthage, we drove into signs of a massive Klan rally and took it in. We watched six lawmen and sixty or seventy rednecks whooping it up at a private party in the woods. I think they might have been celebrating the schoolhouse fire and rape of the Freedom Rider."

Philips kept quiet until they finished. He wrote the names and locations of the White Knight leaders on his notepad. When he finally spoke, it was *loud*.

"I'm astounded by your amateur decisions!" He yelled at them like a drill instructor berating recruits. "How could you be lured off task so easily?"

Neither man had a chance to answer. He glared directly at Tucker. "You may have blown the whole operation."

Defensive arguments were racing toward Tucker's tightly closed mouth.

"This mission has precise, narrow focus." Philips snapped his words. "To secure and confirm identities! A damn school fire and backwoods meeting belong in somebody else's report, not mine."

"The girl might have died—" Tucker tried.

"—I don't care!" Philips cut him off. "Every hour not spent tracking the White Knights left a gap for them to learn we're inside. You two had the names."

Chess and Tucker exchanged a look.

Philips continued, whisper-barking. "How long do you think it takes for a soldier to get word to Bowers or DuPree? Their movement is our sole goddamn purpose for being here!"

Tucker shook off the instinct to defend himself again. There may come a time when their experience at the school and Klan rally mattered, but Philips was right—it wasn't now.

The case officer finally took a few calming breaths. "Oh-six-hundred call," he said with a dismissive flick of his cigar stub. "Get some sleep."

A waitress at the roadside joint next door put blue-plate specials before them, and the men plowed into short ribs and potato salad that was ready to serve hours ago. It might have been the best meal either of them had eaten before if they'd slowed down enough to taste it.

"We'll get CO's confidence back tomorrow," Chess said.

Tucker didn't want to rehash the dressing down. He licked spicy rib sauce off his fingers. "I didn't want to say so earlier, but I knew Underhill…slightly. A friend of mine knew him well. So what else do you know about what went down in Dallas?"

"There's not much anybody *knows* about Dallas. It's all speculation and I just like listening to the talk. The Warren Commission investigators seem to be building their case along President Johnson's insistence that Oswald worked alone. Grapevine is heavy with talk of spooks walking the cat, though. You hearing the same?"

Tucker nodded, grimly remembering the men demanding Carla's diaries.

"Are you a Cowboys fan?" Chess changed the subject to football.

Tucker was grateful. "I am, but they need more practice winning."

"Four and ten last season. Pretty dismal."

A good word for the way Tucker felt, dismal.

Later, Tucker flopped on his motel bed, exhausted, still wearing his redneck costume and, sure enough, the second his head hit the pillow, personal crap filled it up. He started to think about Vincent's promise—to find Carla. Did he? Where were they? Tucker had no idea.

I just want to sleep.

He mentally debated the merits of not sleeping again versus a sleeping-pill hangover. Willing his mind to clear, Tucker closed his eyes and took a deep breath. Feeling the humidity, he got up and turned the air conditioner's knob to high, peeled off his work shirt and jeans and tossed them over a chair before flopping back down on the bed.

Thoughts of Carla with Vincent led to severe agitation once more, though. When Tucker called his brother for help Vincent had said, "Carla's level-headed. She won't go to the ranch if she's that mad at you."

Tucker, straining to keep impatience out of his voice told him, "Yes, well, she's pregnant and unreasonable."

"So I heard," his brother said. "Whose is it?"

How did he—what?

During their big row, Carla had threatened marriage to keep the baby. "I've already proposed to one old friend," she'd told him.

Tucker lit a cigarette and scrambled for thoughts to replace that one.

Recollecting Philips's ass whipping seemed to work. For a superior to consider him untrustworthy had to be remedied. *I will not stand accused of torpedoing the mission.*

Something deep in Tucker rumbled about chances lost and reputations fouled. He got up again and scrounged in his shaving kit, then ran the cold-water tap. The water seemed to smell less repulsive if he ran it at least a minute.

"Are you sure?" he said to his scowling reflection in the mirror.

Carla's face returned to mind and Tucker suddenly knew Vincent was the old friend that she'd asked to marry her.

Tucker swallowed the pill and resettled into bed.

Female expectations outside the bedroom always made him tense, and he refused to endure another sleepless night over the goddamn drama queens in his life a thousand miles away.

TWENTY-SIX

Ivy Jean

Dahl House

Ivy Jean and Debra didn't get far in their plans for a drunken joy ride in Carla's Corvette. Debra's feet had barely touched pink shag as she slid back through the window when her mother appeared in the doorway. Until that second, Ivy Jean's head was still buzzy from the vodka and dope cigarette. Joanne's arms were crossed, and she glared at the pouch in Debra's hand. Ivy wanted to jump off the roof, but she didn't, and Joanne's features softened slightly when she appeared in the window after Debra.

"What are y'all doing on the roof?" she asked, watching her daughter closely.

Debra opened her mouth but Ivy spoke first. "It sure is a pretty night out there. We were just admiring the Milky Way. Have you seen it?"

Joanne's shoulders relaxed a tad. "No, I haven't—"

Expecting World War III to begin any second, Ivy Jean forgot her manners and interrupted her aunt. "Gosh, I'm hungry. Can I make a sandwich?"

Both Joanna and Debra seemed relieved, and Ivy Jean left them to settle it. She went straight for the Hydrox cookies and a jar of peanut butter that she'd seen earlier in the pantry. Shutting herself in the small closet that smelled of cinnamon and fruit and fresh paint, she ate two crunchy cookies at a time.

• • •

Sometime later, and still fully clothed, Ivy Jean startled awake in her room with the bedspread knotted around her middle. She couldn't remember going to bed and just wanted to be in her pajamas. While trying to get her bearings, she untangled the covers. Sweat trickled down her neck causing her head to itch and her mouth was drier than dirt. She went to get a drink and pee. A dream lingered, but she couldn't make sense of it except for a thimble reference that made her remember the roof and giggle. She had drunk liquor. And smoked dope! Her heart quickened with guilt—if Vincent ever knew… But a smug grin slowly appeared on her face. She had adult experience now. And real secrets of her own. It wasn't clear yet why that was important exactly; Ivy Jean just knew it was.

As if a rubber band snapped in her head, she remembered Carla, and the realization that she'd forgotten all about the woman during her antics with her cousin stung. Even more guilt forced her shoulders down. *Good thing I'm still dressed*, she thought. She'd check on her godmother now.

A peek in Debra's room almost caused a belly laugh—the girl snored so loud. Her window was raised up a few inches, and the sheers sucked outward, flapping like little pink flags over the roof where everything changed. Like Ivy, Debra slept in her clothes, and her head was where her feet should be. A clock by her painted toenails read five minutes past five. *It's Saturday.* Disbelief mixed with amusement. She and Debra shared something now—something nobody else knew. Maybe they'd begun to act like real cousins, whatever that meant.

Ivy put on her sneakers and tiptoed down the main staircase. Her stomach lurched when she opened the little door and was greeted by a blast of odor, strong and metallic. She knew instantly that Carla was not better and called out in the dark. Keeping a hand to the wall, she made her way and whispered to God. Carla didn't answer—and neither did God.

Ivy fumbled with the lamp, eventually finding Carla curled on her side facing the wall, her body half out of the covers. A large, red stain on her bottom and the bed linens seemed to grow while Ivy panicked. A water glass on the table was knocked over on its side. It must've fallen a while before since the scarf under it looked dry. She reached to touch her godmother's back and Carla whimpered. Ivy's knees buckled, she was so relieved her new friend wasn't dead. Barely conscious and burning hot, but she was alive.

Could she be really sick, dying sick, and not know it?

Anxiety paralyzed Ivy Jean. She didn't know what to do. She tugged Carla's shoulder gently and suppressed an urge to scream.

"Carla, can you wake up?" Her own voice sounded far away.

Full-blown panic arrived when each tug and each word had no effect, and Ivy Jean screamed with everything in her to wake up the rest of Dahl House.

No one heard her screams, though. Carla didn't even stir, close as she was. Ivy bolted up the stairs and kept going into the darkness outside. Her sneakers slipped on the dewy porch steps, and she almost fell, but she recovered and ran a hundred yards to the bunkhouse, trying to hold back her sobs.

"Daddy, I'm in trouble!" she shouted to the fading stars. The words caught in her throat, and Ivy felt herself coming apart. A voice in her head whispered, *Carla might be dying.*

Light from behind a window by the nearby bunkhouse door made her gasp in gratitude. Apparently she'd been shouting while she ran, as Mr. Haines's door opened just before she pounded on it, and he stood there, dressed and alarmed. Ivy ran straight to his arms.

He pulled her back and made her look at him. "What is it?"

"M-miss Summers won't wake up!"

Before Ivy knew it, Mr. Haines took off like a track star for the main house. Reaching to close the door and follow him, Ivy noticed rifle parts on the table. The gun pieces seemed more high-powered and military, or like movie spies, she thought, instead of cowboy style. *Debra was bragging she knew Haines was a spy.*

Ivy shook it off, pulled the door soundly shut, and ran to catch up.

By the time Ivy reached Carla's room again, the patient's eyes were trying to open. Mr. Haines stood over her but her upward gaze was vacant.

"Can you tell what's wrong with her?" Ivy said.

"Go wake Mrs. Massey. Whatever it takes."

Ivy ran for the stairs, glad Mr. Haines was in charge, grateful for something to do, and wishing she'd paid more attention to emergency drills in Girl Scouts.

In her cavernous suite, Joanne was face up on top of the bedcovers, wearing yesterday's clothes. *Nobody bothered with pajamas last night.* On the night table, an empty liquor bottle lay on its side like a fallen soldier. A heaping ashtray by the chaise explained the stale air. Still, Joanne heard Ivy's call and sprang right out of the bed, paused to focus for a moment, and then stumbled to the bathroom to splash water on her face.

"Mr. Haines is with her now. She was unconscious at first," Ivy said as they rushed down to the little room.

Joanne stopped Ivy at the threshold of the diminutive door, commanding her to wait, so Ivy sat near the bottom of the elegant stairway and busied her mind counting chandelier crystals. Debra must have heard her shouting earlier, too, because she appeared, hair still pillow-tangled, and plopped down beside her. She sneered at the odd little door.

"Now what?" she said.

Ivy tried not to roll her eyes at her cousin's tone. Debra was back to the spoiled-brat mommy-hater.

"What's the big crisis this time?" she asked again. Her green eyes flashed and narrowed. "Don't you know she's just creating drama? She intends to be here when my father comes back and is going to force him to choose."

Defense of her godmother reared up inside Ivy Jean, but she caught a glimpse of Debra as that wounded cub Carla had mentioned. She clamped her teeth together real tight, determined to stay out of her cousin's misery.

"I want my fucking dad to come home," Debra said.

"Me too," Ivy Jean whispered.

Except by then, she had already quit hoping Vincent would rescue her. Maybe he'd never come back, she'd thought once or twice. He hadn't even called to check in. Ivy's hopes now centered on how to get home to Prosperity on her own, by whatever means possible. She intended to ride with Mr. Haines and Carla to Dallas. She could stay in Dallas and care for Carla then take a bus back to Prosperity. Or maybe Mr. Haines would take her back to her house too.

The small door opened and Ivy leapt to her feet. Mr. Haines came out, bent over, and Joanne ducked through the doorframe right behind him. They were arguing in hushed, jumbled tones.

"Mother," Debra stood and spoke loudly. "What is going on?"

Ivy caught a treble of fear in the spoiled demand.

"Not now," Joanne said, not looking away from Mr. Haines. She grabbed at his shirtsleeve. "Please, you know what's at stake."

"It's not wise to move her, Mrs. Massey. We may be too late." He pulled his arm back and went to the front door, shouting over his shoulder to all of them. "Call the hospital in Gatesville and get an ambulance here *now!*"

The lingering image of his face lacerated Ivy's heart as he ran off, leaving them with his instructions.

"But I thought she was awake," she whispered to his back. Ivy went straight past Joanne and hurried to Carla's side. Her godmother's waxy, corpse-like hand was so hot she flinched and fought back tears.

"Carla, it's Ivy Jean."

Carla's pale, cracked lips curved upward slightly and soothed Ivy's fear a bit. *She's alive.* Folding her legs to the floor, Ivy brought Carla's very warm hand to her face and held on. *Dead skin is cold, and this hand is a long way from cold.*

The unpleasant smell from earlier was replaced with the scent of detergent and warm suds. Her aunt and Mr. Haines were in charge now, and the washing machine chugged energetically at the foot of the bed.

"Is this from the miscarriage?" Ivy asked. "Is it normal?"

The miscarriage was her assumption, of course, but she wanted to know the facts. Why did it seem like everything on this ranch was a big fat secret?

Carla's eyes fluttered open, and she settled a sleepy gaze on Ivy Jean, then snorted weakly. Her face wrinkled in a distorted grin.

"Something went wrong, I guess." It seemed hard for her to talk, and her eyes closed again. "I have to go. Please help me get home."

"I will," Ivy said, sniffling back tears. "I promise."

Carla struggled to a sit, and Ivy stuffed pillows between her and the wall.

"Bring me the bag." Carla pointed to a corner on the floor to the stylish weekender she'd carried with her into Dahl House the day before.

Every utterance, every move, seemed to cost her. Ivy delivered the bag.

Was it really only yesterday?

Carla mumbled and rummaged in her things, but she wasn't talking to Ivy.

"I'm sorry, baby," she seemed to reassure the inside of the bag.

Ivy leaned in closer to see.

"Those men are bad, I know. Tucker has to fix it."

Ivy thought maybe Carla had gone all the way crazy, but she tried to grasp her meaning and watched as she tugged open what looked like a cotton flour sack from inside the weekender. She was too weak to lift it out, so Ivy moved to help. Fairly heavy and awkward, it felt like a stack of books. Ivy laid the package on the bed, wondering if Carla brought paperbacks to the ranch, then she remembered what Carla said to Mr. Haines about books. *Her* books. She set the open weekender on the floor.

Keep her talking. That's what they always say. "Want me to help you pack?" Ivy offered.

More of the odd mutterings were scattered between her weak, quiet instructions. When Carla pointed to a pair of shoes, Ivy brought them over and listened to her ramble, weirdly incoherent at times. Ivy rolled and folded and stuffed things back in the weekender. Carla's strength seemed to return when she located and withdrew a particular book from the sack.

"Come here, doll," she said. On her lap a worn, canvas-covered, green book rested; the letters "CSL" printed with a marker pen above the year "1941." Ivy assumed it was a diary and met Carla's eyes, which seemed more alert than they'd been in a while. She held a snapshot out to Ivy.

"Put that in your pocket."

Ivy took the picture and instantly recognized her mom, her breath catching. With a vibrant, young, and slightly heavier face, Carla's smile in the photograph was also unmistakable. Her left arm rested on the shoulder of her pretty friend wearing a school sweater that said "TCU." Ivy studied Gwen's familiar, yet oddly strange, face, captured mid-laugh, and she smiled back at the cheerful image. Ivy had a hundred questions to ask about the photograph of her mother, but she obeyed and simply slid the treasure into the back pocket of her cutoffs just as Carla bolted upright, ran her hands over her hair, and then fell back on the pile of pillows in a gusty breath.

"Tucker knows people, and he'll make them stop," she said with her arm across her eyes. "We'll need a clean sheet, Ivy Jean."

Until that moment, as she looked down at the fully packed bag, Ivy wasn't sure Carla actually prepared to leave Dahl House. Mr. Haines had told Joanne they couldn't move her. *She could bleed to death.*

Carla started rubbing her arms for warmth, and her teeth clattered together in small bursts. *Fevers make you cold.* Ivy pulled the covers tighter around Carla and the woman suddenly grabbed her arm and held her gaze. Ivy felt as if she'd suddenly gotten in the deepest part of the lake, way over her head.

"I'm afraid." Carla spoke just as sound and clear as could be. "We'll fool them." She sighed deeply. "Nobody can know."

What is she talking about now?

"Carla, don't close your eyes." Ivy remembered the Girl Scout guide said to keep a delirious patient talking, with open eyes.

Ivy looked around for Mr. Haines or Joanna, but she was alone in the little room with Carla.

"We have to go. Now." Carla sat up with another second wind. Fishing beside her in the covers, she withdrew a small zippered case and handed Ivy a single key. "Where is my car?"

"In the barn."

"Can you drive it?"

Ivy didn't know how to answer. "Wade has let me drive a few times, but I'm not…" The idea of being in charge of Carla's Corvette both excited and scared her to death.

"We're in danger," Carla whispered.

Ivy stopped to think about how to stall Carla. How long would it take for an ambulance to get there?

"Maybe Vincent is at my house," Carla whispered.

Ivy thought it was more delirium talk but it was a good stall.

"Try to call him there, Ivy. Tell him to come."

"Okay," Ivy agreed. She scrambled for something to write down the phone number with when Mr. Haines blew back in the room. Barely pausing to stoop through the doorway, his hulk suddenly filled the space. He carried a box and motioned his head for Ivy to move. His deep voice was loud and clear when he spoke.

"Carla, I got a dose of antibiotic from the stable, part of an equine emergency pack. You have a serious infection, and I'm going for help. But I need to give you this injection first."

He held a humongous syringe filled with pale liquid to the light. *Equine means horses.* Ivy gasped inside and tried not to show the horror she felt.

"You're not serious," Carla said.

Liquid squirted out the end of the syringe, and Haines turned to the patient. "As a heart attack."

Sweat glistened on his head and neck like he'd been running the whole time Ivy and Carla had been preparing to leave. "Roll over. It goes in your rump."

She draped an arm over her eyes. "Just take me home, Haines."

"How do you know that's good for her?" Ivy whispered.

Like the strong hero of a movie, Mr. Haines turned Carla's limp body as easily as he'd turn a pillow. "I don't."

Carla protested weakly as he jabbed the needle in her backside. Right through her gown he pressed the plunger and a kind of verbal *thud* came out of the patient. Ivy turned her eyes away when a buzzing began in her head. She felt queasy and reached for the wall.

Mr. Haines spoke gentler now, to both of them it seemed.

"We've called for a doctor. It could be an hour or more before they get here." He turned Carla on her back again. "Your infection is out of control, Carla. We couldn't wait."

She didn't groan—or move at all—and her eyes stayed shut. Mr. Haines seemed like a sad giant as he watched Carla.

"Fucking butcher," he said under his breath. "She's gone unconscious again. This shouldn't happen." He shoved past Ivy. "Move!"

She watched him run away again and called after him. "What butcher?"

The buzzing between Ivy's ears silenced as it dawned on her what Mr. Haines meant.

She quickly collected the drawstring bag of books and resumed her place on the floor beside Carla. A horrible chill crawled across her chest as she put two and two together. All the blood, her godmother's tears, and talk of babies lost. Of butchers. Carla didn't miscarry. She had an abortion and something went wrong.

Ivy had read about abortion, *that it's against the law and girls die from it.*

She slunk to the floor to cry. Feeling utterly hopeless, she was desperate to help her mother's best friend, but all she could do was cry and beg.

"Please, God, wake her up."

"Has he gone?" Carla's lucid voice and normal volume jolted her.

"Yes," Ivy said, already up on her knees and wiping her face. She found Carla's hand, thinking how God worked really fast sometimes and feeling immensely thankful. She kissed the warm flesh with tenderness. Ivy hoped with all hope that the horse medicine was the miracle they needed.

Carla raised her head again and freed Ivy's hand, propping herself on an elbow. "Get my car, Ivy. And take that with you." She pointed at the cotton drawstring bag. "Don't let anybody have it."

Then she dropped her head back on the pillow, splaying dulled but still beautiful hair across the bed. Her skin, pink with effort, seemed to drain again to a yellowish gray. She licked her chapped lips and looked at Ivy. "Go, sweetheart. Fetch the car. I have to get home."

Forced to make a decision, Ivy intended to do what Carla asked. "You're sure we should go now?"

"I'm sure she doesn't need to be going anywhere." Joanne's voice came from behind, and Ivy jumped out of her skin. Her flesh riddled with goose bumps so fast it caused her to shout.

"You scared me!" She shoved the drawstring bag out of sight with her foot.

"How is she?" Joanne asked, ignoring Ivy's outburst and looking over the patient.

Ivy thought she saw the slightest smirk on her aunt's face and felt compelled to remark on it, but Joanne's features seemed to soften when she spoke, her question sincere. Ivy felt protective and responsible for her godmother, but it was good to hear concern in her aunt's voice.

"I don't know," Ivy's voice cracked. "She kind of comes and goes. Why is she so sick, Joanne? What can we do?"

Forgotten mascara rimmed Joanne's puffy eyes and she stared at Carla with strangely blank eyes and expressionless features, hands clasped in front of her.

"What we have to do is remain calm," she said in a normal voice despite wearing that creepy, frozen gaze. "You need to go eat something, dear. I'll stay with her. We've spoken to them. They're coming."

"Who's 'them'?"

Ivy wasn't leaving Carla, and she wondered if her aunt was stoned on pills from the way her face still hadn't changed... The mistress-sex-abortion triangle had made enough sense for Ivy to question her aunt's motives, too. What she craved, what they desperately needed, was for someone objective to take charge.

Her father would never let his house get this out of hand.

"Um, the hospital." Joanne drifted and came back. "An ambulance will be here soon. Ivy, can you tell if the shot made a difference?"

Ivy shook her head and her lips turned down just thinking of the needle that was meant for Bella's giant rump. "Where did Debra and Mr. Haines go?" she asked.

"I'm not sure. Debra is supposed to be on the phone finding her father. Haines might have gone to a vet he knows for more antibiotics—someone named Dodd. Go now. Check on their progress. Miss Summers needs rest."

Heat rose between Ivy's bony shoulder blades. "I want to stay here. Did you know she's my godmother?" She sat down on the foot of the bed. "I don't even know what that means."

"Don't test me," Joanne said, directing her glare at Ivy.

If you make me go I'm getting the Corvette.

Carla had begged Ivy to get her away. "We're in danger," she'd said.

"Okay," Ivy Jean said. Acting in a huff so Joanne wouldn't notice, Ivy scooped up the drawstring bag and left, calling back gently for Carla's benefit, hoping she was playing possum again. "I'll go find Mr. Haines."

Back in the foyer, Ivy dug the car key out of her pocket and headed outside. Her godmother needed to get away from Dahl House, and she was going to help.

Imagine Wade's face when he hears I drove a Corvette!

Ivy's brain kept step with her arms and legs as she strode to the barn, hoping no one saw her or questioned the bag. Carla said not to let anyone have it.

Practical details started taking over. *What if Carla is not awake when I get back? How do I get her in the car if she's not awake? I don't even know where the main road is.*

Carla said take her home, but Ivy didn't know where home was.

Ivy realized how delirious she sounded herself. *You're going to the hospital first, stupid.* And if she wasn't awake when Ivy got back, they'd wait for Mr. Haines.

Getting lost or in a car wreck is not fleeing to safety.

Ivy slowed her pace, forcing herself to breathe deeply. Carla had spoken of danger but in the middle of her crazy talk.

There'd be signs for the hospital surely, but could she find her way to Dallas after that?

Standing beside Carla's car, Ivy grappled with a case of nerves but was instantly encouraged to see PRNDL under the gearshift, and no clutch. *Thank goodness.* The windows were down so she tossed the drawstring bag behind the driver's seat. The 'Vette car key pressed on her palm and itched like mad so she stuck it back in her pocket and looked around.

Mr. Haines might chase them in his pickup, she realized, seeing it parked outside.

And Mr. Haines carries a gun.

Looking back toward Dahl House from inside the barn, Ivy paused to notice how peaceful and inviting it seemed. A home built to withstand all the elements and wear and tear of a hundred years. Hushed serenity covered its grounds, still mottled with wildflowers. The lovely picture of it made a deceptive covering of the turmoil inside.

```
PRISTEEN RANCH HIDES TRAGIC SECRETS
```

She moved deeper into the barn with imagined stealth and found the interior door to Mr. Haines's bunkhouse. She knocked. No sound came from inside and, turning the doorknob, she found it locked. Could she get Carla out of there by herself? Ivy scanned the workbench for something heavy or sharp she could use for protection.

Ivy Jean didn't want to believe that Carla might die, and she wasn't at all sure she could do the rescuing. But somebody had to.

Ivy Jean reached for the thickest, heaviest tool on the worktable in the barn. A wrench would do. She chose the biggest wrench she could comfortably wield with some dignity. With a surge of urgency, she headed back to the Corvette and practiced swinging the iron tool in each arm. Carla's drawstring bag sat behind the driver seat in plain view. The sports car only had a cargo deck back there, no seat, so Ivy picked it up and put the bag on the floor of the passenger seat, slid the wrench under it and tucked both items tight against the seat bottom.

Pushing seatbelts aside, she slid into the driver's caramel leather bucket seat and let it reshape around her. The Corvette's dashboard might have been the cockpit of an airplane, for all Ivy knew, and she couldn't find a lever to move the driver seat. But she could reach the gas and brake pedals okay. For once, her long legs would be handy.

Ivy Jean took a deep breath then proceeded on pure adrenalin to rescue Miss Summers. The Corvette growled to life.

TWENTY-SEVEN

Tucker

PHILADELPHIA, MISSISSIPPI

Tucker was sure he'd only slept twenty minutes when Philips pounded on the door to his room Saturday morning, shouting orders to clear out. Stepping out to see what was up, Tucker was stunned to find an army of men milling around the scene like ants on rotten fruit. Most wore suits and others were in shirtsleeves and shoulder holsters. A kind of dirty fog hovered in the pre-dawn grayness, presumably from all the parking lot movement and cigarette smoking.

Looks like a pressure cooker blew somewhere.

Tucker might have expected military tanks and combat soldiers, but this scene perplexed him. Other than their obvious government origins, he had no idea who all these men were. He showered and dressed in the clothes he'd worn when he'd arrived, to blend in, then set his jaw at a stubborn angle and went looking for answers.

Philips's door was propped open again, and Tucker reached to knock at exactly the same moment a hunk of black plastic slammed into a mirror on the wall. A short burst of glass shards made him duck.

"Goddamn yahoos!" Phillips was evidently pissed at the phone. He pushed past Tucker, growling, "Philadelphia fucking Mississippi."

Tucker assumed he meant the backwoods and inadequate phone lines because he stomped toward a pair of phone booths outside the café, barely visible in a sea of men chain-smoking. Tucker watched their case officer plow through the bodies and storm the nearest blue box. He nearly broke the glass with his fist, and Tucker winced in sympathy for the poor sucker on the phone. The motor court manager walked up and paused beside Tucker, then stepped inside the unit, crunching the fragments of mirror on the floor. He didn't say anything to the men still sitting around, but when he glanced outside and saw Philips coming in their direction again, he stepped out to intercept him and stuttered an offer to use his private office phone.

One of the team swept the pieces of glass into the corner with a magazine while their group waited around Phillips's cabin. He eventually got through to his people, but he wasn't saying much upon his return.

"A large-scale exercise is unfolding," he said. "Our mission has changed. I've been told to sit tight in the vicinity for now and await orders."

He dismissed their questions by stepping into the toilet. "Act like tourists," he said closing the door.

Surely he knows more than that.

Tucker and Chess walked over to their pickup, observing the scattered goings on. Large scale had been an understatement. A crowd waited around the door to the motor court's office, to use the phone, Tucker presumed, and a line of men snaked out the front of the café next door. Parking areas of both establishments had become a sea of dark-colored cars.

"These guys are pure Government Issue," Tucker said. "Nothing covert about them."

Just as the sun topped the trees, a procession of five unmarked telecom trucks rumbled into the area, claiming every remaining patch of dirt to park.

"Communication ought to improve now," Chess said.

"The news trucks can't be far behind," Tucker added.

"Who's in charge?" Chess wondered out loud.

The question tapped on Tucker's disenchantment with war games and his cattle-boss fantasy. They split up and walked around smoking like everybody else, pausing to listen. Some conversations were about baseball but most were political. Tucker knew about the constant feuding between the Department of Justice, FBI and Johnson's White House, but these men lived it every day.

"J. Edgar, the old girly man himself, might show up," one guy said. His group speculated that Attorney General Robert F. Kennedy was on his way to Mississippi too, in brazen defiance of President Johnson's attempts to "manage the case."

"Kennedy's striking a power play," another man said. "He's forced a carload of missing outsiders to become *the* most urgent matter on Johnson's desk."

Missing outsiders. *Freedom workers?*

Tucker thought about Julia McPherson, lying unidentified in the hospital. He imagined their mission's targets—Bowers and DuPree—off in the woods nearby, laughing at them, and he decided to approach Philips again directly. The girl, the fire, the Klan celebration in the woods—all those things could be relevant now.

Making his way toward the CO's cabin, he looked around to spot Chess first and see what he'd picked up. Neither man was in sight, though, so Tucker lit a cigarette and leaned against the outside wall of Philips's unit. He watched steam rise from the ground. The Mississippi heat had already reached miserable at barely nine o'clock in the morning.

"Excuse me, Lieutenant Massey?"

Tucker turned toward a guy in shirtsleeves who sported a fresh haircut and shoulder holster and looked like he might be fifteen.

"I was told to find you. They're in the second truck," he pointed, then walked away.

He'd worn a demeanor with that gun and called him Lieutenant.

Haines, back at the ranch, was the only one to call him by rank, and even that was rare. Tucker couldn't decipher why, but had a feeling he should prepare for bad news. He ground out his cigarette and headed to where the aide had pointed. Jumping from one of the telecommunications rigs, Philips glared at him through smoke burping out the stub in his mouth.

"Your orders are to return home immediately," he said.

Tucker thought a semi might have swerved into him.

"Actually, the wire says return to *the ranch*," Philips read.

Tucker tried to speak, but Philips's round, pumpkin head shook sternly.

"Somebody higher up the food chain than me claims family emergency, Lieutenant. You're going home. You got a pregnant wife or something?"

TWENTY-EIGHT

Haines

Dahl House

Seated at the bunkhouse table, Haines hung up the phone and rubbed his head a minute, trying to figure out when Tucker would arrive. His contact in Virginia had just called back to tell him orders were dispatched to Tucker's unit at 0930 Eastern Time to wherever on earth he was. 8:30 Texas time. He didn't want to think of the Lieutenant's response to an abrupt, inexplicable summons home, but it was done.

Carla Summers was not going to make it, and Haines was having trouble thinking. He scrounged around the room, through more random belongings than he'd ever remembered owning, until he found a pack of cigarettes. He smoked, trying to get his head around what the next steps should be.

Infection raged through Tucker's lady with every intention of killing her. The delirium, and her stark, sallow color pointed to kidney shutdown and a fatal stage of dehydration. While human antibiotics were more pure than what he'd used, he was pretty sure pumping more antibiotic in her, of any kind, wasn't going to save her.

Haines felt responsible for not reading signs of septic shock earlier, but understandably, Carla would not volunteer that she'd had an abortion—not here. Even if she'd realized the gravity of her condition, she would never intentionally reveal that information to Tucker's family. And if you knew the people and relationships, like Haines now did, it was entirely understandable why Joanne Massey wouldn't probe or question.

He considered priorities. Concerns about surveillance on the ranch had slipped a notch for the near term. Since he wouldn't be driving Carla to Dallas yet, Haines intended to remain at the ranch until Tucker got back so he could brief him. Soon after that, he needed to relocate until he could figure out who was out there watching them and try to remedy their misinformation. A scandal at Dahl House leaking to the press wouldn't help keep his cover either.

He checked the clock above the fridge. Dr. Dodd, the neighbor veterinarian, lived two spreads north and had been at home when Haines called. He would arrive in roughly ten more minutes. The ambulance would get there in thirty to forty more.

Joanne was showing signs of hysteria building inside her as they waited. Haines didn't blame the lady for feelings of panic. The public life of prestige she'd crafted around Tucker for eighteen years was definitely at risk. She might have to give up some of that status. But she would at least live through it—Carla would not.

Her death is so unnecessary.

Haines had experience with the seedy abortion landscape in America, and he'd formed a strong opinion. Regardless of morality laws, people were still copulating and making unwanted babies. Illegal status was the same as awarding a zillion dollar contract to gangsters. Lawmakers and the mob might as well have shook hands for a press release. It seemed so simple to Haines, and it was maddening that deaths by abortion kept happening.

He'd once removed a foreign diplomat's daughter from a "clinic" in Boston. He was too late and never forgot. Blood-encrusted sheets on the floor infested with cockroaches seemed to boil when the light came on. Carelessly strewn everywhere, rusted tools evoked horrible images. Yellowed antiseptic clouded a jar by the window, and dark-brown handprints covered a wall phone.

And that was during business hours.

Like the foreign diplomat, Tucker could have afforded Miss Summers a safer alternative. Physicians did exist who couldn't stomach imposters killing girls in trouble. They risked it all and priced accordingly. Yet here was Carla, another young woman who sought and paid for quiet termination, forced into being gutted in the manner of a tyke's first catfish.

Haines decided he'd make a few preparations for exit, assuming the law would soon follow an ambulance out there. Depending on what Dodd had to say, he'd do his best to stay out of sight until Tucker got back, then slip out the back after they talked.

If a watcher in the hills truly did pay attention, chances were they'd follow him away.

Stepping outside the bunkhouse on his way to the stable, he changed his mind and decided to move the pickup first. He went back through the bunkhouse to the barn and opened the door.

It took a half second to realize he'd just heard Carla's car start.

Christ Almighty, is that little girl taking the 'Vette? He almost twisted an ankle leaping off the bottom step to chase Ivy Jean.

"Hey!"

TWENTY-NINE

Tucker

<u>Philadelphia, Mississippi</u>

They stood outside a grey telecomm truck tilted half on and half off the highway. Philips handed Tucker an envelope of public travel documents that he did not want to accept. Dozens of sweaty plainclothes agents with guns, badges and cigarettes scurried around them, and Philips's hands seemed small, not to scale with his power-lifting hulk.

"You know everything I do." His round eyes pierced Tucker's demanding glare and dared him to say more. Feeling dismissed from a White House mission smarted his ego.

Tucker knew better than to let his temper show, to force the issue if the man didn't have more information about his family's "emergency." But he felt his composure slipping. He scratched a coarse eyebrow and steadied his voice.

"What did you mean by the pregnant wife bit?"

Torn between ideas of what defined the emergency, Tucker assumed female hysteria. Imagining a range of disasters jarred his emotions. Joanne. Debra. Carla. It could be any of them.

"It's an inside joke," Phillips said, with a touch of sympathy. "Leave the pickup at the airport with the key on the right rear tire. There's a Braniff departure for Dallas at 1650."

"Can I see the wire?"

Philips handed over a torn sheet of paper then turned away and climbed back in the telecomm truck:

```
Return to ranch immediately
```

Four simple words with his ID code attached. That was it.

It wasn't an easy task for somebody to catch up to him, though, Tucker realized. More than one person inside of the president's considerable entourage had to be involved. And they left him no chance to argue.

He resisted thinking on how the summons could impact his future with the president's team and pulled off the road at the first gas station on his way back to the Meridian airfield. He rolled close to a phone booth outside. Flies buzzed around his head when he wrestled the glass door open, and he cursed the stinking, steamy air inside. It made him realize that a part of him felt positively jubilant about leaving the godforsaken land of Mississippi.

Forcing coins into the slots, he held his breath and dialed the bunkhouse number first. *Haines will know what the real goddamned emergency is.*

He stretched the cord as far as he could to stand outside, craning his neck toward the fresh air. Then, holding his breath a moment, he inserted a dime and dialed for the operator.

A dead fucking line.

Tucker slammed the receiver down and stormed off, yanking a cloth from his pocket to wipe his face.

• • •

At least civilian airlines knew how to stock a first-class bar and hire pretty hostesses. After deplaning at Love Field, Tucker went straight for a pay phone to summon his car. Still tight from three single-malt highballs, he opted not to phone the ranch again because he'd be there in two hours and he didn't want to deal with Joanne's nagging.

One of the partner benefits at the law firm was around-the-clock car-and-driver service. With his old man's influence, Tucker had made partner the same year he'd passed the bar, so skinny old Bobby Hart had been his regular escort for a dozen years. Not his confidante—Tucker didn't chat about personal things with the help. Most of them figured out plenty on their own. But his driver operated as a quiet, standby guy—suit and tie, all business. The familiar black Cadillac rolling up was a welcome sight, but Bobby, who was usually so stoic, was clearly agitated. His mouth was going before he parked.

Bobby could be anywhere from sixty to eighty years old, as far as anybody knew, but he leapt from the car like a spry young'un and rushed toward Tucker, putting him off.

"People have been desperate to find you, sir." He threw Tucker's bag in the trunk then opened the back passenger door. "My switchboard service called three times asking if I'd heard from you. Said they were getting calls from all over the U.S."

"Slow down, man." Tucker had never seen the guy so expressive, and he felt his single malt buzz sliding off at the curb.

"They said your daughter Debra called too."

Tucker felt relief over that. "Did anybody say why they were hunting me?"

"Not that I'm aware of, not for sure, at least." The old guy didn't meet Tucker's eyes in the rearview. "But let's get you to the ranch."

They sped away and Tucker settled into the comfort of leather, air conditioning and super-glide shock absorbers.

"Nelda, at the switchboard, she's a talker. She spilled some gossip."

Bobby never shared gossip. That, and his obvious nervous energy, told Tucker whatever Bobby knew wasn't good. He continued watching his driver's face in the rearview mirror.

"Let's have it."

"Nelda said your friend Miss Summers went to the ranch."

Bobby didn't know about Tucker's government work, but he knew about Carla. Tucker's gut sank. *Vincent failed.*

"And?"

"That's all. Girls at your office were the source of that one, according to Nelda."

"Sheesh."

The skyline of Dallas was behind them, flickering into scattered incandescence. Tucker sank back in the corner opposite Bobby's mirror. He took a hat from the back deck—an all-purpose, dignified fedora kept handy for naps—and covered his face. The car radio picked up a Fort Worth station and Frank Sinatra, Old Blue Eyes, crooned at low volume from the rear speakers.

"Call me irresponsible…"

THIRTY

Ivy Jean

Dahl House

"Hey!" Mr. Haines shouted from the doorway, and Ivy Jean's heart raced.

Focus. Carla needed her calm.

But they both needed—and liked—Mr. Haines. Ivy reached for the gearshift, hearing Mr. Haines's cowboy boots stomping the dirt floor of the barn and she started to feel trapped, and chicken. *Now or never, babe.*

"Ivy!"

She turned her head to look. His face wore fury and his stride was determined. Ivy turned off the engine and opened the door. She stood to face him, breathing hard.

The sound of a car arriving outside turned both their heads. A vehicle shot out of the trees, taking the corner in an enormous cloud of gravel and dirt, but Ivy could see it was a pickup, not an ambulance, or her dad's Pontiac.

"Is that the doctor?" she asked.

"I think it is." Haines's left her, striding up the drive.

Butterflies caused a fury in her stomach and stilled Ivy Jean for a moment.

A bearded stranger hopped out of the pickup the instant its wheels quit turning and ran into Dahl house with Mr. Haines on his heels. The man carried a black bag, like Dr. Kildare, and Ivy felt so relieved she nearly sat down to cry. Hope came back with every breath as she looked around. She realized Carla's bag of books was still visible in the car, so she moved it over by the bay doors in the corner of the barn and hurried back to Dahl House.

Inside again, Ivy Jean found all the adults crammed into the little room with Carla, so she raced up the staircase to her bedroom. In whatever vehicle that took Carla away, Ivy intended to be with her. She started packing her things.

Debra intruded. "We need to talk." She closed the door and crossed her arms.

Ivy ignored her and went about shoving clothes in her dad's old suitcase.

"You can't just leave, you know," Debra said.

Like she cares. "Yes, I can. She needs help, and my dad would want me to."

"You're going because of the whore?" she cried.

Ivy stopped to glare at her cousin. She had surmised enough details out of Carla's delirium to know that Tucker was the father of her dead baby. "She had an abortion, Debra. Because your father made her." She held Debra's angry green eyes. "It was a horrible, filthy place, and... and it didn't go right. He cut something." Her voice cracked. "Or didn't put it back right."

Once she understood the reason for Carla's sickness, Ivy could derive a lot from her godmother's nonsensical talk. The complicated scramble of it made her feel so mixed up she wanted to cry, and she was weirdly sad for Debra.

"She doesn't love him," Debra said with an ugly sneer, arms loose now and flailing in all directions. "She wouldn't have let herself get pregnant if she loved him. He is an important man and can't be siring bastards. She knew that!"

"She did so love him!" Ivy challenged. "But she quit! She says she killed their baby for his stupid career." She thought that was the truth, and wanted to wipe that sneer off Debra's face. "Her love for your daddy died when the baby died."

Tears collecting in her throat felt like a pineapple rind. Debra didn't respond at first, and Ivy halfway wanted to take her hateful words back, but she stood there, matching her cousin glare for glare.

"Well, good riddance is all I have to say—to her, the baby, and their so-called *love* affair."

"She might die," Ivy said, intending to shock Debra.

"I've been wishing her dead for a long time."

Ivy swore she heard a cackle. "You make me sick. Have you really wished her dead? Put-a-spell-on-her dead?"

A tiny glimpse of Debra's friendlier side had fooled her into forgetting what a hateful and mean-spirited, rotten bitch she was. *Pure evil*, Ivy thought. *Plotting and ruthless, like Cruella DeVille.*

Ivy couldn't help it then, a dam burst and she shoved past Debra into the bathroom, bawling. She sat on the toilet and sobbed into a towel that smelled like laundry soap, fresh and clean. It made Ivy think of home, and she cried harder.

Where are you, Daddy?

She felt like a little kid for blubbering in front of Debra, but she couldn't stop now. It felt like she was drowning in decisions that had to be made, and that stoked her fury with Vincent again because she was only twelve. It wasn't fair.

"Hey, come on," Debra said.

Ivy spun off a wad of toilet paper and blew her nose. Debra was not going to make fun of her tears to her face.

"Do you mind? I'd like some privacy." Her voice sounded like she had a head cold.

"Look, I know you're not a baby, but you've got to get a grip, kiddo. Whatever is making you cry right now isn't something you can fix."

"I know that!"

"Yes, but what I'm saying is you've acted in a way you should feel proud of. Truly! That was hairy—the plan to bag her car. I was watching. It blew me away."

"You were watching?"

"Yeah, I've got to hand it to you," Deb said.

Ivy dropped her face back to the towel. "She might die anyway." She wiped her face then collected her things.

Trudging back downstairs, she put her suitcase next to the library wall, by the front door but out of the way. Carla's sack of books were still in the barn and would need retrieving if they took her away. Ivy was mapping a plan to fetch them when the small door opened and Haines came out, casting a scowl in her direction.

Maybe her defiant look back put him off because he didn't say anything about the car and just walked past her. Then Joanne came out, her skin looking mottled, an angry red on sickly white.

"Don't leave me alone with that thing," she growled, chasing Haines.

Ivy's stomach tumbled. *Thing?* She took a few steps toward her aunt and thought her head might have stayed behind.

"What is it?" she said. "Aren't we taking Miss Summers to the hospital now?"

THIRTY-ONE

Vincent

<u>Dallas, Texas</u>

Sunlight filled Carla's apartment in Dallas on the later side of Saturday morning. Vincent had been snoring on her couch, surrounded by yellow throw pillows. After the reporter gal left the night before, he'd been flat unable to turn his mind off. Finally desperate at 1:00 a.m., he'd rummaged and found a bottle of Sominex in Carla's bathroom cabinet. He took two, restacked sofa pillows under his head and fell into a deep sleep, clothes and boots still on.

The phone had jerked him awake and the bright sun shocked his senses.

Carla.

He jumped to standing pretty quickly, having forgotten the head fog that lingered after Sominex, and nearly fell on the coffee table. Swearing at the late hour, he rubbed his face and reached for the phone extension on the kitchen wall, clearing his throat.

"Hello?"

Nothing for a beat, then a female voice spoke hesitantly. "Is this the man who called me yesterday?"

She identified herself but neither the name nor the voice clicked with Vincent's memory. He looked around but couldn't spot Carla's address book and bluffed.

"Yes. Hello, again. Do you have something new?"

"I was hoping she had come back," the woman said. Then, almost mumbling, "Because I wasn't all the way truthful when you called."

"Okay," he said when she paused.

He pictured a glass-walled phone box and perhaps a hanky over the mouthpiece distorting the voice intentionally, but it rang familiar now. She'd been one of the short conversations yesterday morning, when he'd been dialing people listed with just numbers.

"It's true that Carla called me last week and we met for a drink," she said. "What I didn't tell you was that I put her in touch with a guy I know, who said he knew somebody who could help her. That might be where she went."

Vincent felt his heart slow down. "Who's the guy?"

"You know she's pregnant, right?" she whispered.

Vincent didn't hesitate. "Yes."

"Well, the mister won't allow her to keep the child. And she won't leave him."

Oh, God. Abortion.

It was a dangerous subject, and Vincent knew why the caller was being so vague with him. "Where do you think she is?" he said.

"I can't, I don't want to—" she backpedaled.

Vincent interrupted, impatient. "Listen," he said. "Carla is missing. You're her friend—" He caught himself. "I know you care because you called me back."

"I just gave her a number," she said. "A phone number, that's all. I want Carla to be okay, but you can't tell *anybody* this came from me. No way, no how. These people don't mess around."

Confused, Vincent wanted to demand that she explain but was terrified she meant someone untouchable.

"I promise," he said. "Just give me what you gave to Carla. What's the guy's name?"

She took in air, then *click*... The dial tone answered his question.

If Carla had gotten an abortion, she could be hurt somewhere, alone. The idea now being a possible reality made Vincent nearly frantic. He wasn't a single step closer to Carla than when he first blew into town.

Failure.

After a moment of seething frustration, Vincent went to the bathroom and washed his face. The nagging pain between his shoulder blades didn't ease up any, but some water on his face and a damp comb through his hair and eyebrows helped appearances. He scrounged for coffee fixings in Carla's kitchen, found his cigarettes and paced and smoked while the coffee perked. Why didn't he just ask for the damn phone number? She'd said "a guy I know," and he must've pushed her in the wrong direction.

He grabbed the phone again and dialed the number at Dahl House, from memory this time, while finding his calm, daddy voice in case Ivy Jean answered. A busy signal sent him looking for something to throw, though, and he imagined his reflection exploding on the patio doors, leaving bits of brain and guts dribbling down the glass. His stomach growled at the idea, and he dug the bottle of chalky liquid out of his shaving kit. Food would be wise, but the mystery caller might ring again. He could not leave the apartment.

He found a notepad and pen and put them by the phone, brushed his teeth, and had just picked up Carla's address book when the phone rang again.

"Look, all I know is a guy's nickname," she said without preamble. "Lenny. That's all I know. And here is the number I gave Carla."

Vincent wrote fast but, before he could read it back or even thank her, she'd clicked off again. He tapped the switch hook for a fresh dial tone and rang the number she'd given. No answer. He redialed it in case he made an error. While the phone rang he imagined a professional voice answering, "Doctor Leonard's office."

Better yet, "Good morning, Underground but Sterile Abortion Clinic."

Fifteen rings later, he gave up a second time, hopes dashed.

Light taps on the front door surprised him then, and he yanked it open without caring. Carla's spiritual-guide neighbor stood there smiling at him in all her flowing layers and woodsy scents. He was so glad to see a familiar face he nearly hugged her. But she confirmed his fears in short order. Tea leaves or star alignment or something had the lady convinced "our Carla" had met with trouble. Her accent was thicker than ever.

"More than once I receive message through energy connect to Carla. Means fear."

Vincent thought all methods of prognostication were a bunch of hooey. "What do you mean? Did you consult Ouija?"

"This is not joke," she said, unaffected by his insult. "I see much blood."

A tidal wave crashed in his ears. *Much blood.* An irrelevant memory of Ivy Jean flashed, her chubby little leg cut deeply from trying to get over a barbed wire fence, her tiny polka dot dress soaked in crimson. In a twisted way, the imagery equated to Carla, at the ranch, with Ivy Jean.

He said goodbye to the neighbor and didn't pause to second-guess his instincts. He tried calling one more time but the damn line still rang busy so he quit trying. It took him ten minutes to gather his things and secure Carla's place. It was time to go.

THIRTY-TWO

Ivy Jean

Dahl House

Clinging fiercely to all the hope she could muster, Ivy Jean walked toward the bed where Miss Summers laid. Firelight seemed to flicker in the room, but it was just the shadow of Dr. Dodd moving around Carla's still form.

Joanne had called her a "thing."

Please, please, please, don't be dead.

Darkness shrunk her peripheral vision and Ivy steadied herself with a hand to the wall. She gulped down two breaths and went to her godmother's side, desperate to prove everybody wrong.

"Carla," she leaned in close to her ear.

Dr. Dodd had his back turned at first. Then he nodded at Ivy with a folded sheet in his hands, and like he was making the bed, gently shook it free of folds over Carla. Ivy Jean watched. Her lip began to tremble as he covered Carla's head.

She was dead.

Pressed squares in the fabric sectioned her unmoving figure. Ivy's eyes trained on the doctor, studying his movements, because right then she could not look at the bed where a pale, unfeeling dear hand poked out from under the sheet.

The sudden absence of promise felt like someone just dug inside her and scooped it out. A precious connection to her mother came and went in a day. Ivy's tears dribbled and fell.

She would never go shopping with her mother's best friend, or make a family picnic for Wade and Daddy with her, or ride horses together, or roller skate. All the stuff she'd dreamed up since yesterday was just taken back, like fate had only been teasing.

Ivy ached for the strong arms of her father and the tenderness of Wade. She longed more than anything to turn back time.

At some point, someone led her out of the room. She didn't have to be carried, but somebody had to take charge and tell her to go. Nothing made sense. Ivy's head felt detached and she marveled at the sensation, feeling oddly grateful for the haziness it rendered. Reality was soothingly unreal. She could hear people's voices, but she didn't care what they said.

Ivy chose the library for a retreat; she wanted space to think, or something. Dragging a massive chair to the window, she worked to turn it just so, facing a peaceful, ordinary meadow beyond the steadfast shelter of the barn. She noticed, again, one of the bluest skies she'd ever seen. Leathery smells in the library comforted, evoking memory of her father's closet. A cardinal trilled from its perch outside, such an innocuous reminder that it was summer. But, as Ivy started reconnecting to reality through her senses, suspicion snuck into her thinking, and brought a chill. She wished for a sweater.

She wished for someone to blame and didn't like thinking that way.

Joanne could have killed her.

Sensible Ivy Jean was hiding somewhere else because, sitting there in Dahl House, her imagination popped with ideas of wrongdoing. It happened all the time on TV... Weak patients get smothered with a pillow... and no one knows.

```
        MISTRESS OF RANCH MURDERS
           MISTRESS OF HUSBAND
```

Joanne and Carla were natural enemies.

Ivy Jean knew this was disturbed, nightmare thinking, probably inspired by Debra's venom. She replayed enough of the recent events to regain common sense, but right then Dahl House felt unsteady and adrift, and Ivy's stomach reacted with queasiness. She wanted her dad to come back.

Thoughts of Vincent brought more heaviness and she administered a silent but hysterical lashing out at him, making every other word obscene on purpose. Trying to curl up in a ball and somehow lose the weighty burden of being, she realized that sleep was what she craved. That pleasant, happy feeling whenever she woke up in the backseat of the car to see she was safely home and totally missed the boring drive. She strained to swallow.

Out the window, Ivy watched Mr. Haines walking to the barn. His cowboy image was reassuring, but his big shoulders sagged today. Was it horse feeding time? Despite the tragedy, they'd still need tending. She couldn't see the animals from where she sat, but she noticed that darkness crept into view in that direction. Thunderclouds were collecting over the hills in the west.

The door to the library blew open.

"I hate you!" Debra shrieked at her mother so loud it hurt Ivy's ears. That had to be the rudest intrusion ever. Ivy rolled her eyes and tucked her legs under her butt, trying to be invisible.

The door to her quiet place slammed shut and privacy escaped. Ivy peeked around the oversized chair back to see her cousin pacing back and forth in a scheming posture like Groucho Marx, throwing off a kind of energy Ivy didn't know what to do with.

As if reading her mind, Debra spoke of conspiracy, "They're in there, you know, studying all the angles. They've got to convince the law, and the papers, that there is not a crime and not a story in any of this."

Ivy clung to her common sense. "I thought doctors swear or take an oath or something."

Debra scoffed. "Sweet naiveté! Doctors respond to money and power just like every other breathing human, oath or not." She plopped down in a nearby chair and scooted it around so she faced Ivy, then abruptly stood and resumed pacing.

"Sons of bitches. I'm going to have my say about what happens. If they don't think I'll blab, they're more stupid than I thought."

The hairs on Ivy's neck stood up. "Blab about what? They didn't kill her."

"Of course, they did! But that's not the point."

Even if Ivy had momentarily imagined Joanne smothering Carla, this talk of the adults making a pact of secrecy made Ivy sick. "What do you mean 'of course they did'?"

"Well he impregnated her, then forced an abortion, right?"

Did she mean the great Tucker Massey?

Ivy tried to make sense in order to argue. "That doesn't mean he killed her, not like he stabbed her or shot her."

"We could have a lot of fun making the case."

Ivy shuddered. "Do you actually think that would be fun?" She didn't even try to grasp that. "What about your mother?"

"That's the best part. She *knew* what was happening and deliberately kept the poor woman here." Debra leaned toward Ivy, one eyebrow arched. "Fed her sedatives." She sat back with a thoughtful look on her face.

Ivy stared at her cousin in utter amazement and disgust. She'd had enough.

Debra went on, excited. "And she summoned a *veterinarian* instead of a *physician*! A goddamned horse doctor."

"You are so full of it! You don't want to make that kind of trouble for your parents."

Now both of Debra's eyebrows pointed, daring Ivy Jean to think about what she'd just said. Loud pounding on the library door sounded like cannon fire and they both screamed.

In an eerie coincidence, Dr. Dodd breezed in. "Where is the telephone, miss?"

Ivy took advantage of her cousin's surprised fury, slipped around the new intruder, and left them.

THIRTY-THREE

Haines

Dahl House

The death of Carla Summers, in Haines's mind, made it urgent that he redirect whatever trouble loomed in the hills. The damn Kennedy business felt so far from the ranch right then, but he knew if sanitizing was underway, he could very well be a target. And snipers don't talk things over first.

He left Carla's corpse with Dodd and Joanne, intent on engaging a set of precautions. He moved the ranch pickup out of sight first, taking it behind the barn, facing the pasture. After crossing the pasture, he'd take the first hill to a low water crossing near an old wagon path that led back to the road. He strained to remember if it had rained the last week.

The realization he might never get to come back once he left crept in his thoughts, and he shook off the foreboding in favor of keeping in motion. With the pickup in position, he took long, hurried strides to the stable, pleased to see the livestock returning from the pasture on their own. Haines made sure the cows and horses had adequate sustenance, assuming Tucker would return within twenty-four hours. He stole a moment with Bella, like the old days when he'd go off on a mission. Any more time than that made him sad. The Masseys were horse people; she'd be fine in their care.

His task, now, was to keep out of sight.

Back in the bunkhouse, he gathered his duffel and rifle case and snuck back outside to stash them in a separate place from the truck, in case he had to take off on foot. That way, any obvious traces of identity went with him. Standard procedure. On the river-facing side of the barn, but still in sight of the pickup, he found a clump of cedar growing low to the ground by a boulder. He slid the items underneath the lowest branches.

From three corner points of the barn, he scanned the immediate area with binoculars, anticipating signs of "the Florida connection," as he'd taken to calling it since the cigar wrapper. But he'd seen nothing detectable all day, so far. Skilled watchers would have seen the commotion. Would it scare them away, or provide opportunity?

In the bunkhouse again, he sat down to review his next steps.

Mrs. Massey was terrified of scandal. She'd begged him to remove Carla's body from the ranch before Dodd arrived. Tucker and Joanne both were monitored for news across the state of Texas. Their affluent circles, charitable deeds and glamorous images drew certain members of the press, and Haines knew if those parties got hold of an honest-to-goodness soap opera like this they'd never stop digging. Like a sweet, south-Texas onion, this story had a hundred tasty layers. It would be worse for the Masseys if the gossip press decided to spice things up with an old CIA guy in hiding.

What disturbed Haines so deeply was that none of the so-called investigating press, or their vigorous "digging," would be focused on the bastard who killed Carla. None of it. Death by abortion was a tired, common story and he knew it was terribly dangerous to meddle in a favored business of the mob. Mafioso, gangster, whatever you called it, underworld operations were intentionally comprised of deep and tangled tiers, ruthlessly guarded, so *identifying* the illegal abortionist was impossible, much less nailing him.

THIRTY-FOUR

Ivy Jean

Dahl House

Midday shadows filled the foyer as Ivy snuck away from Debra and Dr. Dodd in the library. The shiny floor reminded her of the gym at school and she longed for a basketball and no worries. Already overwhelmed by experiences she'd never expected, Debra's scheming truly made her sick with worry that this could all somehow get worse.

Ivy's head felt foggy as she returned to the inner part of Dahl House. Carla was dead, *really dead*. And Ivy had to say goodbye.

For the first time, a hinge creaked like a scary movie as she opened the door. The lamp was still lit beside Carla's sheet-covered body and they were alone. Ivy's feet felt weighted with bricks, but she made her way bedside and stood there, hands together and head bowed, trying not to think about the tent in the sheet made by Carla's pretty nose.

Hands shaking, she timidly lifted the sheet away from Carla's face and draped a fold down, mindful of the original creases. She remembered the first time hearing Carla say "Ivy Jean." It'd been so familiar and perplexing.

Ivy tentatively touched Carla's cheek, somehow not repulsed by the chill of her skin. Ivy coughed to release pressure in her throat and the sob that was stuck there released, allowing all her pain to surface. She dropped to the floor, hugged her knees, and surrendered to all the sorrow she felt.

Irrational but aching guilt compounded Ivy's grief. Carla might be alive if Ivy had gotten her away from Dahl House when she'd asked the first time. Hot tears poured out of her, unrestrained, until after a while the room got cold. Worry about what was going to happen next began to fill her head and dread weighed on her heart. An ambulance was still on its way to the ranch. Ivy knew she had to leave Carla's side if she wanted to avoid other people, which she did. She stood up and covered the body again, knowing her godmother would not want others to see her that way.

To erase the vision of Carla's lifeless gray face, Ivy settled on the one of her smiling like a toothpaste ad, saying, "Very nice to meet you, Ivy Jean."

"I promise to remember your perfect smile and gorgeous hair, Carla Summers," Ivy whispered as she silently left the room.

Scouting the foyer before exiting, Ivy tiptoed across the gleaming wood floor, being careful not to make any noise, and slipped out the front door. The porch completely wrapped all four sides of Dahl House like a frame around a picture. She picked the north side, closest to where the road entered the property but out of sight from everything else. Scanning the hills, she recalled Debra's insistence that hunters were up there, after Mr. Haines. Peering more carefully and detecting no such thing, Ivy chalked it up to her cousin's dramatics.

House wrens hovered and hopped around a bird feeder in the yard and drew her there, near the oak tree that swept the porch roof where she and Debra had laughed, unaware of what was to come mere hours ago. Carefree, silly.

Judging by the shade and shadows, Ivy guessed it was around five o'clock. Maybe she could eavesdrop on the bird's chatter and take her mind off things. The wicker furniture in that spot seemed the farthest from any doors, too. Ivy dragged a chair close to the house. She curled up her legs the best she could and settled in, trying to decide whether she would just hang out and wait for Vincent to come back, or hide, or what.

To her right, an ambulance flew around the bend in a cloud of dirt, just like the doctor's car had earlier. Ivy got up and walked the length of the house to see it pull up to the steps. Road dust settled on the white wagon with red crosses on the doors. Two guys dressed in white got out and entered Dahl House, unaware they didn't need to rush since the patient was dead. They carried a folded-up stretcher on its side between them.

Ivy didn't want to follow them. Instead, she returned to the north side of the house, to her wicker perch. Dusk arrived while she kept an eye on the road, intent on willing her father's green Pontiac to appear. Long shadows served to deepen Ivy's sense of separation from the goings on inside the house. She felt completely alone and, right then, it was a welcome sensation.

A little while later—she didn't know how long—a cop car drove up, too, and parked behind the ambulance. Ivy returned to the front corner of the house to check it out. It was a brown-and-gold cruiser with a bubble light on top and a round badge decal that covered the side. It said "something-something-sheriff" on it. Two giant radio antennas bent backwards from the roof, and attached to either corner of the rear bumper like wings on a bug.

Ivy supposed the slight man who got out was the sheriff. A wink of sunlight flashed off the badge on his chest. Stepping onto the great porch, he removed his hat and tucked it under his arm. Did he already know the patient was dead? Will they have to wait for a coroner, too, like in the TV shows? Ivy mulled over questions, hoping that crazy cousin of hers didn't really try to convince anybody that Joanne killed Carla.

The idea of people fighting over Carla's body sat heavy on Ivy's heart, but her tear ducts were dried out. And as much as she wanted to feel sorry for herself, Ivy figured she should probably hear what was being told to the officials. She decided to follow the sheriff in, having no idea what to expect but knowing that, if it turned out anything like Perry Mason, she'd be a star witness.

THIRTY-FIVE

Vincent

<u>Dallas, Texas</u>

Stepping out of Carla's apartment, Vincent set his things down to lock the door just as two men topped the stairs. They had long sideburns and wore dark, polyester sport coats. The larger man had his shirt unbuttoned, showing off chest hair and a gold medallion. The other wore a gold ring on his pinky. Vincent hoped they weren't looking for him. As they approached, he pocketed the apartment key and the pair shifted into single-file, making room for him and his valise to pass.

"Evening," Pinky Ring said.

Vincent gave a small but polite nod and kept moving, careful not to make eye contact. When he reached the stairs, he looked back to see them disappear through a door. After tossing a bag of garbage in the dumpster, Vincent eased into the Pontiac. He looked around the parking lot for sign of Sims and seeing none, turned the ignition, anxious to get away.

"Where you off to?" Carla's reporter friend called out her car window as she pulled up beside him. He tried to relax his brow so it read cordial, and he smiled at her.

"I was in the area," she said. "Stopped by to see if you've heard anything."

Vincent marveled at her timing.

"Nothing new." He shrugged, thankful the late-afternoon shadows hid his lie.

They exchanged pleasantries then said goodnight. Vincent didn't say he was giving up, going to fetch his daughter, getting the hell out of Dodge.

"See you later," he added with a half wave. As calmly as possible, he drove away, stifling the thrill of leaving violent, destructive, Dallas behind.

Slightly more than an hour later, near Cleburne, he slowed the car and pulled into a gas station to use the toilet. While there, he grabbed a bag of potato chips and a cola from the icebox, leaving money at the unmanned register. He got back on the road and had barely taken a sip of the beverage when it hit him like a slap. He'd just passed an unmistakable tail, sitting dark at a rest area. How could he not have noticed the gold-colored VW Bug before now? It was just like the one the reporter gal had been driving. There probably weren't ten Volkswagens of that color in all of Texas.

Headlights appeared in the rearview mirror and his heart sank with affirmation. Vincent recalled details, tried to settle into believing there was no reason for Carla's friend to go covert and follow him into the country. Unless she'd picked up the scent of a story.

Which would serve Tucker right.

Vincent contemplated pulling over again or even turning around, but he let miles roll by as he formulated a plan. Who knew what his brother, or his brother's wife, had in their closet? He couldn't care less. They had crafted a public life for themselves and, by default, invited public scrutiny. Not so with Ivy Jean. The *Times Herald* rep needed to be confronted and sent home—he would not knowingly bring a reporter to the ranch.

As he approached the next crossroad, he slowed, turned his blinker on, and took a farm-to-market road on the right. Fifty yards later, he rolled to a stop and cut the Pontiac's headlights.

Sure enough, he watched the Bug slow and make the same turn.

He took a breath and opened his door. Standing tall, he faced the glare of the vehicle's close-together headlights. It struck him that he needed something to say on the off chance it wasn't the reporter. But there she was behind the wheel, looking straight at him, quizzical. Vincent put his hands in his pockets and leaned over to her level.

"What on earth are you doing?"

Her long brown hair was pulled back to a ponytail and she wore glasses, looking bookish. "I thought maybe you'd found Carla," she said. "You were leaving and I followed." She kept her eyes on his face. "So, did you find her?"

He employed the scowl his children feared most and addressed her. "Didn't I say I would call you?"

She looked in her lap, chastised. "I'm worried, Mr. Pritchard. That's all."

He wanted to believe her. "Go back to Dallas. I haven't found Carla. I've given up. I'm going home."

"Really? Where's home?"

"Why do you think that's your business?"

"I'm sorry."

She sounded sincere, but Vincent had been living the private investigator life for two days and paranoia and suspicion came with the job description.

"Listen, I'll give you a call when Carla resurfaces," he said, patting the roof of her car. "Now, go home."

He walked back to the Pontiac and her engine continued to idle, sounding like a wind-up toy. Facing her again, he stood his ground until the gears shifted and she headed toward the highway. He watched the Bug turn back east and take off toward Dallas. Lighting a cigarette, he smoked until her taillights disappeared and waited in the darkness until he was sure she was gone.

Imagining Tucker's face if he showed up with a reporter did bring a smile, though. He knew Tucker's soft spot. *He's a big, fat fraud. With a gift for pushing himself into your life before you realized he was there.*

Vincent maneuvered the Pontiac around and returned to the highway, turning west. He flipped on the radio but only got static, so he let the white noise blend with the wind as he smoked another cigarette. Driving into Hico, he slowed to make the merge onto US-281. A mile later, headlights appeared behind him again, and he had to fight an urge to stop his car and wait for the other car to pass.

The headlights stayed a quarter mile behind him, keeping pace. The turn off to the ranch was coming up, and small goose bumps accompanied the admission that Sims could have followed him away from Dallas just as easily as the reporter had. Vincent felt like a useless amateur.

Who gives a damn? He hit the steering wheel for emphasis. His brother's obsessions and secret women were not his, and neither were Tucker's enemies. Vincent whipped the wheels left, too fast onto the county road, almost missing it. The back tires spun out on the gravel and fishtailed several yards before he got the Pontiac under control again.

THIRTY-SIX

Ivy Jean

Dahl House

The sheriff had just entered the house. Ivy was about to follow him to eavesdrop when another car sped up the drive. She snuck behind one of the corner columns and watched a black Cadillac park by the ambulance. The car was sleek with chrome trim and the windows seemed to be painted black, too, like a celebrity was inside. Instinct told her it was Tucker Massey…and that her father was not with him.

The back passenger door groaned open and a pant leg and cowboy boot came out, then a man larger than her father emerged, stretched his back, and leaned into the car to say something. She didn't know Tucker Massey, but the way this man held himself, so confident and in charge, it had to be her father's half brother. He looked vaguely familiar, too, but he had a lot more hair than Vincent. Ivy wondered what he knew about the happenings at Dahl House, where he'd been, and if he knew where her father was.

The man she assumed was Tucker slammed the car door shut and looked toward the barn. Ivy could see Mr. Haines at the edge of the deepest shadows behind Carla's car. She couldn't make out his face but could see his light-blue work shirt easily, and every now and then his shaved scalp caught light off something. Then Tucker looked in her direction and Ivy froze, but he turned away quickly. She let out her breath, pretty sure he hadn't seen her. The Cadillac's engine never cut off and, as her uncle started up the porch steps, his car made a U-turn and left.

Ivy slunk back into Dahl House in Tucker's wake. She took advantage of the homecoming scene her dramatic cousin made to grab her old suitcase from the foyer. She didn't know how or when she would leave Dahl House, but Carla's drawstring bag of books would go with her. She needed both bags in one place. As she hurried to the barn, Ivy noticed that the foreman was gone but the window on the side by the bunkhouse was lit. In her mind she counted heads and realized Mr. Haines must be alone.

His connection to the ranch seemed more like hers than anybody else's, like they were both outside the tornado but getting beat to shit by the hail. Haines wouldn't turn his back on her—at least that's what Ivy told herself—and she needed someone to tell her what to do.

She found Carla's bag in the corner of the barn where she'd left it and slid her suitcase underneath. The Corvette seemed deeper inside the barn than before and she felt for the key in her pocket, wondering if now was her chance to get out and go home...

```
YOUTH CRASHES STOLEN DEAD GIRL'S CAR
```

It would be horrible for Wade to hear about her in the news like that, all the way over in Asia. Or Vincent, Ivy supposed, though with less sympathy. Her father's keeping Carla out of her life was inexcusable and a hundred tiny deceptions nagged at her. *It's even his fault I don't have Wade.*

A certain kind of solace came from knowing the Corvette key was in her pocket representing a quiet, secret power that might come in handy. Ivy decided then to combine the two pieces of luggage for an easier get away. She tried to just shove the bag of books in her suitcase, but it wouldn't close with the extra volume. So a wad of garments came out and made room for the diaries. Ivy stuffed the excess clothes behind a rake and returned her now much heavier suitcase to the corner for easy grabbing.

Something else seemed different about the space around her, Ivy realized suddenly. The pickup was gone. The whole time she'd been there, it had sat just outside the barn, off the drive. Ivy leaned to look outside and double-check, feeling uneasy. She had seen Mr. Haines watching Tucker arrive from the barn, but she hadn't noticed if the pickup was there then.

The door inside the barn to the bunkhouse was closed, but light seeped around the edges like a beacon of safety. She made her way there, staying close to the wall to avoid the blackness and unknown hazards in the middle.

Please be here.

Ivy tapped and turned the doorknob at the same time and, before she could call out for him, she was facing the foreman. He stood by the red Formica table, arms out, poised for greeting, she guessed. His shoulders relaxed when he saw her, in relief or disappointment she couldn't tell, but there was no question about her own tremendous relief. She almost hugged him.

His arms relaxed and his left dimple deepened. "Hey, kiddo," he said.

Ivy smiled. "Where you been?"

He shrugged. "Around."

Ivy could see the ends of four bunk beds to her left and all four had a naked mattress rolled up on top. She thought it was an odd way to make a bed. Scanning the living area she didn't see any suitcases, but the place seemed extra tidy, like it had just been cleaned—emptied of personal things. "Did you know Uncle Tucker came back?"

Coffee cooked in a pot on the little stove behind him, the pungent smell reminding her of home and causing a little ache.

"Yes, I saw his car come and go," he said. He turned the flame off under the burner and, using a towel like a potholder, poured the hot black liquid into a mug. Dark circles padded his eyes like he hadn't slept recently. Ivy noticed a briefcase on the floor beside the outer door.

"What do you think is going to happen?" she asked.

He responded with a reassuring smile. "Nothing you should worry about." He leaned his big, shiny head down to her level and stared in her eyes. "I mean it, okay?"

Mr. Haines sat down at the table and took a careful sip from the steaming mug. The heel of his boot bounced under the chair but quit when he caught her looking.

"Aren't you part of things at the big house?" he asked. "Why are you here?"

Ivy liked that he came straight to the point, but she wasn't sure whether to admit her fears or tell him he wasn't like the others and, by default, her ally, because clues were adding up that he was leaving.

She bit her lip and then answered honestly. "I don't trust them."

Mr. Haines let out a big sigh and studied the inside of his cup, like answers were written in there. His head reflected the light bulb over the table, grayish fuzz visible so close up.

"Well, aren't you going to say anything?" Ivy said. "Doesn't anybody tell the truth around here?"

She'd put the same question to Debra earlier and, like she had then, she damn well knew the answer.

"Sit down," Mr. Haines said. He pushed a chair away from the table with his foot. His tone made her hopeful she'd done right coming to him and she couldn't avoid the catch in her throat when she spoke next.

"Why did Carla have to die?"

He visibly softened and Ivy blasted him with borrowed words.

"Can't you find those butchers and kill them? Debra says you're a spy. Tucker can pay y'all to find them."

His eyebrows raised in surprise as she continued with her emotional questioning. Desperation was taking over.

"She was my godmother. Did you know that? What's going to happen to me now if my father doesn't come back for me?" Tears started to fall down her face.

"Hey, now, hysterics don't help anybody."

His chair scraped along the floor and he knelt beside her. She fell into a hug and he waited until she'd cried all she could, patting her head with a gentle "shh." When her tears finally eased, he returned to his chair and his coffee.

"Now, the best I can figure, your father is looking for Miss Summers in Dallas. He'll probably show up here very soon."

"How do you know that?" Her tone sounded accusing and she wished it didn't.

He just stared at his damn coffee mug again, though, and evidently didn't see her answer. His quiet fueled angry thoughts about being dumped there and worries that he was leaving too.

"What are you hiding from anyhow?" she demanded, now sounding like Debra.

His mouth turned up slightly at that, but again he didn't answer. He seemed a hundred miles away.

"Are you a spy like James Bond?" Employing the absurd brought him back to the bunkhouse. "Debra said you're a hired killer. Did you know Lee Harvey Oswald?"

Ivy felt herself spinning out.

Haines put his hands up. "Whoa."

He made an ordinary chuckling sound and got up for more coffee.

Ivy made up her mind to stay put. If he was leaving, she was going to make him take her with him, one way or another. Her hands were on the table, clasped.

Mr. Haines noticed and the slightest flinch and furrow appeared between his eyebrows, but it was thoughtful rather than angry. "Listen, little girl—"

"—Don't call me a little girl."

She was both surprised by his term and by her hasty, but honest, reaction. But she probably would never think of herself as a little girl ever again.

A slow grin appeared on Mr. Haines's face, both dimples showing. "Sorry, Ivy."

Something in her melted. Never before had she known dimples to be so charming.

"Listen to me," he said, watching her to make sure she listened. "It's probably best for you to just get pissed off, like you're doing right now. Pissed off beats afraid any day."

It sounded like worldly advice, but it didn't answer her questions.

"Why did you say that about Daddy showing up before? Have you heard from him?"

"No, I haven't." He clipped his words short.

Ivy thought she might have finally overstepped because he unloaded. Not explosively, but matter-of-factly.

"I think your father went to Dallas to find Miss Summers for Tucker. Anytime now, he's bound to figure out that Carla is here, or at least that she's not in Dallas. You've been here what, two days? Are you really afraid he's abandoned you and left you with Tucker Massey in such a short time?"

Yeah. She kind of was.

Mr. Haines laughed and the atmosphere lightened. "That would suck." He watched her face. "Nah, I'm just kidding. Tucker is good people. He's just not too skilled in the daddy department, but you seem like a girl who has had capable fathering. Your daddy wouldn't leave you out here."

"How do you know that?" She met his gaze and hoped he knew what he was talking about.

"By looking at you, watching you. Your daddy is obviously a competent parent. You already have the stuff to stand on your own. He seems like the kind of father who would never abandon his little gi—" He smiled and then winked. "I mean, his *daughter*."

She took his words for what they were and felt a swell of gratitude. Maybe he was right. Maybe she should wait for Vincent after all.

"Are you leaving?" she asked.

What he was hiding from or if he had to leave the ranch wasn't her business, but Ivy itched for answers about so many things.

"Nah." He poured himself some more coffee. Her father told her drinking too much coffee made him jittery. Maybe it was having that affect on Mr. Haines too. His foot was bouncing again.

"So are you a spy?" she asked again.

He didn't deny it. Just looked at her with a half-smirk, like he dared her to believe Debra. She looked away and pressed more.

"Debra's the one who said you're hiding." She knew she was repeating herself but he had ignored her the first time. "Do you know the man who killed President Kennedy? Oswald?" Ivy met Mr. Haines's gaze, which didn't look so forgiving at the moment. She shrugged her thin shoulders in a manner daring him to dispute Debra's claims.

"Where do you suppose that girl gets her stories?" he said. He laughed easily, a surprise response that felt honest and Ivy relaxed, laughing too.

"She comes up with some doozies!" Ivy admitted.

Their laughter left an echo.

Still smiling, he said, "Tell me, Miss Pritchard, why would you worry over something like Kennedy's killing?"

Miss Pritchard. She never thought of herself that way. And when had she told him her last name? She shrugged and felt a chill cross her arms. He'd avoided answering her questions, again. She wondered if he would have to kill her if she knew the truth.

THIRTY-SEVEN

Tucker

Dahl House

Tucker was astonished to learn that Dahl House hid a secret core. The windowless, musty space felt like the bowels of a palace. The air cloyed, and a single lamp spotlighted a shrouded corpse.

The heartrending loss he felt facing sweet, dead Carla buckled his knees. All the strength inside him unraveled at the sight. He had known war, witnessed unspeakable atrocities, seen children blown to bits. He thought he'd known heartache. But no experience prepared him for the utterly devastating sense of the life being sucked from him that he felt as he drew the sheet away from her face.

His beloved's hair clumped dully around her pretty head. Her perfect, milky nose, no longer breathing, had turned a putrid grey. The absence of her vibrancy, her breath, literally took his own away. Tucker bowed his head and let his agony crawl out in a slow moan from deep inside. Pain of regret, huge and heavy, came into the room growling, turning into a cry for mercy, then to pitiful, shameless sobs. His anguished frame crumpled on the floor, helpless.

"I didn't mean for this to happen," he cried. "Please wake up. You're the only one who ever really loved me."

• • •

Eventually, the weight of responsibility forced him back on his feet. There were lawmen outside and Joanne chewed her fingernails over scandal and publicity. She'd be frantic this would foul up everything for Tucker with the president. The unraveling sensation returned and crowded his heartache. He needed information…and a plan.

Regaining composure, he took a handkerchief out of his pocket and blew his nose. He gently re-covered his love with the cloth, first kissing the tip of her cold nose.

"I'll be back, baby," he said. When he stood, a giant shadow leapt to the walls.

He turned, postured like he was facing a jury, and reentered the foyer. Crossing the threshold, he silently acknowledged that by reentering the house, all thoughts of Carla must remain in the catacombs. He'd shut her back in there alone. The scent of coffee brewing and sound of low voices came from the hallway. Joanne, the dutiful hostess, had corralled people in the kitchen and bar area. He'd take advantage of her distraction to get the story from Haines.

Near the banister he caught sudden sight of his daughter and jumped. Debra glared at him, arms crossed.

"What are you doing?" He snapped.

"Waiting for you." Her tone was defiant.

Tucker forced himself to be patient. "What is it? I told you this is going to be a long night. I've got a lot of ground to cover, Deb."

Debra's red curls reminded him of the young college student in Mississippi, which piled on more regret. His daughter just stared for a beat and then stunned him with her next words.

"Don't you think we should get the corpse out of here?" She spoke offhandedly, as if detached, sounding just like her mother. It shook Tucker on several levels and he would have laughed if the situation hadn't required reason.

"Why would we do that?"

"I don't know… It makes sense you'd want to cover your tracks. I'm just trying to help."

Debra's assumption inflamed Tucker. "I think you don't know what you're talking about."

"I know she was your lover." With her Tucker-like chin tilting upward, his daughter stared down her Joanne-like chiseled nose. "She came here looking for you. To destroy our family."

Various kinds of discomfort stirred in Tucker. "That is simply not true."

With a dismissive gesture he blew her off and strode to the front door, fearing he had little time before the sheriff demanded his full attention. He wanted to hear details about what happened from Haines.

Joanne's voice came from behind just as he opened the front door. "She had an abortion, Tucker. Killed your boy."

He had not seen her come down the hallway and her message stupefied him even further. "How do you know that?" he spat, angrily.

"Which part?" Debra snarled from behind her mother. "The abortion? Or that it was a boy?"

Both parents shot her an angry scowl and Tucker snapped. He threw his hands up and his voice sharpened. "Listen…both of you. We're not talking about this now. Not like this. Joanne, you need sleep."

Joanne sniggered. It was sloppy and he ignored her.

"And Debra, where's your cousin? Find her and you two…go watch television or something."

He walked out, leaving the door ajar.

THIRTY-EIGHT

Ivy Jean

D̲a̲h̲l̲ ̲H̲o̲u̲s̲e̲

Haines glanced at the bunkhouse clock above the sink and Ivy Jean followed his gaze. If he were a spy hiding out at Dahl House, she'd bet he couldn't get mixed up in an investigation about Carla's death.

"Are you waiting for someone?" she asked.

He nodded, no.

Being around Haines seemed to feed a sense of safety for Ivy and she wanted to tell him everything. She wanted him to confide in her too. Maybe they could help each other. Looking him straight in the eye, she said it. "Take me with you, if you leave."

He smiled at her again, dark eyes sparkling.

"Just to Prosperity," she added quickly. "I can wait at home for my father."

Mr. Haines started to speak when hurried footsteps sounded outside and Tucker blew into the room without knocking. His eyes locked on Ivy, surprised, and her initial sense of defiance turned to cowardice in a snap. The man was only slightly taller than her dad, but he had a lot more bulk and seemed to suck all the air from the room.

Tucker said, friendly-like, "Well, hey, there, Ivy Jean." His face turned serious and, after a look at Mr. Haines, he ordered her "to the house."

But Ivy was not going back to Dahl House, not yet.

She opened her mouth, intending to speak her mind, when a realization stunned her silent. The man standing there might become her guardian if her dad really didn't come back. Before she could fully grasp the terrifying idea of Tucker Massey being in charge of her, Mr. Haines locked eyes with her and nodded, solemn-faced. She obeyed his signal and left the way she had come in, through the door in the barn.

Dawdling around the workbench just outside the door, Ivy worked on getting pissed off, like Mr. Haines had said. She liked saying, "pissed off," it meant the same thing as "really mad" only described the feeling so much better. Her short list of reasons to be really mad kept circling back to Vincent's secrets, primarily the ones about Carla. She couldn't figure out her father's motives for keeping her from a godmother's love, from knowing her mother's friend. It got Ivy plenty hot but seemed utterly useless.

Tucker and Mr. Haines's voices rose form inside the bunkhouse and she could hear the emotion in their tones. Ivy's uncle wasn't quite shouting, but he was not happy. She couldn't hear Haines much at all and assumed he refused to fight. That made sense to her—he did not strike her as an angry man. She would've put her ear to the door except one of them could open it and knock her off the steps;

she didn't want to be caught listening, especially since Tucker had banished her to the house to watch TV. He obviously didn't know there wasn't a single TV on the ranch. *How dumb is that?*

Ivy spied a light switch near the workbench then, but she had no idea what it worked. She needed light, yet brightening the whole barn would draw people's attention there. Feeling around the worktable for a flashlight, she landed on a cigarette lighter, the heavy chrome kind a motorcycle guy like Steve McQueen would carry. She dropped it into her shorts pocket with the car key. Now she felt equipped, ready.

Ivy walked with care along the outer wall again. She'd just reached the Corvette when Debra came sashaying down the lane from Dahl House.

Shit. Ivy dropped to the ground, intent on avoiding her cousin.

Debra came through the bay doors taking big, quiet steps and walking hunched over, acting covert. If she'd seen Ivy Jean it didn't show in the direction she moved. Ivy stayed down by the exhaust pipes, wishing the redhead away.

"Ivy," Debra whispered loudly. "Are you in here?"

Ivy craned her neck to see her cousin moving toward the door to Mr. Haines's rooms, arms straight out like Frankenstein.

"Ivy!" Debra whisper-called again, but it was fainter than the first time.

Ivy crab crawled around the car to the passenger side, wiped her hands on her shorts, and slipped out of the barn. *Supremely* covert, she stayed close to the wall and low to the ground, stopping at the riverside corner. She hugged the old barn a moment more to make sure Deb wasn't onto her.

Imagining a football field, Ivy judged the distance between the barn and the river's tree line to be about thirty yards—*thank you, pep squad*. An easy run, except her mental and emotional exhaustion felt so heavy she didn't think she'd get that far. Besides, she could see a minefield of rusting farm contraptions in her way.

Ivy just wanted to be alone to think. A nearby clump of bushes would hide her for now, she decided. She darted around and settled in the foliage, training her ears back toward the barn doors.

Up the lane, the big house looked eerily normal, quiet even, despite all the lights and cars. The wind was cooler coming off the river and the mosquitoes weren't biting yet, thank heavens. Looking southward to where the river bended, a light glinted off something metallic and Ivy ducked, certain she was about to confront a killer. She kept very still and counted to twenty, her eyes sweeping the dark as best she could, while crouched in a bush. She felt around and found a dry branch and snapped it. Nothing stirred. After staying put another minute, she moved toward the shiny object, wary. Two feet into a cedar grove, by a boulder, she knelt to feel with her hands.

She let out a small gasp when she found Mr. Haines's rifle case. When she came to his luggage, disturbance buzzed in her brain. He *was* leaving.

Weight settled on her shoulders. She was going to be left behind. Leaning her head around the rock, she spied Mr. Haines's pickup angled oddly behind the barn. *His get-away ride.* It was backlit by the pole light down at the stables and she could see it pointed toward the pasture.

Ivy started scheming—she had to hide in the truck. But first she needed her suitcase with Carla's books in it. Seeing no sign of her pesky cousin, she snuck back to the barn and grabbed it. She'd forgotten the books made her suitcase so heavy and had to hoist it in both arms, making a beeline back to Mr. Haines's gear in the cedar trees.

If Ivy had anything to do with it, Carla's diaries wouldn't be discovered at Dahl House. "Tell no one," she had said.

Gooseflesh pimpled up as it dawned on Ivy that what she held in her arms like a baby might be a treasure chest of stories about her mother. Taking a seat on the far side of the rifle case, out of sight, she peered in all directions, checking to be sure she was truly alone, then sat thinking about a green book with "1941" written on it. Hands shaking, she took the chrome lighter out of her pocket and soundlessly unlatched the suitcase. Ivy worried about being seen while digging, pulling the wrong book out each time as she hurried, flashing the lighter too much. Maybe "1941" was still beside Carla in Dahl House. She gave up the exact moment she found it, though, and, closing the lighter, she thumb-fanned the pages checking for more pictures, letting her eyes adjust to the growing darkness. She flicked the lighter back on to look more closely. Carla's writing was messy and there were sideway notes on some pages, like afterthoughts.

It took her a moment to notice that voices had intruded again. Male voices. She slapped the lighter shut and dropped it. Her mind raced in fifty different directions, shoving "1941" in her waistband, snug against her back. That book belonged with her.

Ivy knew Mr. Haines would never voluntarily take her, or the suitcase, with him, so she lugged it to the truck and heaved it through the open passenger window. Reaching inside, she slid it to the floorboard so maybe he'd get far enough away before noticing it. She paused to contemplate whether she had time to hide in the truck's bed, but turned back first to see about the voices and ran toward the corner of the barn.

Oof! Ivy jumped with a stifled yelp. Something had slammed hard into the ground near her foot and she pressed her back to the old wood. Was she just shot at? With bullets? Breathing hard, her brain bounced between disbelief and figuring out her options. It was too fast for a peashooter, and it felt deadly, but she hadn't heard a gun shot. She couldn't be sure, but thought the projectile had come from where the truck faced, across the pasture.

Ivy swallowed her fear—deep trouble lay out there...*with a silencer.*

In a crouch, she sped to the front corner of the barn, fighting her panic by being pissed off. If what hit the ground beside her had been a bullet, and the voices coming from Dahl House were the law, then Mr. Haines had guns coming at him from both directions. He deserved to be warned, even if it meant she'd be stuck at the ranch. *At least Carla's diaries will be safe.*

The sheriff's deputy and the taller ambulance guy were on the porch, smoking cigarettes. Ivy hurried along the face of the barn as one of them tossed his cigarette and gestured toward the gaping bay doors. Good and mad now, she made up her mind as she slipped back inside the barn. She didn't think her heart had ever pounded so hard. The bunkhouse door was still closed and she peeked back at the big house just in time to see the men move off the porch.

Touching "1941" at the small of her back, Ivy rounded the front of the 'Vette and, in one slick move, dropped into the driver's seat and clicked the door shut, holding her breath.

THIRTY-NINE

Tucker

Dahl House

Tucker motioned to a whiskey bottle on the bunkhouse shelf. At that moment, he felt an intense urge to cast blame, fair or not, and he needed to calm down somehow. Emotion persisted in tiny explosions of grief as he worked to separate Carla's death from everything else.

Haines grabbed a fresh coffee cup and poured from the bottle for Tucker. Sliding the drink across the table, he nodded to a chair. Tucker sat and took a sip of the liquid courage, rolling it around on his tongue to ease the burn. He breathed in deep and exhaled slowly. No matter the trouble, he wanted Haines at his back.

"Christ, buddy," he said, fighting a tremble in his voice. "What fucking happened?"

Haines wore a look of pity. "She surprised us Friday morning, looking for you, and went down in twenty-four hours. No one knew why, until it was too late." He looked at the coffee in his cup.

"She didn't volunteer that she'd had an abortion. I don't think she even knew she was cut and bleeding out."

Tucker hung his head over the table. "A beautiful life, so brutally...oh, God." He breathed purposefully to maintain composure.

"I always enjoyed the sparkle of Carla," Haines said.

After a moment, Tucker looked at him and grinned. "She did sparkle."

Haines held his gaze. "There's more we need to talk about."

Hearing urgency in his voice, Tucker nodded at his friend of eighteen years.

"You've heard the talk, I'm sure—the Kennedy job didn't turn out like it was supposed to, and even the most unwitting assets near Dallas that day are in danger."

Tucker sank back in the chair. A botched job and the tactical erasure or extreme distortion of all ties back to the truth was textbook CIA.

"Shit, man." Tucker remembered discussing this speculation with Chess, his partner on the mission in Mississippi, an ex-Company man. "Do you think our own guys took out the President? Like someone gone rogue?" he asked. "They can't possibly think they can cover that up."

Solemn faced, Haines shrugged. "I don't know who, and I damn sure don't want to believe the Company was involved, but it looks like I've brought them, whoever they are, to the ranch. I'm sorry, Tucker. Horace Ortiz saw me in Dealey Plaza when everything went down that day and it got me on a list somewhere."

Haines continued. "We don't have time to solve anything, though. I found evidence the ranch is being watched and I need to divert them away from here."

Tucker trusted his friend and the man's belief was enough for him.

"Leave the pickup in Lampasas. Where will you go?"

"My best shot at deep cover, for the short term, is Mexico, I think. I'm not taking chances while I figure it out. Especially with everything going on with…well, you know."

Haines's was right. His presence at the ranch could add unnecessary tangles to the already supremely messed-up business of Carla's death.

"Carla told me a pair of shadowy goons came to her apartment," Haines added, "with accents like thugs. They scared her. Do you think it could be the same guys who've shown up here?"

"I'm not sure." Tucker shook his head, alarmed, but unable to say. "All I know is that last fall, at my father's behest, I joined Lyndon Johnson's personal, off-the-record, security crew. November twenty-second had me scanning crowds around his limousine during the motorcade, carrying a walkie-talkie."

"Inside chatter is lively about cleanup, but I've not heard your name so far."

Tucker felt relief at that, but fear for his friend—and his family—remained. "The deputy in the house right now is asking questions and I suspect he'll come knocking out here any minute," Tucker said. "You need to be gone before he does."

Without hesitation, Haines quickly briefed Tucker on matters of his ranch. Someone would have to fetch the heifers in Waco next week and Tucker hadn't laid eyes yet on the chestnut, Blade.

He wrapped it up. "Joanne will fall in love with Bella, given the chance."

"Your horse is part of this outfit, my friend. I'm sickened it has come to this, but I'll handle it here. And I plan to get you back on the ranch, pronto."

The men shook hands and gave each other a squeeze and backslap apiece, then stepped apart. Haines tipped his head and Tucker opened the door to the barn—then abruptly held up his hand. Another cruiser had arrived. Without looking at his old friend, he whispered sternly, "Go."

FORTY

Ivy Jean

Dahl House

"Boo!" Debra's head popped out of the darkness of the barn on the passenger side of the Corvette, and Ivy almost peed her pants.

Unnerved, she watched her birdbrained cousin open the door and hop into the passenger seat.

"The light!" Ivy whisper-screamed, inserting the key in the ignition.

When another pair of headlights swept around the bend and sped onto the property, both girls ducked. Easing up, they saw another squad car slide to a stop.

More police! Choruses filled Ivy's head and thoughts sparked in every direction like fireflies as she pressed the brake pedal, ticking through her intentions. She glanced over her shoulder just when the bunkhouse door opened and filled with Tucker's hulk. She turned the key and brought on the rumble.

In that fragment of time, Ivy did not fear bodily harm. In her mind she had nothing to lose and everything to gain if Haines got away. It felt like another chance to save Carla.

The music in her head swelled, along with pressure on the gas pedal. She revved the accelerator and dropped the gear to "D," barely discerning Tucker's swearing and pounding footfalls getting close. As the Corvette plowed away, it nearly clipped the right side of the barn door and Debra screamed, but Ivy held onto the wheel and the rear end of the car straightened out.

Debra squealed with pure glee.

"Shut up!" Ivy snapped.

With her eyes set on a narrow patch of drive between two of the cars in the driveway, she applied even, but deep, pressure on the pedal. The hot rod zipped past the collection of stunned men and sliced through the parked cars like a cartoon sequence.

"Wahoo!" Debra cheered. "We made it! Way to go, cousin!"

"Now what?" Ivy shouted over the noise, glancing backward.

She didn't see the other car emerge from the woods until nearly slamming into it. Both her feet jumped to the brake, and Ivy pushed with everything she had while steering to get out of the way. In slow motion, her father's Pontiac rolled past and Ivy glimpsed Vincent's terrified face as the Corvette's wheels locked, throwing both girls forward with such force that Ivy no longer controlled the machine. The car's rear end slid out, tossing them right, sideswiping an oak. Debra's squeals and the roaring engine fell abruptly silent in the crash.

FORTY-ONE

Haines

DAHL HOUSE

Tucker's order—"Go!"—had come across plenty urgent to Haines and he acted fast. Having already taken leave of emotional attachments, his physical departure from Dahl House ranch had only required a sequence of one foot in front of the other. He'd heard Carla's Corvette roar into action as he slipped out through the side door, thinking *Bravo!*

It looked like the girls had picked a perfect moment for ruckus.

Staying close to the outer wall, as he'd rounded the back of the barn to collect his gear, he'd caught a glimpse of Ivy finessing the 'Vette past the jumble of cars very capably. It had all the makings of a fine distraction. Amid the racing engine noise and spinning tires, Debra's voice had whooped it up as he trotted to the pickup. Sincerely grateful for the quick-thinking girls, he'd smiled and pressed the clutch to roll start the truck.

Hearing the Corvette hit something solid had made him jerk his head around to look. Then he thought he heard a bullet drill the air by his ear and ducked. His instincts assured him the car crash wasn't deadly, but professional snipers didn't usually miss. Haines had sped up to make the truck a bumping, erratic target.

Now, as he reached the pavement, Haines could slow his speed to see if he was being followed. A gunman in the trees would have seen him leaving, but also would've had to reach his own vehicle to come after him.

Come on, you bastards.

The point was to draw them away from the ranch, although he didn't plan to confront the enemy until he identified them. He backed the truck into a cutaway and sat awhile unseen. After five minutes spent with no other vehicles coming along, Haines drove on. He kept to the quiet back roads, skirting the massive Fort Hood, passing through towns like Pancake and Bee House with the truck's speed just below posted limits, so as not to draw any attention. He had the window open and cracked the corner vent to minimize cross draft.

With nothing to do but get lost in thought, he admired Debra and Ivy Jean's take-action style and wondered how much of young Ivy's deed had been for his benefit, really. Carla Summers would have admired her gumption and the stunt.

The domino effect of events over the past few days were overwhelming. He wasn't even sure what day it was anymore—*Saturday, maybe?* He replayed the days in his mind. First, Joanne and progeny had shown up unexpectedly and then Tucker had gone on his LBJ mission. Haines thought through Moss's warnings from the next night, the mysterious arrival of another young girl, and Carla's appearance on Friday. It was a literal cascade of smaller, manageable happenings seeming to mash up over a single weekend to doom his retirement to Texas. Now that he had a moment for self-pity.

Dwelling on poor Carla Summers as he traveled southward, he thought about how timing could be such a harsh enemy. Swift and deadly. But it was pointless for him to resent the forces of change. His whole career in espionage had been about affecting or enforcing change. He craved static existence, but it clearly wasn't in the cards. Not yet.

A lot could happen in a short period of time, though, as he'd just been reminded. He thought of Ivy Jean and Debra's experiences in the context of Carla's death, knowing they would be the most resilient of everyone, by default. Young people bounce. Ivy Jean would give the clearest account, too. Tucker's domestic problems would eventually settle and the Kennedy hit could be exposed any day, calling off the dogs.

Public digging and prodding at the assassination continued, enough to indicate not all Americans were accepting that Oswald acted alone, or that Jack Ruby wanted to "spare Mrs. Kennedy his trial." Who knew? As long as he was dreaming up miracles, though, he figured why not hope that the whole world would just suddenly accept the lone gunman pap?

Barring that, Haines figured he'd be gone awhile. It would take tedious, deep-cover investigation to find out who was chasing him and he didn't have all the same connections as an outsider, a retiree. He rolled up the window, turned on the radio and found a Spanish station out of Austin.

Might as well ease back into the culture.

FORTY-TWO

Vincent

Dahl House

Vincent had crawled along the final stretch of county road in low gear because the entrance to his brother's ranch was easy to miss. At the grove of cedar elms that signaled the river bend, though, he'd picked up speed, anticipating answers and the sight of Ivy Jean's sweet face. Carla's tan Corvette had suddenly come out of nowhere, barreling straight at him.

Braking to avoid collision, he took in everything at once: Ivy driving, Tucker's house lit up, squad cars, an ambulance, uniforms—then a sickening crash as fiberglass met oak. Without memory of stopping or exiting the car, he jumped from the road to the wreckage, holding his breath. Pressure whined in his head and the white caliche dust of the road impeded his sight and breath. He tried to swallow and call out.

"Ivy Jean?" It came out quieter than he intended, but her little head turned to his voice and he stifled a sob at the blessed sign of life.

There was considerable blood on that adorable face, though. Debra's body had flown against her and their mass was just now untangling, both girls uttering whimpers. Debra's cheek had hit something hard, he could see right off, but Vincent only felt relief.

"Take it easy, girls. Don't get out yet. Let's be sure nothing's broken."

He helped Debra sit upright on the passenger side so he could reach Ivy Jean. Others ran toward them and he left both car doors open before checking Ivy over. The girls were coming around alright and Vincent silently thanked his lucky stars.

The mob descended then from all directions and he choked back a sob at the sight of his daughter being tended by the medic. Everything slowed in the loud and urgent atmosphere. Vincent saw Tucker then. His brother reached Debra's side of the car, wearing an expression Vincent had never seen on him before. *Human.*

He realized Carla wasn't in the crowd, though, and walked over to Tucker, who stood watching the other medic work on his girl.

"Where's Carla?" Vincent inquired, looking away from Joanne, who seemed horror-struck as she stayed away from the Corvette.

Tucker looked at the ground and spoke so Vincent couldn't see his mouth. The wind rustled leaves and he thought Tucker had said she was *dead*. But that couldn't be right.

"What?" he said, confused.

Taking one look at his brother's big, bowed head, his lack of response said it all.

Every ounce of breath in Vincent's body left him. He processed and rebalanced as a growing wad of sorrow connected his throat to his belly. That his brother was wholly and completely responsible was the only message getting through.

"How?" he managed to ask, fearing the answer.

Tucker looked around at the other people near them. He turned away from the car with his face scrunched up in pain. "She had an abortion. And they killed her." His shoulders heaved.

Vincent's fists balled up instinctively as he mentally dared his brother to sob, but the medic interrupted them.

"Sir?" he said, looking at Vincent. "Your little girl needs a few stitches." He held a finger to the outer edge of his left eyebrow. "But she's going to be okay. Her rib cage and right knee are going to be bruised and sore for a while, but that's all."

A welcome lightness of fortune overtook Vincent's distress over Carla and he nodded humble thanks to the man.

The medic turned to Tucker. "Mr. Massey, your daughter was even luckier. Soreness is about all, some swelling around her right cheekbone where she hit the dash." He looked from one man to the other. "Too bad they weren't wearing them newfangled seatbelts."

A guy wearing a badge stepped up to Tucker then, excusing the interruption.

"Sheriff Hansen." He extended a meaty hand and Tucker shook it. "Can we have a word? My deputy will help sort this out with the missus and your daughter. Those girls sure were lucky."

The medic spoke again to Vincent. "We have a dead body that needs to get to the morgue, but I can have the deputy take your girl to get stitched up or you can take her there yourself."

Vincent nodded and confirmed the nearest hospital while Ivy waited in the bucket seat of the Corvette, so frail and vulnerable. Tape and gauze covered the gash on her brow, and Vincent felt a jolt of vicarious pain akin to nails scraping on a chalkboard. Nothing mattered but her.

He tried to carry her to the front seat of the Pontiac, but Ivy Jean wriggled free to stand and hold onto him instead. Vincent surveyed the scene around them and imagined striding over to issue a straight-on punch between Tucker's eyes. Beyond the initial surprise, his brother would stomp his butt in the dirt. But it would feel good for a couple of seconds. Getting his girl stitched up and back home where she belonged would feel even better. And Vincent really didn't think he'd ever need to say another word to Tucker Jack Massey for as long as he lived.

FORTY-THREE

Ivy Jean

<u>Dahl House</u>

A weird, thick silence between Ivy's ears had muted all the outside noise. The chalky heat swirled around her and made it hard to breathe, too. Her father was close—she could smell his aftershave—and he was real flesh and blood and she wasn't dead, because his squeezing and prodding didn't feel very good. He kept asking questions then holding her face in his hands and examining every atom of her.

He helped her get upright and out of the car, but her legs felt floppy and her bangs were in the way. Only they were red and wet bangs. She shuddered at the idea of blood soaking her hair, vaguely recalling the volumes of blood around her godmother. Vincent seemed very glad to see her, though, so he didn't know yet about the vodka or pot at least.

"I'm glad you came back," she said to the middle of his chest.

"I never went far," Vincent said. He peeled her away from him and held her at arm's length, studying her again like he was seeking the truth of the universe.

When he attempted to carry her, Ivy remembered Carla's book in her waistband and protested his help. That piece of her mother's life belonged to Ivy Jean now. If her father found it, she'd likely never see it again. So she had tried hard to steady her legs and feet and, drawing his arm to lean on, she offered a weak smile.

Soon after, the familiar smells of their good ole Pontiac had overwhelmed her senses with a rush of normal. Reclined on the backseat, "1941" mashed into her back, and she weakly slid it under the floor mat. In the process she'd bumped her knee and, with a bolt of pain, tears came gushing out just as Vincent drove them away. Since the Pontiac didn't have air conditioning, the windows had been open and her dad hadn't noticed, she thought, until he pitched a handkerchief over the seat. The cotton smelled like him and she'd blubbered into it.

As they entered the Gatesville hospital, a doctor and nurse quickly tended to her, Vincent standing guard, in a room with bright lights and checkered floors. The nurse wiped her cut and it stung. The doc came at her with a needle and she flinched, but instead of feeling the needle go in her skin, she heard it. A weird straining sound, of her hide, resisting puncture. Then they all watched her respond to flashlight beams and toy hammers and the doc made her stand and walk, like she was a chimpanzee experiment.

"Take a picture of that knee," Vincent ordered the doctor. "I don't care what it costs."

Ivy's fuzzy disconnection made the whole time there dreamlike. Her head was woozy, and lost hope for Carla squeezed her heart and brought numbness everywhere else. Memory of bullets firing after Mr. Haines made her breathe fast, too. She just wanted to be home, to be safe, and away from it all.

The rain waited until they were back in the car then washed down on them with all the racket of a freight train. Ivy was glad to have the excuse not to talk. She found a bag of potato chips on the front seat and shoveled them in her mouth without thinking. The salty, oily flavor seemed to settle her stomach and felt satisfyingly *ordinary*. Then she fell asleep, until the sound of the turn signal brought her around and the car slowed to a stop.

Home.

Finally.

The house looked different than she'd remembered. She felt almost like a stranger, except she'd only been away two days. Nighttime and a dewy mist made it appear less ragged but eerier, and the kitchen's bulb must have burned out because all the windows were black.

Ivy and Vincent entered the house without words between them and her dad flicked on the lights. Her heart quickened when she saw that the inside looked exactly the same as always.

At least some things don't change.

FORTY-FOUR

Haines

L̲a̲m̲p̲a̲s̲a̲s̲, T̲e̲x̲a̲s̲

It wasn't until Haines had secured a motel room that he discovered an extra bag on the floor of the truck—a small, well-used Samsonite suitcase. He stood in the open door of the pickup and placed it on the seat, carefully unsnapping the latches to a rush of Carla's fragrance. And a drawstring bag filled with books. *Carla's books.* But it wasn't Carla's valise.

She'd told him she intended to hand the diaries over to Tucker, but Haines pondered how they got in the pickup. Carla had pled with him, "Don't let anyone have them."

He'd still believed she had the flu then.

Ivy Jean must have rescued the books. The case was hers, too—the clothes shoved inside were too small for anyone else. Plus, Carla would not have revealed the diaries to Joanne or Debra. And if Ivy Jean put them in the pickup, it explained her timing in the scene with Carla's car. He hoped the tragic weekend didn't bother the little girl's head too much, and smiled at remembering her asking how much she had to grow to be a ranch hand.

In the light of day he would more closely examine the extra cargo and make decisions then. Just in case he was being tailed, he moved the pickup because it looked obvious in the motel parking lot. He parallel parked it on a residential street between two other vehicles so the plates weren't easily readable.

Haines planned to purchase a used car for the trip to Mexico, but he woke up to Sunday and closed car lots. Very few establishments in Lampasas did not observe the Sabbath, despite its Wild West reputation of the olden days. He could research bus and train schedules, or lay over another day. He opted for that. It would give him a chance to peruse the parcel Ivy entrusted to him.

• • •

The journals Carla had so fiercely protected were very private, but harmless in his opinion. He understood why she'd fight strangers accessing them, though, and he supposed she might have already gotten rid of anything incriminating in terms of Tucker or the assassination. Most of the chronological assemblage was just filled with flowery prose on a gamut of subjects. The earliest dates were pre-war, during Carla's college years. A whole volume was filled with stories of her best friend Gwendolyn's wartime romance with their "guy pal," Vincent. Both women speculated for pages over whether it was real love or fear of being alone. Love won.

Haines soon got a clearer picture of why Carla and Ivy Jean clicked. Vincent and Gwen were the girl's parents. Ivy Jean's father was also Tucker's half brother—Haines hadn't been sure, as Tucker had never confided in him about that. The phrase "tangled web" came to mind.

There were a few racy parts in the sequence after Tucker entered the picture, in both events described and the language Carla used. Evidently his old friend didn't mind using his mistress—and a close circle of her friends—for ready-made partying whenever he wanted.

Don't let anyone have them.

Haines couldn't bring himself to destroy the books. He thought about leaving them in the pickup for Tucker—Carla probably wouldn't have minded that option—but then Tucker would only have to dispose of them himself. Haines liked a second idea developing better—giving them to the girl. Racy parts be damned, by the time Ivy Jean read them in five or six years, cartoon rabbits would probably be sucking cock on TV. Her dead mother dominates most of the pages, anyway, and her parents' obvious importance in Carla's life made them Ivy's now.

First thing Monday morning, Haines donned a mustache hidden in his kit with some theatrical glue, put on an Austin Senator's baseball cap and set out to find a car. He paid cash for a '54 Plymouth that had at least one more road trip in her and transferred his things from Tucker's pickup. Per the plan, he parked the truck in the bus station lot, hid the key atop the back tire, and walked away.

Before leaving Lampasas, he parked in front of a squatty stone structure near the county courthouse with lettering on the window that said LAW OFFICE. He'd looked up an "estate attorney" in the Yellow Pages. The plan was to bring a new stranger into his personal network, someone who had no reason to pry further than what Haines told him, so he could get the diaries to Ivy Jean. Haines wanted her to receive the parcel sometime in her sixteenth year, which he'd calculated to be '68. She would be past the trauma of Carla by then, any connection of the books to Haines would be long forgotten, and she'd be about the age her mother was in the earliest volumes. He entered the law office with the drawstring bag and left without it a little while later, sliding the lawyer's business card in his wallet. The random choice had felt right; the guy had been discreet and capable.

Jetting now down US-281, the limestone outcroppings and oak groves of central Texas molted into an arid landscape for a bit. The sun was low in the sky as he approached the valley region of the Rio Grande River, lush and tropical, marking the border with Mexico. He'd spend the night on the U.S. side and make the four-hour drive to Monterrey in the morning. Nomadic living was familiar and easy enough, so Haines didn't stress himself with looking backward. Already translating thoughts to Spanish in his head, the language shift would feel natural in no time.

January 1965

Seven months later

FORTY-FIVE

Haines

Ciudad de Asuncion, Paraguay

Haines's head of hair grew quickly when left unshaven, most of it grayer than he wanted to admit. He'd gone from bald to unruly and wore the coarse, wiry mass bound with a rubber band at the nape. From what he could glean stateside, the tail on him never reappeared at the ranch, but evidence of sanitizing continued to appear in the news to trouble him. He had made his way deep into South America and the sprawling capital district of Paraguay, at the border of Argentina.

The national language was Spanish, though he brushed up on the local's Guarani, so he found cover easy enough. But he didn't know enough or blend enough to really *live*. He'd taken a second-floor flat in middle-class housing near Calle Palma, fond of its traditional architecture, but Haines truly missed country living. It is what defined *real living* for him now, and he wanted it back. Horse breeding was big business in Paraguay, too. He'd found one place that specifically bred Palominos, providing the local vaqueros sturdy rides for the enormous farms.

Paychecks had piled up into a tidy sum ever since he graduated West Point, always split by thirds then deposited in three different foreign countries where his identity was royally protected. As a result, he didn't have to work, but he couldn't stand idleness or even too many hours cooped up in his room not sleeping. So he'd taken a job loading semi-haulers by the river. That heavy lifting, plus a boxing gym he'd found near his room, kept him fit.

His shift at the docks ended at 7:00 p.m. and he always detoured on his way to the bus stop, giving the smelly crowds time to thin. Icy refreshment at a small cantina allowed him to readjust to being alone in a crowded city.

The cantina's air was mechanically cooled and, unlike Mexico, offered frigid beer, which he thought had never tasted so good. Over the past few months, he'd staked out three or four well-iced beer establishments along the way home at night.

Haines took a deep pull from his beverage. It had been seven months since he'd left the U.S. and he still found himself recalling plans he and Tucker had made for the business of Herefords and thoroughbreds. Longing for the ranch, or rejoining Bella, forced constant re-steering of his thoughts—because feeling cheated was for whiners.

On more maudlin days, though, he'd admit investing in Tucker's damned cattlemen scheme had just proved once and for all that he wasn't meant for civilian life.

Too bad. The illusion had felt so right.

Haines stayed tuned in to the Kennedy controversy as best he could but, after the Warren Commission's official conclusion that Oswald acted alone, highly visible news coverage subsided. And because so many dots connecting back to Oswald, or Ruby, had been rubbed out, there'd never be enough evidence to make anything else conclusive. Most recently, a pilot from New Orleans—ex-CIA with supposed ties to a Chicago plot to kill the president—had fallen out of a high-rise to his death. The rate of coincidence on these small news items had passed bizarre already, and every time Haines thought it might be over, another suspicious case would catch his eye or ear. Like a reporter found dead by a karate chop to the neck; he'd been in Jack Ruby's apartment the same day Ruby shot Oswald. Haines knew the events were not all flukes.

All those curiously missing inroads would surely inspire conflicting theories forever. It chilled Haines to think of America's vulnerability if our own military and intelligence leaders had President Kennedy iced. The country's security apparatus would collapse, rendering the U.S. an opportune target for overthrow. Somebody in a high place was surely calling the shots on the cover-up business, he knew. There was no trail, the mainstream press scoffed at the notion of internal conspiracy, and tons of records were being systematically shredded or sealed. He'd given up identifying whom, half afraid of what he'd learn.

So whoever it was, as long as they were out there distorting the truth, he was still presumably on their list and wouldn't go back.

• • •

Back in his flat, Haines turned on the TV and opened windows for some fresh air. A news clip about race riots in America came on, followed by a story of students protesting Vietnam, distracting the world from JFK's killing, of course. Everybody was tuned to a hundred other things.

Tired of looking over his shoulder and weary of stateside speculation, Haines admitted he needed the countryside for his soul and a solid rock flank. In a magazine story he'd read, a tribe of monk-like Indians dwelled high in the Chilean Andes. Meditative and self-sufficient, they comprised a village and led rugged but deeply meaningful lives among gardens and astonishing natural beauty, literally hundreds of miles from modern civilization. The article had called it "transcendental living."

Before overthinking the idea, Haines dug through a pile of paper for a very specific map and prepared to go in search of a mountain.

FORTY-SIX

Vincent

Prosperity, Texas

Vincent tried his darnedest to resume a normal existence after he and Ivy returned, except he'd quit reading newspapers and watching TV news. He was flat unwilling to risk stumbling on something related to Tucker, or even Wade William, who was now entrenched in Vietnam. Jarring, raw imagery was the trend with news people lately and the war in Asia offered plenty of it. On-screen or on-page violence disgusted Vincent; he'd been to war, seen it up close. Imagining Wade in that reality hurt him, and blatant visuals concerned him as to younger minds. What did it convey to kids like Ivy Jean when they were forced to confront live deaths captured by a camera?

Carla's death and that horrible weekend had shaken his little girl enough. The impact of it seemed to translate to extreme moodiness and hours spent alone in her room. He admitted the behavior could be hormone driven, but either way, Vincent felt sure that what Ivy Jean needed was a dependable routine.

He'd bought her a basketball, hoping to inspire more time outdoors. Probably not a mother's choice, but Ivy Jean had responded to it well. From the open window by his desk upstairs, Vincent read his history books and watched her moving up and down the concrete drive, the ball becoming surer in her hands every day. Pinging off the driveway, it made pleasant background noise. *Dring, dring, dring, dring, whoosh.* He'd installed a hoop over the garage door the same day Ivy joined the junior-high girls' basketball squad. She showed good form and lots of promise, and Vincent knew she'd excel if she practiced.

As for the impact that awful weekend had had on him, Vincent thought he was pretty much the same. Sweet Carla Summers had reentered his life true-to-form, brightening and stirring things up in a hurry. He'd enjoyed the hope of reconnection and couldn't escape some degree of guilt mixed in his sorrow, because he'd hurt her and she had died before he could correct it.

As Vincent peered out the window, he scratched a quick note to Mrs. Polk, reminding her to take Ivy Jean shopping. The girl sprouted more and more each day and the poor kid needed a woman's counsel. He didn't know how he could ever be enough.

• • •

One rainy Thursday at the bank, Vincent was working in the lockbox vault when a colleague entered quietly and tapped his shoulder.

"There's a woman here to see you."

He started, struck with a sense of déjà vu, and his heart skipped. What he would give for another chance with Carla…

"I'll be right out, thanks."

His pace slowed on entering the granite-tiled lobby to get a look at his visitor. He thought she might be a new client the bank president had mentioned and extended his hand to the attractive stranger.

"Vincent Pritchard. How can I help you?"

"You don't remember me?" Her smile grew with a mischievous twinkle in her striking, dark eyes. *That* he remembered and a grin crept onto his face.

"Cassidy, right? From the *Dallas Times Herald*. What are you doing here in Prosperity?"

Her hair was tied back from her face with a strip of colorful fabric. She wore a slender black skirt and cream-colored sweater. Vincent permitted a discreet peek at her ankles and saw she wore boots with high heels that made her even taller. He motioned for her to sit and caught a whiff of her fragrance, recalling a night at Carla's apartment that felt so long ago now. The woman had been easy to talk to then.

"As you might expect, I'm working a story," she said. "And when I found myself here, I thought I'd look you up."

People didn't often "find themselves" in Prosperity, but he was pleased nonetheless.

"What's the story?" Then adding too quickly, "Does it have anything to do with my brother?" He wasn't even sure if she knew that Tucker was his brother.

"Nah," she said with a knowing smile. She placed a hand on his desk. "Listen, Vincent, I'm sorry about Carla."

They both had lost a friend. He met her eyes. "Yeah. Me too."

"How's your daughter?" she asked, changing the subject.

He didn't know why she'd ask after Ivy Jean, trying to remember if the two of them had met or if he'd even mentioned her to Cassidy.

"We're good, thanks for asking. But really, what brings you to Prosperity?" he repeated. "I'm pretty sure the scoop isn't new electronic calculators at First Cattlemen's Bank."

She laughed softly and crossed her legs. "I'm nosing around the rural parts, trying to get a read on average folks' impressions, now that everybody's had a chance to study the Warren Report and digest the official 'conclusions' on JFK."

It was his turn to laugh, feeling pretty sure not many residents of Prosperity had slogged through the tome. "Interesting," he said. He considered the angle, wondering who cared what rural Texans thought about the Warren Commission anyway. "Where do you get your ideas?"

"My stepfather was a newspaperman. He's been a strong influence."

Vincent noticed her face light up with the mention of her mentor and he pictured a burly elder, a cigar-chomping newsman who never quit working. "You mean, he gives you leads and you do the legwork and write the story?"

She smiled. "He's dead, so no." She didn't lose her grin and one deep, round dimple drilled her left cheek. "He's the one who taught me to go for the sensational stuff."

She winked, then leaned in, and in a gruff Texas drawl said, "Ya have to get your name out there first, Cass. Get their attention! *Then* you can make 'em listen to your ideas for real news.'"

They both laughed. A thrill zipped through Vincent when he realized that this lovely lady could be flirting with him.

Cass. He liked the sound of that.

She pulled away and folded her hands in her lap as he pulled a stack of papers toward him and looked around. No one seemed to notice them, but it felt like they were sitting in a fish bowl.

"Well, don't get me started on the Warren Commission," he said, all business. "Who have you talked to around here? I'll bet everybody is glad to render an opinion."

"You're my first victim in—whatever county I'm in."

Now she *was definitely* flirting—he saw it in her eyes. This whistle stop at the bank was no accident. Something shifted at the core of Vincent at this realization and he grew bashful and prayed she didn't notice him blush.

He said, "Come on, nothing I have to say is sensational."

"Maybe not, but I'm predicting that anything related to Kennedy's murder will always be sensational news. In Texas at least. And I want to get an early snapshot of the state's collective opinion of their government's handling"—She held eye contact and showed him white, slightly crowded teeth—"of the *sensational* matters of political assassination and cover-up."

Oh, yes. He would read her stories.

"You're right. The assassination will always be sensational," he said. "Johnson probably had that in mind when he established the committee. Keep it a mystery—and thereby benefit glorious Texas, for the tragedy that made us look like gun-toting yahoos."

Cassidy's eyebrows rose and she let go a hearty laugh.

He said, "Seriously, we'll never know who really killed Kennedy. The government has concluded we can't handle the truth." Suddenly he hoped with all hope that she didn't quote him, and changed the subject. "Do you specialize in politics?"

"I have aspirations," she said. "Big changes are happening in the political press and it's exciting times."

"What do you mean?" Her manner of speaking placed her as Southern, but it was hard to decipher a Texas region.

"Uppity, liberal D.C. and New York papers shaped political news…before. And shaped the rules. I don't think reporters today are accepting the word of so-called insiders, or official press corps, so willingly anymore. The rules of play are changing and conflict sells papers. No more holding back, even for the President of the United States."

Vincent was impressed with her confidence.

She said, "It's hard for a girl to break into serious news that's not fashion or recipes. I'm still hunting down my breakthrough story."

"This Warren Commission pulse thing has potential," he said, meaning it.

She awarded his sincerity with a mischievous look that wrinkled the skin around her eyes and allowed him, he thought, a glimpse at her soul. Then she shocked him with her next words.

"Do you want to have supper with me?"

He shouldn't have been surprised by Cassidy's assertiveness. He knew social proprieties had changed, but he was still taken aback.

She was too young for him and these new, looser rules of courtship were unfamiliar. He was completely out of his league but accepted her invitation to dinner, anyway.

Prosperity offered no dining options besides the truck-stop café on the highway, so they settled on barbecue, served up at the VFW on Thursday nights before the band started. It turned out Cassidy danced quite well and they moved nicely together around the floor. Vincent didn't step on her feet once. And that evening was just the beginning.

Cassidy took a room in nearby Lampasas, calling it headquarters, while she interviewed. Vincent snuck around, making excuses at home and at work to see her. He'd never called in sick to his job before, not once in his professional career. In a matter of eight days, and a lot of internal arguing, he admitted he was head over heels.

Vincent had never had such aggressive, bawdy sex before either. She seemed so raw with her passion. Both of them completely wanton, they explored pleasuring like he'd never imagined. He told himself it was just a fling to her and she'd be gone any day now.

But she stuck around. And after he got past being amazed by that, Vincent started reading newspapers again. Then, on one fine Saturday morning, Ivy Jean asked him about Carla. About her abortion and her death. About Gwen, and the rest of her and Wade's family. They'd held each other and cried. Things were truly changing.

Vincent came to realize that stories, family stories, of good times and hard times past, were a kind of nourishment for his kids. By example, the experiences of kin taught them what they're made of, how their character and their family's character, survived and celebrated. Gwendolyn knew this. How did he forget that piece of her and not carry on the tradition with her babies?

Gwen, Carla and Vincent, as young adults, had established their own family unit. Rejection of their parents' values is what had drawn them together in the first place. Pep talks for each other, much of it through stories, had been a staple activity. Vincent hadn't contributed much, but the girls had plenty of material. Their musketeer sort of arrangement became its own treasure trove of shared experience. There was a lot his children didn't know about him, and even more they didn't know about their mother.

Later that same Saturday, Vincent took one of his drives in the country and owned up to a lot of guilt. Then he settled at his desk upstairs and wrote a letter to Wade William, to say what needed saying long ago. *I love you* was true, and easy, but inadequate. *Watch your back,* trite. The right words came once Vincent allowed himself to get inside and imagine his boy in a wet, rotting jungle, struggling for rest in a mildewed sleeping bag, hugging an M60, and peeling leeches off his bare skin—for some imagined, patriotic reason that Vincent knew had died months ago.

"I've been there, son. It grieves me to recall that aching loneliness in context of my boy," he began. "My war was different than yours, but war is war, and it is hell. You wrote about your buddy, Jordan, and I hope to meet him someday. Mates are a vital piece of getting through your time in hell. I remember my closest chum, Dallas, from North Dakota. He was a strapping farm boy who liked to gamble, always getting into dice game scrapes and causing us both trouble with the MPs…"

Vincent quit at five pages, encouraged that he'd found a way to connect with Wade, even from nine thousand miles away.

Then he arranged for Cass to join him and Ivy Jean for supper at their house.

I bet they'll be fast friends.

FORTY-SEVEN

Tucker

Dallas, Texas

It had been a thrilling moment when President Lyndon Baines Johnson called Tucker at his office. Over a million people had attended the inauguration and everyone else had watched it on TV. Tucker would have guessed it was Elvis on the line from his secretary's excited behavior.

Known as the gentle conspirator, LBJ put Tucker at ease right away. In his trademark manner, he spoke as if to a boy, saying how much he'd loved Tucker's daddy and admired his pretty mama. Tucker normally perceived LBJ as a caricature of the schmoozing politician, but right then it was Lyndon, their trusted family friend, calling to say hello.

"Thurman and I go back to when Christ was a carpenter, you know. I'm sorry I had to miss his funeral," Lyndon said.

Warmed by the sincere tenor of his voice, Tucker responded, "We all understood, Mr. President. Ladybird sent a lovely floral spray, and her kind message meant a lot."

Tucker heard a tussle on the other end of the line, and Johnson put his hand over the mouthpiece to utter something. *In the Oval Office.*

Coming back to the conversation as a confidante, Johnson said, "Things kind of blew up for you in Mississippi, son."

Tucker didn't know what to say. Not long after his time in Mississippi, disturbing news surfaced about the mutilated bodies of three missing freedom workers found in Neshoba County, near Philadelphia. According to one newscast, an anonymous phone tip had led federal officers to the bodies, hidden deep inside an earthen well. Although he hadn't researched the precise locations and dates involved, Tucker was pretty sure he and Chess had witnessed the Klan celebrating the murders. Maybe Chess had even made the phone call.

Tucker cleared his throat. "Yes, sir. Seems they did for you, too." He cringed—because that could have been said better. Again, Johnson covered the phone and spoke to someone else, his voice unclear.

When President Johnson came back on this time, he sounded hurried. "Now, I'm sending someone to Dallas to talk to you," he said. "He'll be there tomorrow. Listen to what he says, do you hear me?"

"Yes, Mr. President," Tucker promised. "I'm glad you called, sir, because I—"

"—I'm sorry, Massey," Johnson said, issuing further muffled orders. He came back with a heavy sigh. "Listen, son, duty calls. You understand."

Tucker understood, all right. But it smarted. He'd imagined his first interaction with Lyndon to be less awkward, somehow, and chided himself for not assuming a stronger position with the old politico.

The president had said he was sending a man with orders. And sure enough, his representative flew in from Washington, D.C. the very next day and scheduled a meeting with Tucker at 11:00 a.m. sharp. That meeting didn't go much better than the clumsy phone call with Lyndon himself.

Tucker and the man met alone in a vacant office at the federal court building, three blocks away. There was an empty desk between them and on a credenza under the window sat a telephone, wrapped in its severed wires.

After cordial introductions, the president's man said coolly, "You should stay out of the news."

Tucker thought Johnson had probably heard about his mistress's death at the ranch, and disapproved of the tabloid speculation over the coroner's investigation. It had been a routine matter from the start, except paperwork got bungled at the county level and those delays stirred the gossip mill two weeks too long.

"I can do that," Tucker said. "But what is this really about?"

Excessively thin, LBJ's man had a congenial, brotherly style of speaking. "Mister President advises that you take up residence at your ranch and assume a quiet country life." His brown eyes locked on Tucker's. "And watch your back."

Tucker realized this wasn't about bad publicity or Mississippi, as he'd thought after the president's "things kind of blew up" comment on the phone.

D.C. guy seemed sincere, and even concerned, but he spoke doubletalk. "Activities underway pose a threat to certain individuals, and there's reason to believe you're on their list."

Tucker's mind scrambled for meaning. Haines's had mentioned a list before he'd left Dahl House. The pesky investigators who were hounding Carla came to mind, too, and his stomach lurched. They hadn't been around to see him since she had died. Tucker sucked in a breath, remembering a news bit from a few weeks earlier. One of Jack Kennedy's regular babes had been shot and she had bled out on the tow path of a canal right in the heart of Washington, D.C. Tucker's inside sources were sketchy, but he'd heard she kept a diary somebody wanted.

He forced calm and cleared his throat. "Is this because my lady kept a diary?" D.C. didn't reply. Tucker pressed, "It sounds like, in the president's mind, I'm burned. Does this have to do with her somehow?"

D.C. still didn't speak, but his head wagged a slight "no." Then he stood up and looked around at all the corners of the borrowed room, high and low, and stooped to peer under the desk. When he picked up the telephone base, Tucker realized he was looking for bugs. This wasn't about Carla.

"I don't understand." Tucker said, bluntly.

"We've got a serious image problem," the man started, "and it's exposing the country as weak. Mister President is pinned to the wall."

Tucker nodded soberly. He didn't grasp the relevance of the words but continued to listen.

"Some semblance of order and security must be regained, and Mister President is sorry, but Kennedy is dead, and the current administration can't address bigger threats if the assassination keeps churning public mistrust."

Assuming they weren't bugged, Tucker mentioned his only connection. "Are you here because I was watching Johnson's limo during the motorcade? What did you mean about operations posing threat? What list?"

D.C. held his hands up in a "slow down" motion.

"Mister President has very private opinions about a conspiracy. Any intelligent mind would. But the matter must die with Oswald. Too much suspicion points directly at elements inside."

Tucker was starting to get the doubletalk and shouldn't have felt so stunned at his conclusions. He'd been weighted with skepticism since Johnson appointed Allen Dulles to his Warren Commission, even after Kennedy had fired him. Of course, Dulles engaged his favored "plausible deniability," meaning information that can't be traced is withheld, avoiding blowback on senior officials. And without substantial evidence to the contrary, it settled the case on Oswald.

"At certain levels, the CIA is untouchable," D.C. guy affirmed. "The president is trying to corral rogue activity both in the field and at Langley."

Tucker shuddered. *Obviously Jack Kennedy was not untouchable. If America's enemies know there is such internal strife as to suspect our own, we'll be at risk indeed.*

Walking away from their meeting, Tucker tried to get his mind around what had just happened. He'd been told to get out of the way and lie low. "Activity," he supposed, meant the sterilization of the crime, beginning with the murder of Oswald, which rendered any prosecution impossible. Haines had feared the participants of such activity had tracked him to the ranch. But there hadn't been sign of those watchers again, so Tucker had assumed they'd followed Haines away. So whose list was he on?

I may never know.

On the one hand, he felt relieved of the pressure to fashion a career out of Lyndon's rise to power. Joanne wouldn't like it, but he felt lighter, deep inside, at the idea. On the other hand, he'd never been fired before, and that's exactly what it felt like had happened, and it smoldered, angry and defensive. All record of his government service beyond 1946 was vapor now, of course. No record existed of participation in Lyndon Johnson's private security detail, on November 22, or ever, and anything that did exist would be destroyed. Any debts owed his father were either imagined, or died with him.

• • •

Later that night, his wife didn't act too pleased, as expected, when he called to tell her Dahl House was to be his permanent residence, at the advice of Mr. President. She'd vacated their house in Dallas as soon as attention to her ranch died down, and preferred the two of them living apart. The news of Tucker moving in might have gone down easier for her, or come out of him better, if he hadn't been so stinking drunk from "celebrating." But he took up residence in the bunkhouse over the course of a few weeks, anyway, and she just ignored him.

The cowboy quarters were quiet and isolated and suited him fine. Joanne didn't give him as much thought as a horsefly, but he felt thankful they had a place to lick their wounds and maybe reinvent their life.

Things with their daughter seemed to be looking up. Her grandmother pulled strings to get Debra accepted into the eleventh grade at a fairly prestigious school in Kentucky. Tension between Joanne and Debra remained pretty volatile and it was probably best to have a thousand miles between them for now.

He thought of the young girl in Mississippi often—Julia McPherson of Connecticut. Remembering the awful way Carla died, Tucker wondered whether the brave young Freedom Rider had gotten pregnant by that redneck rapist? Could her family afford to fix it? Like so many other concerns, Tucker swept away thoughts of looking into it, with apparent ease. His field of worries had been greatly narrowed by LBJ's orders, and he didn't mind. He had other things to deal with. Livestock on the ranch had grown to six head and he'd need to find another foreman soon.

FORTY-EIGHT

Ivy Jean

Prosperity, Texas

Ivy played basketball and kept to herself most of the time while the hurtful memories from her weekend at Dahl House abated. The diary she'd kept of Carla's had helped a lot. And on starry nights, when she found herself sending dispatch to Vietnam from the porch roof, or the hood of the Pontiac, she also talked to Mr. Haines and Carla through the moon.

A whole bunch of news, right after school started again in the fall, stirred memories of things Debra had said, about Haines being at President Kennedy's assassination. The 888-page report of President Johnson's Warren Commission was not studied in seventh grade, but Ivy couldn't avoid feeling conflicted about certain related stories on TV. So, with Vincent's help, she grasped the concept of conspiracy in context of the report. Coach Dan, in third period Civics, had brought the topic up as a current event, but no one acted the least bit interested. Only two kids had piped up with puny questions and Coach Dan had said the world would speculate for years but that the truth had died in Dallas.

Ivy chose to believe what President Johnson and Justice Warren said—basically that Oswald did it and now he is dead and life goes on. She also took the same position as Coach Dan, that news reporters might have been reading too much spy fiction.

Taking in the moon a couple of nights during those days, she had earnestly prayed for Mr. Haines's safety. And she'd sworn the moon told her that what she'd felt on the ground that last day at the ranch had not been a bullet. Maybe it had been an acorn. She'd asked the moon where Carla's other books were, if Mr. Haines still had them, but she hadn't gotten an answer on that one and had to accept that she couldn't know everything.

Ivy had read "1941" from cover to cover at least six times. Her godmother's writings were a schoolgirl's account of her freshman year in college, mostly lighthearted and sketchy on details. In the opening five pages, Carla Leah Summers became lasting friends with her very first roommate, Gwendolyn Jo Haslett. Ivy had lingered on every detail about her mother. Holding the smiling picture of them, she'd imagined Gwen's young face having different emotions, like one Sunday during second term when she'd had a fever with a toothache. Carla had worked the phone until she found a dentist in Fort Worth to treat her roommate—the father of a friend of a friend's cousin. It had taken some doing.

When Vincent entered the pages, Ivy smiled knowingly at every insight. According to Carla, he'd liked her first, which surprised Ivy. But Gwen's more quiet ways had won him over, which wasn't surprising at all, knowing her father.

One day, as she turned the pages, a curious piece of notepaper, stuck in a fold near the back of the book, fell out. It was a small lined sheet like the ones that tear off a pocket-sized notepad and read:

per Patsy: LHO > JR > T. Dealey??

It made no sense to Ivy. She went back through the entire journal looking for a reference to Patsy, T. Dealey, or anyone by those initials. *Dealey* rang a faint bell in her memory, like a department store name or something. She returned the sheet of paper to the journal and forgot about it.

Considering where best to hide her prized memento—her solitary remnant of her mother and godmother—it dawned on Ivy that she'd never felt such comfort from an object before. It required an exceptional hiding place so that no one *ever* knew of it unless she offered to share it with them.

The diary fit in an ordinary cigar box that held her old crayons, so Ivy got a piece of wax paper and lined the box, then double wrapped it shut with a rubber band. She pitched the crayons and returned her treasure to the old toy box in the corner of her room, under a stuffed bunny, bear, and a bubblehead Barbie. Not even Wade would know of it.

Her brother had been in Vietnam for months now. He'd write of rations and supplies and a new friend from Memphis. Wade never wrote of danger or being afraid, but it was plain as day in the news everywhere what was going on over there, and he must have been living those things. Ivy had started several letters back, sharing how far away from home *she'd* been, in a lighthearted way. But the first page kept going in the trash. It felt like she was trying to make sense of a thousand-piece jigsaw puzzle without a picture on the box—which reminded Ivy Jean to install her cherished photograph of Carla and Gwen in the small frame Vincent had given her.

The picture was the only thing she'd shared with Vincent and she'd been adamant, and probably unfeeling, but it was her picture and it belonged where she slept. A loving and loveable connection to her dead mother had been cruelly removed, just when she'd discovered it. The raw unfairness—that a brief moment was all she got—hurt with every breath she drew on some days.

After she set up the photograph, Ivy dug in her closet and reclaimed a little girl's diary that Mrs. Polk had given her one Christmas years ago. With a felt-tip marker, she wrote on the flowery cover, "I.J.P. 1964."

The exercise of putting down *her* stories—of Dahl House, of Carla, of the daring escapades with Debra—had taken a few weeks of stolen moments, but she felt much lighter afterward. And one Saturday morning at breakfast, questions she'd wanted to ask her father, things that she'd bottled up, just blurted out.

"Why did Carla have to die?"

Vincent froze with a spoonful of cereal in one hand, the *Star-Telegram* folded neatly in the other. That question combined a whole lot of troubling ideas. *Could be a Pandora…*

"Only God knows the answer to that, honey."

Ivy was surprised he brought God into it, but that was another discussion.

"Will the police go after the butcher who killed her?"

Vincent frowned at the word she'd used. He sat back in his chair and looked at her, sympathetic.

"I don't know if they can possibly find the person responsible, Ivy Jean. Do you understand what happened to Carla?"

Ivy Jean squared her shoulders, more than ready for truth between them. "Yes. She got pregnant and got an abortion. Something went wrong." Some of the matter confused Ivy still, but she wholly understood the basics.

They looked at each other until he spoke again.

"An abortion is a very dangerous surgery. It requires advanced medical skills and a sterile environment. In America right now, abortion is against the law, so doctors who perform it are 'underground.' Do you know what I mean by that?"

"I know a little. An article out of *Redbook* got passed around Health class."

True Crime magazine was the real source, but the lie came so easy.

He seemed relieved to speak plainly and didn't talk down to her like a child. He didn't even ask how or what she knew about getting pregnant.

"When a medical procedure is illegal, licenses aren't involved and real names aren't used, which means anyone can pose as a doctor." He took a breath and the tension in his voice eased. "So then it becomes a money-making operation for criminals. Women in trouble like that are easy prey for shysters…and psychopaths."

"Can't real doctors break the law and do abortions in a hospital? Just not tell anybody?"

He seemed to think it over. "Most legitimate doctors won't risk it, honey, because if they're caught they'd never get to practice medicine in America again. Besides, girls in a situation like that are so desperate for a solution, they don't ask about medical license." He dipped his chin, looking at her eye to eye. "Neither do the babies' fathers. They have responsibility in the decisions too."

Ivy didn't know what he meant by that exactly, but she didn't want to give up control of the conversation. "But why is it against the law if it just makes money for bad guys?"

"It is a complicated subject, Ivy Jean, one that's being constantly debated by the best legal minds. Some people see it as murder because at any stage of development, abortion is taking a life. Others think, just as strongly, that the courtroom isn't allowed to make health decisions for people."

Like Carla.

Her father was right about it being complicated. She asked him, "How do you feel?"

He surprised her by answering, "I'm neutral because it doesn't affect my life." Holding Ivy Jean's gaze again, he added, "Except you're growing up, and it might affect yours. In which case I think sterile abortion can *save* lives. Girls in trouble shouldn't have to die." He cleared his throat. "And sadly, not all unwanted babies get adopted."

He reached for the next newspaper in his stack, like he wanted to get back to it.

Ivy pictured a dark house full of unwanted children. She had only seen orphanages on television and movie sets, or read descriptions in books like *The Littlest Princess*, but she hadn't really thought that far yet. The whole subject just seemed too big and disturbing.

After a bit, Vincent finished unfolding and refolding a news section to read, then set it aside and looked at his daughter again.

She thought she saw him struggle for words, so Ivy broke the awkward silence.

"She was my friend." Her voice broke. "Did you know we had become friends?" Her hands flew to her face, but she couldn't stem the flood of tears or mute the wailing that came with them. Her father pushed his chair back and actually picked her up and brought her to his lap like he used to do when she was five. Ivy allowed the warmth of his arms to soothe her and she finally wept without holding back for the loss of her godmother and friend. At some point, more questions came out.

"Did you love her?" She moved back to her seat, a smart move because it seemed like hours of listening followed that question.

"Not romantic love, like a man has for a wife," he said. He looked embarrassed, and saddened, by the admission.

Ivy felt tremendously sad for Carla, but it had to do more with remembering Carla's delirious ramblings about Tucker's love, than her father's answer.

"If she was your friend, why didn't she come to our house?"

"I was coming to that."

"If she was our mother's friend, our *godmother*, how come me and Wade never saw her? Or even knew about her?"

Vincent leaned back in the chair, staring at the ceiling and holding his palms up as if to stop her. He gave a huge sigh.

"After your mother died, I wanted my children far removed from the non-stop party scene that revolved around my brother back then."

Ivy didn't understand what Tucker had to do with it. "You mean you didn't want Carla to love Uncle Tucker?"

"I thought he wasn't good enough for her," he said, and faced her. "I made judgments, Ivy Jean. I'm not proud of some wrong ones. You and Wade had just lost your mama and"—he stopped for the right words—"well-meaning relatives wanted to take you away from me."

Ivy gasped inside but didn't stop him.

"My mind wasn't clear about anything except raising you and Wade William far from that city, and that meant far from everything Carla clung to."

Ivy had a sick feeling but had to be clear about this. "Did Tucker have something to do with our mother's death?"

"No. No, but in my twisted thinking at the time, Dallas and that world of flashy money and my brother's distasteful conduct surely did."

Before Ivy could interject another question, she heard the words she most needed to hear come from his mouth at last.

In his words, her father explained how her mother's death had blinded him to all reason. "She died with such violence." Wade had told her about the bank robbery, probably when she was about six years old. She remembered him saying, "It was her time to go. We didn't like it, but it was her time to go."

All kids have hardship, Ivy knew. Some kids are hungry or don't have a safe place to live. Her and Wade's hardship was not having a mother.

While her father shared painful memories, Ivy caught a glimpse of him as a man who had been bloodily wounded and still soldiered on. Heroic stuff. She imagined that it must break a man in half to witness the brutal end of his world like that. Vincent became a different man in her eyes that day over breakfast.

• • •

Ivy had changed too, and it was easy to see, even in her mirror. Thanks to basketball, her gangly legs were getting surefooted, for one thing. Plus, she and a girlfriend from school had finally plucked and tamed her awful eyebrows. Most exciting of all was when Coach had said she could play junior varsity next year if she wanted it bad enough. That had marked the second time her long legs felt like an advantage.

After things opened up between her and Vincent, she thought maybe it was time to take her role in the family more seriously. She'd heard the term "female head of household" and realized it's what she was, though in her private thoughts—and in her diary—she expressed deeper desires, to play and explore and never grow up. Basketball kept her thoughts on the happier, optimistic side of things and she relied on the activity a lot. Eventually, she hardly even thought about the journal titled "1941." She didn't want to be the "female head of household," yet. She hoped for a family spot in-between where she could fit.

One weekend, Ivy was practicing under a forgotten hoop at an empty house across the street. She pretended it was an away game, a foreign court, and she had just made the winning basket when a late-model black sedan came creeping down the street and rolled to a stop in front of her house. Parking the basketball on her hip, she watched two guys get out, dressed alike and looking kind of thuggish. Dark suits strained around big muscles—or fat rolls—and they wore black neckties, hats and sunglasses. Like it was practiced and timed, both of them removed their sunglasses at exactly the same moment, turning toward her house then slipped them in their pockets. Odd...

James Bond would call them goons.

Something told Ivy to warn her dad but not to act overtly. She dropped the basketball and skipped across the road. She was almost a teenager now, her skipping felt rusty and she felt pretty stupid as she lifted her legs up in forced cheer. But she reached the front porch ahead of the men.

"Company!" she shouted into the house through the window screen.

As soon as Vincent appeared, one of them got right to the point. They weren't police because they didn't present a badge or papers, and they gave all-purpose names of Smith and Jones. Ivy was ignored.

They were looking for Mr. Haines. Not that he'd be in Prosperity—they said they were interviewing everyone who'd recently interacted with him. Nobody had come around looking for Mr. Haines before. Suddenly, the overheard conversation between him and Carla came to mind. Hadn't she said some thugs with accents had come asking her questions? That was before she came to Dahl House. They had pressured her about the books. Ivy hoped fiercely these men weren't looking for Carla's books.

She sneered and tried to distract them. "Where're y'all from?" she asked in her most syrupy voice.

"Our office is in Dallas," said one goon, who had the busiest hands she'd ever seen. He'd shoved them in and out of his pockets twice, checked his wristwatch and wiped his head with a hanky in the last thirty seconds.

"Really?" she said, carrying on the act. "You don't sound like Texans."

He ignored her dramatizing and her remark. "When was the last time you saw Haines?"

"Me?"

They looked sinister and acted snotty and, for some reason, inspired her to make trouble. Ivy pushed away snippets in her head about Mr. Haines's other life as a spy but then wondered if the men had guns. Vincent was heating up, and it seemed mostly directed at her. But too bad, this was her show. He didn't know Mr. Haines.

"I don't remember, exactly," she said. "Before the car wreck—but it's fuzzy. Is Mr. Haines in trouble?"

Her dad intervened, calm as a cucumber like Atticus Finch. "Why are you looking for this man? Has he committed a crime?"

"No, sir," the other goon said. "He worked for us and stopped showing up. We're concerned, that's all."

Busy Hands asked her dad, "When was the last time you saw Haines?"

"I never encountered the man," Vincent said. He held out his hand. "Leave me your card and I'll be happy to call if we see or hear from Mr. Haines."

They walked away without leaving a card.

It was peculiar and Ivy wondered again about Carla's journal sitting in her toy box. She stayed on the porch in the shade and

Vincent returned to the house. Watching the black car leave their street, it felt like they had somehow dodged a bullet. She had no idea where Mr. Haines went, or if he was safe… That was what bothered her most. She really wished she knew more.

As if she needed a distraction, a moving van appeared on the street and parked in front of the vacant house across the road. A bike was the first item carried out of the long trailer and Ivy stood, wondering if new kids were moving in. Then she heard the distinct pings of a well-aired basketball—*her basketball*—and she strained to see around the humongous trailer. She didn't want to come across snoopy, though, and chose not to leave the porch yet. A boy appeared then, guiding the unpacked bicycle around the moving crew, weaving through boxes and furniture.

Skinny, with lots of dark hair, and glasses, he looked like he was in seventh or eighth grade. Her basketball rested on his hip. When he noticed her watching, he pedaled in her direction. Ivy put up her hand in a half wave. He kept going to the stop sign, passing her right by. Turning around, he rode past her house again in the other direction. She thought he'd made the slightest nod, but he kept on around the curve and disappeared.

Ivy sighed and went inside. She didn't want to scare a new neighbor with her eagerness, but the ladies at church always welcomed new folks with food and pamphlets. The only thing in their kitchen that appealed to her was graham crackers, so she took a fresh wax-paper package from the box.

The boy was back from his ride around the block when she walked outside again. Both he and the bike leaned against a tree, her basketball on the ground between them. The sidewalk from her porch to the street wasn't very long, but it seemed to go on for miles as she moved toward the new kid. She thought for sure he had frozen in terror, seeing her come at him, so she held out the pack of sweet crackers, let him know she's friendly.

Pushing away from the tree, he shrugged, then remembered and picked up her basketball.

"Hi," she said.

They exchanged the basketball and graham crackers.

"I'm Ivy."

Jason Hamilton was younger than Ivy Jean and slightly shorter, like all of them were. He was still eleven and would join the sixth grade at her school.

Jason liked James Bond okay and playing medieval kingdom. He loved the creek. And because he'd lived in lots of places, he was smart about geography and his descriptions revived Ivy's interest in things far away. Jason's dad was retired military, employed at Fort Hood, like several other households in town. They had actually lived in Germany, Spain and Florida. It was no surprise that they became everyday pals.

Ivy Jean waited to confide in her new friend about *her* trip to another land. Dahl House didn't come up until weeks later, and she didn't give up any secrets when it did, not even names.

"Sounds like a nutty place," he said.

No joke. They talked about their own ideas of being rich and agreed the whole Massey family acted spoiled.

Jason said, "You don't have to worry about them anymore, do you?"

Ivy thought about what troubled her most, whether Haines got away or what happened to Carla's journals. "Not really," she said. "My uncle didn't charge me for the car wreck." She shrugged. "It wasn't his car to begin with."

"Good. You shouldn't have to worry."

Jason sounded like her brother just then and she swallowed a lump.

He said, "My dad says we need to be kids as long as possible and be glad of the chance. Do you want to play Battleship?"

"I'll take black," she said with a smile.

They sat cross-legged on the Hamilton's front porch, studying their positions and making moves without comment. Jason was the first to notice a little foreign car sputtering up the street. It came from the direction of the highway and—*surprise!*—pulled over quickly at Ivy's house. Her shoulders dropped at the idea of more strangers showing up to dig at the wounds she was trying to heal.

The car was one of those German jobs called a Bug. A long pair of legs swung out the door first, then a lady stood, smoothing her dark hair and the seat of her dress. She walked toward Ivy's porch.

"Huh," was all Ivy Jean could think of to say.

Jason's eyebrows arched twice, miming *ooh la la,* and she rolled her eyes and punched him in the arm.

Ivy Jean's wiry eyebrows knitted in concentration. Vincent had been smelling different lately, a new cologne or aftershave, she'd guessed. But a few other details hadn't added up, until this mystery woman appeared. She watched her climb the porch steps and knock on their front door.

Ivy Jean reached for her new slip-on Keds and with a quiet "See ya," left Jason to put away the game. It was time to find out what was going on.

Heartfelt gratitude . . .

To my husband, our children, and our pets, for all the love that sustains me. And to my family and friends, for all the support and encouragement throughout this endeavor; you have made completing it possible. Writing stories is what I am meant to do, and your reflection of that truth has made this adventure my new reality. I wish every human on earth could feel as loved and blessed. This has been a learning process from the start and I have benefitted from the influence of many gifted minds that I hope will be a permanent part of my circle now.

Made in the USA
Lexington, KY
06 October 2013